D1551619

GROUND ZERO, NAGASAKI

GROUND ZERO, NAGASAKI

stories

SEIRAI YŪICHI

Translated by PAUL WARHAM

Columbia University Press New York

This book has been selected by the Japanese Literature Publishing Project (JLPP),
an initiative of the Agency for Cultural Affairs of Japan.

Columbia University Press
Publishers Since 1893
New York   Chichester, West Sussex
cup.columbia.edu

Original title: *Bakushin*

Originally published in Japan by Bungeishunju Ltd., Tokyo

Library of Congress Cataloging-in-Publication Data
Seirai, Yuichi.
[Short stories. Selections. English]
Ground zero, Nagasaki : stories / Yuichi Seirai ; translated by Paul Warham.
pages cm.
ISBN 978-0-231-17116-8 (cloth : alk. paper)
ISBN 978-0-231-53856-5 (e-book)
1. Atomic bomb victims—Japan—Nagasaki-ken—Fiction.
I. Warham, Paul, translator.
II. Seirai, Yuichi. Bukushin. English. III. Title.

PL861.E345B3513 2014
895.63'6—dc23   2014014498

Columbia University Press books are printed on permanent
and durable acid-free paper.
This book is printed on paper with recycled content.
Printed in the United States of America

c 10 9 8 7 6 5 4 3 2 1

COVER DESIGN: JULIA KUSHNIRSKY

CONTENTS

GROUND ZERO, NAGASAKI

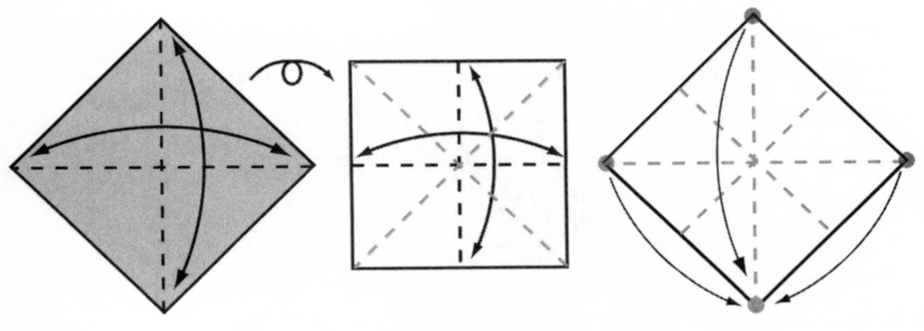

NAILS

The snow that had been falling all afternoon had stopped at last, but patchy clouds of black and gray still covered the sky like warts on the walls of a limestone cave. It looked as though it might start snowing again at any moment. My wife stood with her head hung low, her fingers knitted together over her chest. Her silhouette shaded into the thick gloom of the evening.

The domed belfry of the cathedral was still just about visible over the crest of the gentle hill that stretches out in front of the house. My wife has always claimed that this plot of land, with its views of the church windows glinting in the morning light, is a sacred place. She's prayed here every day, morning and night, since we were married. It broke her heart when she had to stop going to church after what happened with our son.

I hurried across to the cottage storehouse on the grounds, with the crowbar and mallet in one hand. The mud had frozen solid, and the ice crunched beneath my sneakers.

"You found them?" my wife called out, unlocking her fingers slowly and letting her hands fall to her side.

"Under the veranda."

The crowbar was flecked with red rust like scales on a fish. I'd felt a shudder run through me as I took the bar in my hand. I was about to expose what our son had gone to such efforts to hide. It made my heart ache. He insisted that he had never meant to do Kiyomi any harm. He just wanted to expose the truth, he said. But sometimes revealing someone's secrets is harmful enough. I thought of the ancestors, martyred when the secret of their hidden faith had been exposed, and felt more deeply than ever how wrong it was. Secrets weren't something one should ever reveal, no matter whose they were—even if they were sinful things.

The house stands on a level plot of about a quarter of an acre, surrounded by a thick stone wall to prevent it from sinking. No doubt our relatives were right to say that the property was much too big for two elderly people living on their own. Probably we would have had to give up the house anyway sooner or later; but to be driven out, as we had been, from a place where our ancestors had quietly yet firmly kept the faith for three hundred years brought regrets that seemed unlikely ever to heal.

Fancy Western-style houses dominate the slope today—all of them built behind high retaining walls with gaps set into them for garages. The whole hillside is like a fortress; there's not much grace or elegance left now. In the old days, terraced fields with stone boundaries rose in steps from the bottom of the hill to the very top. The deep green leaves of sweet potato and radish plants shining in the sun seemed to flow down the hillside. From here, the hill had looked like a stone-built church that had gradually taken shape over the years as the pious people who lived there cultivated the land. The thought made my chest swell with pride.

Standing still, I felt the cold creeping up slowly from my feet. I took the bar in my black leather–gloved hands and pressed the hoof-shaped tip against the edge of the iron plate that held the locks fixed on the door. I started to hammer at it with the mallet.

I was a little worried about the noise carrying to the Sasaki house next door, but they must have realized by now that we were back. We returned last night after a long absence. They probably would just watch from the windows. Our neighbors didn't talk to us any longer. After what our son did, I suppose we had no right to expect anything else. But with the Sasakis, who had always gone to the same church as us, the rejection was even harder to take.

The tip of the bar bit into the wood. I held the other end of the bar at an angle and pressed down with all my weight. The metal plate crumpled without resistance, and the four nails that held it in place came away like wispy roots.

The locks were of an old cylindrical combination type consisting of three round rings engraved with numbers. The door was sealed with six of them altogether—eighteen numbers to match correctly or the door wouldn't open. I had asked our son about the numbers when I went to visit the hospital that afternoon, but he refused to help. "Can't remember," was all he would say. I tried guessing: Kiyomi's birthday, their wedding anniversary and so on, but I didn't manage to get a single combination right. My wife suggested calling a locksmith, but you don't call in a stranger to deal with a door that has been bolted with six combination locks.

By the time I had broken in, I was breathing hard. The cold air stung my lungs when I took a deep breath, and I felt weak at the knees. More and more often recently, I've noticed how weak I've become since I quit my job at the printing company when I turned sixty. Probably if our son hadn't done what he did, I'd still be in good health. My energy and morale have taken a real battering over the past sixteen months. Even my present job, as a live-in delivery worker for a newspaper subscriptions business in Oita, takes a lot out of me now.

I dropped to a crouch and noticed the red fruit of a nandina shining amid a patch of bluish darkness. In a warm region like this, snow rarely stays long on the ground, even in the depths of winter. I have a vague memory of using nandina berries once for the eyes of a rabbit we'd made out of snow. The nandina has always grown wild in this area; when it's in leaf you tend more or less to forget about it. It melts into the background of the garden, to return to prominence when winter arrives and the plant produces bright red fruit again. As a symbol of purity and long life, it helped me now to struggle to my feet, using the bar for support.

The framework of the old building had warped with age, and the sliding door would open only halfway. From the darkness inside came the smell of mold. I felt with my fingers for the switch where I remembered it on the earthen wall to the right of the door and turned on the fluorescent light.

A mattress folded neatly in three. An electric fan by the window. On the corner of the desk, a pile of gardening magazines with photos of orchids showing on a cover. There was no sign of any disorder—which was typical of him. But the room was practically empty and had a bleak and chilly air. The mental hospital where he's a patient now has much more warmth to it.

He lives in a closed ward. He isn't free to come and go as he pleases, but there are no metal bars or anything. Members of the staff tap numbers into numerical pads to open and close the glass doors; inside, the patients are quite free. There is parquet flooring, which is kept shiny and clean, and comfortable sofas in the visitors' room. They have television, as well as newspapers and magazines. It's more like a decent hotel than a hospital, really—fully equipped with heating and air-conditioning. What's more, the place is built way up on a hillside overlooking the port, and one wall of the dining hall is made entirely of glass, apparently giving a fine view out over the city at night.

I'm sure it's a good environment for the patients, but the thought of what Kiyomi's family must be going through meant that I had to say *something* to him about it, and as a result we'd fought again during visiting hours that afternoon. Dr. Kato has advised me repeatedly to keep off the subject, explaining that our son is sick and can't help himself, but when I think that a word of apology or remorse from him might bring Kiyomi's parents and brother some small consolation, it is impossible for me to keep quiet.

The hardest thing to accept is that he still refuses to believe that Kiyomi is dead.

"So you're in on it, too—my own father!" he told me. "I know what she's up to, the slut. Probably out there screwing anyone who wants it," he said, unashamed of slandering the dead. He doesn't have hallucinations or hear things. Most of the time, in fact, his mind is quite clear. But as soon as the subject of Kiyomi comes up, something flips and he starts ranting and raving, driven by an uncontrollable jealousy.

I took off my shoes and stepped up onto the worn tatami. I felt something clinging around my cheeks and nose. I held my arms out in front of me but they didn't touch anything. Broken strands of cobwebs hung in the air, thick with dust.

Flicking through the gardening magazines, my wife came across a photograph that had been left between the pages.

It was a picture of the two of them cutting the cake at their wedding reception. Kiyomi was holding a knife decorated with a bouquet and ribbon. Our son stood with his hand resting on top of hers. The blade of the knife was just touching the white icing on the cake.

The photographer must have been crouching down, his camera pointing up at the couple. The newlyweds were looking at the blade, their plump faces downturned, illuminated diagonally from below by the flash of the photographer's bulb. Although they looked slightly flushed with drink, their eyes were focused on the same spot. There was no hint of what would happen just six months later.

Dressed in a white tuxedo, our son was standing behind Kiyomi, so you could see him only from the chest up. His left hand showed lower down in the picture, wrapped firmly around her waist. Even this one photograph was enough to convey a sense of how infatuated he was.

I think any man would have picked up on Kiyomi's natural appeal. She seemed to have been born with the power to draw men toward her like a magnet. Whatever she was wearing—whether it was a wedding dress or jeans and T-shirt—always sat tight on her body, so that her pale, ample flesh looked ready to burst out of her clothes. The photo also showed the mole to the left of her mouth, the slightly upturned lips, and the look in her eye when seen at an angle—any of these things, I suppose, could have been interpreted by some men as a come-on. As a man myself, I could just about understand what it was that made my son phone her constantly from work throughout the day and what had stoked his insatiable desire for her morning, noon, and night.

Before the wedding, I took Kiyomi to one side and asked her what had first attracted her to him. "A ladybug landed on my arm once," she told me. "And he picked it up and carried it out in the palm of his hand. He was so gentle. He walked all the way to the greenhouse door and let it go. He said he didn't like to kill them, even if they were pests." So he'd had a gentle side to him too. And Kiyomi, despite what you might have expected from her appearance, had an innocence about her that responded to this kindness. But just two months after the wedding, she moved out of the apartment. The change that came over him had obviously been quite sudden and quite severe.

It must have been more than ten years since I last went into the storehouse to throw things out and generally clear it up. I had a memory of hoes and spades and mortar stones and the pump we used back in the days when we still drew our water from the underground spring. The only things left behind now were probably a few old chests and trunks.

After she left him, he just collapsed. We managed to calm him down sufficiently to get him to a psychiatric clinic, where he was diagnosed with delusional schizophrenia—a diagnosis that came as a real shock. He was there for three weeks and then discharged himself. Convinced that it was just a matter of time before she came back, he announced his intention to return to the apartment they had briefly shared. Eventually, we persuaded him to abandon that plan and come home instead, though he didn't want to live under the same roof as us and agreed only on the condition that we let him live in the old storehouse set apart from the main building.

After he moved in, he refused to allow anyone inside. He shoved everything we'd stored there onto the porch and did all the cleaning himself. Neither my wife nor I ever once set foot in the building in all the time he was there.

The whorls of age rings lined the warped wooden boards of the ceiling. I remember lying on my back looking up at them when I was a child. High mountains, huge mystical trees, ripple patterns, the skin of molting snakes . . . More than half a century ago, the cottage was home to my father's older sister, whom we called O-Ryo-san. Normally, I suppose, I would have called her Oba-san, or Aunt, but my mother called her O-Ryo-san and, following her example, I did the same.

O-Ryo-san had come back to the family home after the house she had married into in Yamazato was destroyed in the atomic bombing. It was in this cottage that she had recuperated alone. When she started to feel a little better, she often used to invite me and my sister inside. She had lost four children of her own, and it may be that she found some echo of them in her nephew and niece.

O-Ryo-san had a faded scar on her cheek. I remember her standing under the persimmon tree gazing out at the remains of the ruined cathedral. When late autumn came, she would peel the bitter persimmons and hang them from the eaves to dry. I used to enjoy watching the fruit change color, from the shade of a person's skin to a deep orange flecked with black where patches of the peel still remained. We would hold our hands, tingling from the cold, over the hibachi and nibble on the dried flesh of the fruit, bursting with sweetness, as O-Ryo-san told us stories of long ago.

Stories of distant ancestors who had gone, praying, to their deaths, burned alive at the stake; or of the narrow cages in which the faithful were imprisoned when whole families were forcefully removed to Yamaguchi in the final days of prohibition. She told us of the heat of fires that seared the flesh and the frost that streaked the ground during the bitter winter of captivity, her face wrinkling with pain and sorrow as if she had lived through these events herself. Between the stories, she would poke with her tongs at the whitened ash in the hibachi. The fire would crackle into life, and a deep red glow would emerge from deep within the ash. O-Ryo-san told us how the ancestors had hidden an image of the Virgin and Child in this cottage and how they had prayed here in secret during the years when our religion was outlawed. There's no way of finding out for sure now, but I suspect this is the reason why my grandfather left this building untouched when he had the main house rebuilt back in the early years of the twentieth century.

Our son didn't cut himself off entirely. For a while he continued to go to work at the garden center, and he joined us around the table in the main house for breakfast and dinner. "So long as he keeps taking his medications, he should be able to get on with daily life. It's not as if he's having hallucinations or hearing voices, after all." Dr. Kato's words were like a weight off my shoulders, and although I didn't know much about the illness, I had begun to feel reconciled to the situation and occasionally even optimistic about the future. There were periods of sun and cloud in everyone's life, after all, I told myself.

But then he was summoned to the family court for divorce negotiations in September last year, and his condition abruptly took a turn for the worse.

"She's screwing around," he started saying quite openly, albeit in a voice that was close to a whisper. "The only way to stop her is to catch her in the act." If anyone said it was just his imagination or tried to plead with him or calm him down, he'd get stubborn and angry and, with bloodshot eyes and flecks of spittle at his mouth, start swearing through clenched teeth: "I can't believe she wants a divorce. We were so good together. She said there would never be anyone else. She said she loved me!"

It was around this time that he put the six locks on the door. He stopped going to work and taking his medications. He spent his afternoons on aimless walks around the city, and later we would hear the sound of him hammering away at something in the cottage until deep into the night. Sasaki-san from next door came over at one stage to say, politely but with an unmistakable note of complaint in his voice, that the noise was making it impossible to sleep. At that point we didn't realize he had a knife, but we were sufficiently worried by his behavior to contact Kiyomi's family to warn them to be on their guard. As if they weren't wary enough of us already . . .

I went to the police for advice as well, but the fat man in charge of public safety just shook his head and said that since our son hadn't made any explicit threats, there was nothing he could do.

"He's not stalking her, and no official complaint has been filed. We can't go arresting someone and infringing on his rights just because he's not right in the head. The fact that he's refusing to take part in divorce proceedings is not a police affair. It's a civil case."

Besides his gardening books, the only things in the small, self-assembled steel bookcase were a few paperbacks, several dictionaries and reference books from his student days, and the children's hymnals and Bible stories they handed out at church. He had never been much good with words. Ever since he was a child, he had struggled to express himself and his feelings. At school, he was hopeless. Awkward. We were quite worried about him for a while, but then he found the job at the garden center, which seemed to suit him. He seemed to find peace in the slow-moving hours he spent looking after the plants. "Orchids don't go on about stuff all the time. So you can relax," he said once in his whispery voice. How relieved my wife and I were to hear him say this! If only everyone could find their right place, I used to think—somewhere they could settle down and live in peace. If only everyone could live their lives without getting twisted out of shape. Becoming successful, making a lot of money . . . these things aren't important. Living the right life, that's the only thing that really matters. After sixty years of life, that's the one thing I set more store by than anything else.

On the bottom shelf of the bookcase were three batches of documents in a thick paper bag. The documents were bound together with a black cord, each file an inch or so thick. On each envelope and each front page was the name of a detective agency—three separate agencies in all. My wife and I gave a gasp of surprise and dismay when we saw them.

"He hired detectives to follow her," she said.

So now we knew what he'd kept hidden in here. Chances were that it would provide a clue to whatever lay at the root of his mental problems.

Along with the documents were receipts from the three agencies, coming to a total of more than two million yen. I knew that he had taken out a credit card loan for around that amount, but since he'd refused to say anything about it, I hadn't known until now what the money was for. Together they gave a detailed record of Kiyomi's daily movements between May and September. It was a shock to discover that he had hired these people to watch her immediately after they were married. Even more puzzling was that he'd paid them to continue their surveillance even in the evenings, after he was home from work. He must have felt their eyes on him all the time as he sat at home with her.

We turned on the light above the desk and sat for a time reading the reports, shivering with cold. There were no grounds for suspicion anywhere in Kiyomi's behavior. Even when he went to Okinawa on an orchid-collecting trip, there was no hint of anything suspicious. After she fled from their apartment, she had gone straight back to her parents' house. After a while, she had apparently started taking on bits of part-time work at the broadcasting station where she'd worked as a reporter before they got married.

All three reports concluded that there was no evidence of any relationship with another man. Far from explaining the cause of our son's delusions, they were like testimonies to Kiyomi's faithfulness and decency. The fact that he had continued to suspect her even after getting detailed information like this, and had even threatened her with a knife, made it hard to avoid the conclusion that he had actually wanted her to betray him.

Why had he put all his passion and energy into doubting rather than trusting? When had his love turned to hatred? Was he the last of our family line, which has continued unbroken for three hundred years—the one unbeliever, in whom everything came to an end, undoing all the virtue that has kept the faith alive from generation to generation?

"Maybe there was something wrong with the way we brought him up," my wife said faintly, her hand on the cover of the last closed report.

"No, we did nothing wrong. We taught him to believe in God. It's an illness. There's nothing anyone can do about it."

"But no one on either side of the family has ever had an illness like this before."

"Don't you remember what Dr. Kato said?—it can affect anyone. The seeds of it can be lying latent in anybody, waiting for stress and physical strain to trigger it."

"I know that. But if it could have happened to anyone, why did it have to be him? Why not me? That's what's so hard to accept."

I knew what she meant. People have probably always asked the same questions when some disaster has occurred. Our martyred ancestors, our dead parents, O-Ryo-san—all of us at some time in our lives have turned our eyes to Heaven and asked: Why?

Maybe we're the descendants of Job and, like Job, beloved beyond all reason and therefore subject to tests and trials. But we aren't strong like Job . . . and some of us, like our son, are crushed by the experience.

"But he loved Kiyomi so much. What could have made him do a thing like that?"

I had lost track of how many times I had heard the same sighing question from her since the incident.

"Because he's not well. That's why." What else could I say?

A towel was hanging in one corner of the room. It had been a year since he left the place, without returning, and the white fabric was shriveled and dry.

Eventually we got to our feet.

"There's nothing useful in here at all," my wife said, rubbing her feet through her thick socks to get the circulation going after sitting so long on the floor. I put the books and the reports into a cardboard box off in a corner and sealed it with tape. Then I picked up the towel. "Let's throw it out," she said. "It's useless now." The cold crept up into the small of my back. I could feel the sensation of warm urine collecting behind my belly.

"What on earth was he hiding, putting six locks on the door like that?" my wife said.

I nodded. If the detectives' reports had contained a record of wrongdoing—something that made it possible to trace the path leading from love to hatred—perhaps then we might have had some kind of understanding of what he had done, even if there was no forgiving it. But the surveillance merely made Kiyomi's innocence clearer than ever. The fact that our son had caused her death in spite of this just made the workings of his confused mind all the more distant and mysterious. How did deep feelings get distorted like that? It wasn't something the good people of this area, with their simple moral code, could ever have understood. And what, I wonder, was going through his mind as he found himself pushed, kicked, and punched on the ground by passersby?

"Anyway, none of this will bring her back now," I said with a sigh. My wife frowned and looked straight at me.

"He didn't *kill* her, though. Maybe he was planning to threaten her or frighten her, to find out the truth. But he never meant to kill her. That boy loved Kiyomi more than anything in the world."

She was right. He'd pinned her in a wrestling hold in the street and threatened her with a knife, but passersby had grabbed him almost immediately and pushed him to the ground. Kiyomi escaped from his grip but lost her footing when her heel slipped, and fell back toward him, where the crowd was holding him by the head. It was then that the knife still in his hand had cut her on the neck, severing the carotid artery. They rushed her to a hospital, but she died soon after. The cause of death was given as shock and loss of blood.

"I remember something he said once," my wife said. "About marrying Kiyomi. He kept saying it was a miracle."

"A miracle?"

Already in his thirties, our son was shy and awkward, an unremarkable person who looked after orchids, bougainvillea, caesalpinia, and other tropical plants in a greenhouse that was like a sauna in summer. When Kiyomi announced that she'd fallen in love with him shortly after visiting the nursery in the course of her work as a TV reporter, the news was difficult even for us parents to believe.

"It was the night before the wedding," my wife went on. "He said it was like hitting the jackpot on the Dream Jumbo. He looked perfectly sincere. Then he said that for someone like him, marrying a girl like Kiyomi was a kind of miracle. I told him it's not a miracle, and it's not luck. It's a reward, I said—a reward for the way our people kept their faith through all the hardships they had to suffer. You're getting the reward on their behalf. He just laughed and said in that case maybe he should start going to church more often."

It's possible that no one was more shocked by her death than our son himself. Even now, he couldn't bring himself to believe that it was true.

"Kiyomi's dead. If he hadn't done such a stupid thing, there would still have been so much to look forward to. Her parents would never have suffered so much pain, her brother would have been spared all that anger, and we—we wouldn't have been forced to give up the house and move away from the land handed down to us."

She started to sob quietly. Life is hard on mothers. They can't help feeling love and pity for their children, however stupid or useless the kids might be. She was weeping openly now, as she often did these days, the sort of tears that never dry: a mother's tears for her child.

Whether our son intended to kill Kiyomi or simply to threaten her made no legal difference now that he had been absolved from responsibility on the grounds of temporary insanity.

"In a case like this, everyone's a victim," the lawyer had said. "In a sense, your son himself is a victim of his illness and of an unlucky accident. As his parents, you can certainly be considered victims too, given the way you've been treated by the community around you."

I appreciated his attempts to comfort us; but if what he was saying was true, then no one had committed a crime; no one should take responsibility; a mere illness was to blame for all the grief and anger her family felt. They had lost a daughter they'd cherished, somebody they'd raised lovingly for years—how could they be expected to accept that the whole thing was just an unfortunate accident? With a daughter of my own, I could imagine only too well how they must be feeling.

My wife and I managed to get as close as we could on the day of the funeral—though of course it was out of the question for us to attend the ceremony itself. Feeling wretched and uneasy, we found a spot within sight of the funeral home and stood praying in the rain under the willows on the riverbank. I thought back over the events that had led us to face such misery in our waning years; it was a living nightmare. My sense of myself had become thin and indistinct, like a ghost. People came over to warn us off. "You'd better not show your faces around here," they told us. But we could think of no other way to make up for what had happened. All we could do was pray.

To raise funds for compensation was only part of the reason we had to sell the house and land: we also felt that uprooting ourselves from somewhere our family had lived and prayed for generations might bring us at least a little closer to the suffering that Kiyomi's relatives were enduring. Several times, we'd even discussed the idea of dying together, but that would only have been running away from the test we'd been given. And in our faith, it is a mortal sin.

"That's enough tears now, Ma," I said, patting my wife on the shoulder. She tried, but they still kept coming.

"I wish you'd stop calling me that. I'm not your mother."

"Then who do you mean by 'you'?"

"You, obviously, Pa."

Her face, wet with tears, broke into a smile. We had often had similar silly exchanges since our son did what he did. We'd been "Ma" and Pa" to each other for what seemed like ages now.

She looked out of the open window and beckoned me over with her hand.

"Quick, Pa—come and look."

“You’re doing it, too, now.” But I fell silent when I got to the window. It was snowing heavily, in a way it rarely does in this part of the country. Christmas was already over, but the house up the hill was still decorated with the little flashing lights that are so popular nowadays. But other than the flickering glow of green, red, and yellow, there was only the darkness and the snow. Somewhere off in the invisible distance, a siren wailed.

“Looks like we’re in for a real storm,” I said.

“What about tomorrow—the movers?”

“If the road up the hill freezes over, traffic might not be able to make it through.”

I knew from the evening news that the highways were closed to traffic and that the lights were out in some places because the power was off. I still had a couple of days left till I was due back at my job in Oita, but I couldn’t afford to take off more time than that over the busy New Year period.

As I breathed in the cold air that blew in through the window, I was reminded again of my swollen bladder. The nearest lavatory was back in the main house. I wanted to finish tidying up the cottage as quickly as possible.

“When they come tomorrow, let’s have them take away the desk and fan along with everything else,” I said. “Let’s face it: he’s never coming out of that hospital.”

“Is there nothing we could sell as antiques?”

“He tossed out all the old stuff when he moved in here, remember?”

I wondered what had happened to the blue-glazed hibachi where O-Ryo-san used to warm her thin fingers. I had a vague memory of seeing it here the last time I came to tidy up. But more than a decade had passed since then.

The panels on the door to the box room were blackened with age, and the small hollow that served in place of a handle shone dully with the grease from fingerprints. The door was stuck in its groove, and though I managed to get the thing half open by rattling it hard, I couldn’t force it any further. I shoved my way into the opening and pushed against the door with both hands. Something finally gave, and it slid open.

The light from the other room illuminated the floorboards. A single hammer lay abandoned on the floor. Something long and narrow stood in one corner. A stepladder. That was all. From farther inside, I caught a whiff of iron.

I felt for the bump of the light switch. What I saw when I flicked the switch sent horror running through me.

The walls were covered in hair—at least, that's what it looked like at first. Or was it some kind of mold? They seemed raised, as if with scar tissue. As I stepped inside, I felt my skin crawl. The surfaces of the walls bristled with iron nails set close together and sticking out half an inch or so. There must have been tens of thousands, or hundreds of thousands, of them. They covered the three walls and extended right to the edge of the ceiling boards.

Three burlap sacks had been left in a corner of the room. One of them stood open, full of nails about two inches long. So this is what he'd been working on, night after night.

I turned around to find my wife silhouetted in the electric light behind her, her blurred outline shaking in the glare.

"What is this?"

I had no answer.

"Why? . . . What does it mean?"

I stood and stared. I felt a shortness of breath and a crushing tightness in my chest.

Our son had stopped shaving after being admitted to the hospital because he was allergic to electric shavers. They took him for a haircut every two months, and the barber gave him a shave then; but otherwise, since even safety razors were forbidden inside the hospital, he just let his beard grow.

During my visit that afternoon, he had sat on the sofa in the brightly lit visitors' room, his right hand slowly stroking the beard on his cheeks and chin. After asking if there was anything he needed—any food he wanted his mother to bring the next time she visited, or something else—I told him we had come back from Oita to take care of things at the house.

I had already informed him that we planned to sell it, but this was the first time he'd heard that a prospective buyer had been found.

"What will happen to the house?"

"They'll probably tear it down and put up something new. The real estate people say they could build three separate buildings on a plot that size, easily."

He said nothing in reply, just bit down on his lip.

"We're going to have to sort things out in the cottage where you were staying. We'll need to get inside. Did you leave anything valuable in there?"

He was silent for a while, then said in his whispery voice, "No, nothing." On the day of the assault, he had been carrying a daypack containing his bank savings book, name stamp, medical insurance ID, and various bank and credit cards. Probably he'd been planning to head off somewhere.

"You won't mind us going inside, then, if there's nothing in there."

"But you'd better be careful, in any unopened room."

I could get nothing out of him other than this cryptic remark.

"What do you mean, careful?"

He just bit down on his lip and stared fixedly ahead.

"What's the combination for the locks?"

"Can't remember."

"What are you talking about? Without the numbers, you wouldn't be able to open the locks yourself. You must have written them down somewhere. Either that or they're connected with something—a birthday, phone number, whatever."

For a while, he stroked his beard slowly as if deep in thought. But when he finally spoke again, the answer was equally unhelpful. "They didn't have any particular connection."

"In that case, we'll have to break the locks and force the door."

His pale face remained locked in silence. It was then that, ignoring my wife's word of warning, I began pleading with him again to write a letter of apology. My idea was to hand over the compensation money with a letter from him. I thought a heartfelt apology was more likely to console the family than money alone.

"Kiyomi's off doing it with some guy. The bitch!"

His cursing the dead like this was hard to take. Even though he'd hurt everyone around him, he still went on saying things that caused only more pain. I couldn't help it, it made me furious, though I knew it was just his illness talking.

"Kiyomi never did anything wrong. It's a delusion," I told him. There was a ragged edge to my voice.

He reached out a hand for one of the cream puffs his mother had sent and munched at it petulantly, his bearded chin bobbing up and down as he chewed. While he ate, he gestured that he had something to say. My face was red with anger—but still I leaned close. His breath was sweet with the smell of the food. He brought his lips close to my ear.

"Tell me, Daddy: Do you believe in God?"

My body stiffened, and I sat bolt upright. What kind of thing was that to say? I began to shout.

"Of course I do! This family has always believed. Our ancestors gave their lives for the faith!"

With his long fingernails, he wiped away a spot of yellow cream from the corner of his mouth and licked it as he spoke.

"And you call me deluded?"

Suddenly the light in the cottage began to flicker, and we were plunged into darkness. I reached for the switch, but nothing happened. The power was off. The pitch darkness brought the bristling nails closer. It became difficult to breathe.

I took my wife's cold hand in mine, and we brushed past the gruesome walls and stumbled toward the door. Outside, the snow was up to our ankles. Obviously quite a wide area was affected—the Christmas lights were off at the house on the hill, and the windows at the Sasakis' place were dark. But even the faint white of the snow was like brightness after the box room and its nails. I crouched down in the doorway to tie my shoelaces and reached out to touch a bunch of nandina berries near my feet, testing the cold with my fingers.

"What does it mean?" my wife said. "All those nails . . ." She sounded on the verge of tears. But I was just as mystified. What meaning could there be in what he had done? What had made him hammer all those nails so precisely, so regularly, into the wooden walls? What had he been hiding—what was this secret that we had exposed to the light?

My wife slumped down at the edge of the garden, crossing herself and folding her thin, wrinkled fingers together over her chest.

The only thing we could still vaguely make out was the crest of the hill. The cathedral and the city beyond were sunk in darkness, and heavy snow fell in flurries through the air all around. I remembered when Pope John Paul II visited the city—more than twenty years ago. It was snowing then, too. My wife and I had heard Mass outdoors in the stadium with our young daughter and son. The snow fell steadily on my forehead throughout the service, the cold eating its way deep into my body. We remembered the long years of persecution of those who came before us. I was overcome by a feeling that the people standing in line to receive the pope's blessing weren't people from this day and age, but our ancestors. The thought provoked a surge of emotion in me. Whenever I say my prayers, I can feel their shadowy presence by my side. Prayer is never a solitary occupation. This was why the faithful were able to endure the trials they had.

But my son's question made my head spin. "Do you believe in God?" I went to church on Sundays, and I took pride in the beliefs that had been passed down through the generations. But would my own faith have stood firm if I'd been threatened with being burned at the stake? I couldn't say. I had mumbled the prayers for as long as I could remember. But I hadn't simply been mumbling to myself. Somewhere, I believed, He was listening. I clung to Him the same way our son had clung to Kiyomi's body, as helpless and insignificant as an insect.

Is it too much to expect an answer? All those nails . . . Will we ever get an explanation?

"Pa? Are you all right?"

I stumbled and felt a stabbing pain in my lungs. My wife took my hand as she stood beside me, her hair white with snow. The wail of a siren sounded again somewhere in the distance, and I remembered with a shiver that I needed to pee. I started off toward the dark, crouching bulk of the main house.

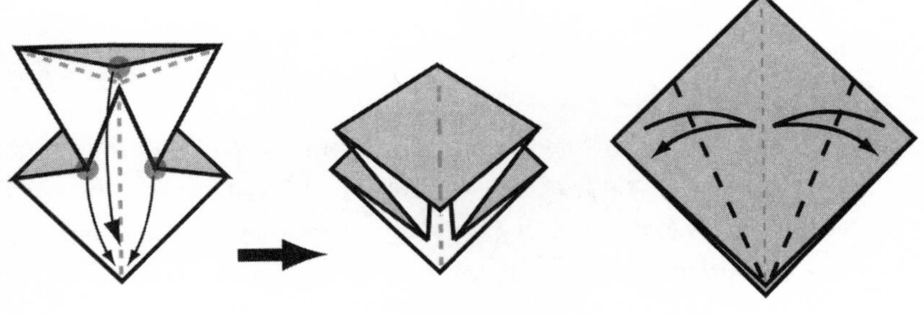

STONE

Even with my eyes closed, I could feel the light from the chandeliers twinkling against the back of my eyelids. I quite liked being here in the lobby.

"Are you waiting for someone?" a man's voice said. He wasn't one of the staff, so why was he giving me that unfriendly look? I felt like giving him a talking-to. I should have told him: *It's not your hotel*. But it would only cause trouble if I made a fuss, so I decided to let it go. You know how it is. You're just sitting minding your own business when one of these people appears and starts asking nosy questions. Maybe it's just one of God's little tests. You can't really complain. But it does get annoying sometimes.

"I'm waiting for Kyu-chan," I said.

"Kyu-chan?"

"That's right. He arrived a few minutes ago in a long black car. Surrounded by reporters—flash, flash, flash. Then he went downstairs."

"Do you mean the politician, Mr. Kutani?"

"That's right."

What was he was getting so worked up about, anyway? Why shouldn't I wait for someone here? That's what a hotel lobby's there for. I even had a necktie on, like everyone else, though my mother made a face when she saw the one I'd chosen. "Why on earth did you have to buy such an awful tie?" she said. But the salesgirl with the pussycat eyes had smiled and said it suited me.

"Excuse me for asking, but do you happen to have an appointment?"

"Yes, I do."

"He's an acquaintance of yours?"

"We've known each other since we were kids."

Kyu-chan is a high flier, but one of the good guys. He went to La Salle High School in Kagoshima and then Tokyo University. He's supersmart—the exact opposite of me. My mother says if you put us together and divided us into two equal parts, you'd have just enough to make two normal people.

I took out my phone from the inside pocket of my jacket and showed it to this pest of a man.

"Is something the matter with it?"

"It has GPS. So my mother will know where I am if I go wandering off. She's in the hospital."

He twisted his head to one side with a little scowl as if he'd just eaten something sour. I didn't seem to be getting through. What a dummy he was. This is why I find it hard to get on with people who aren't Christians. At church they're always telling us not to put people down. This guy obviously hadn't heard the news.

"Does that have some connection with Mr. Kutani?" he asked.

"Obviously. I want to give him my number."

"Ah yes?"

I could feel myself starting to get upset.

When I get worked up, my blood starts to feel as heavy as molasses, and my body goes stiff. I don't want to talk, don't even want to breathe. My jerky heartbeat wants to stop altogether. I get rigid, like I've turned to stone. People start calling out to me, worried about what's happening. Everything feels far away, like I've been catapulted into space. It's a very lonely feeling.

"I believe this gentleman is waiting for me," a new voice said suddenly.

It was a woman with a big black camera over her shoulder. Who was she? I didn't recognize her face. She had glasses and long, wavy hair that made her look supersmart and sexy. There was a faraway look in her eyes.

"And you are?"

"Oh, come on. Surely you remember me," she said.

She showed me the square card that hung from her neck. I usually carry my medical card and my bus pass around my neck when I go to work, but they were in my jacket pocket today since I was wearing a tie.

“Are you with the press, madam? Does this person have some business with you?”

“Well, actually I came here to interview Mr. Kutani. But I thought I’d include this gentleman too, since he’s an old acquaintance.”

“You had an arrangement to meet here?”

“That’s right.”

“I see. In that case . . .”

The man slunk off, suspicion still written all over his face. I was glad to see the back of him. I felt my whole body loosen up.

“Do you mind?” the woman said, sitting down next to me. Her white coat fell open, and a lovely scent drifted toward me. I may not have much in the brains department, but my sense of smell is as sharp as a dog’s. I can sniff out a woman from a hundred paces away.

She smelled beautiful. What if . . . just if . . . she made me an offer, here and now? What would I do? If she took all her clothes off and got into the shower, and just . . . you know . . . let me have *sex* with her?

Here we were, after all, in a hotel lobby. Maybe she was going to *seduce* me and take me up to one of the rooms.

“What’s wrong? You’ve gone all red.”

“Oh, nothing.”

“I know what it is. You’re angry about that man just now. It wasn’t nice of him to treat you like that.”

“The thing is I’m a little bit . . . shy. I get flustered when I meet a pretty girl. And you’re *very* pretty.”

She put her head back and laughed. I suppose there really is something funny about me, as my mother is always saying. The expression on my face, the look in my eyes, the way I move—I’m not like other people. There’s something a bit weird about me, I suppose.

“I understand you and Mr. Kutani were childhood friends. I’m sorry; I couldn’t help overhearing what you were saying just now. I hope you don’t mind.”

Maybe she was one of Kyu-chan’s fans. Kyu-chan was always popular with the girls. On Valentine’s Day, February 14, 1973, he got chocolates from seven different girls. I helped him eat them all up.

“We used to be neighbors. We were in the same year all through elementary school and junior high. I was in the Sunshine Group, though. Kyu-chan was class president.”

“By the way, my name’s Shirotani. I’m sorry, I don’t think I caught your . . .”

“I’m Adam. Kyu-chan is Thomas.”

“So you’re both Catholics? But that must be the name you got when you were baptized. What’s your usual one?”

Today I felt like being Adam for some reason. I can be quite stubborn once I make up my mind about something.

“I’m sorry. Adam it is. I take it you’re waiting for Mr. Kutani? Have you been in touch with him?”

I shook my head. “I don’t have an appointment. But I signaled to him with my eyes just now when he went past.”

“With your eyes? To say that you were waiting for him here?”

“Right.”

“Do you think he’ll understand what you meant?”

“Oh, I think so.”

“You know, I’m not so sure. I mean, apparently there’s a cocktail party first . . . and then he’s going to be busy meeting his supporters. Are you sure he’ll have the time?”

“Good things come to those who wait.”

“OK . . . Look, why don’t you let me give a message to his secretary just to make sure? What should I say, that Adam is waiting outside?”

“And my phone number too, please.”

The woman took a ballpoint pen in her pretty fingers and wrote my cell phone number in her notebook.

“The latest model, I see,” she said.

“It has GPS and everything. That way, my mother will know where I am if I get lost. So I can’t get into any mischief, she says. Have you got it too?”

“What? GPS?”

“Right.”

“Actually, no. I don’t, but . . .”

“In that case, no one will be able to help you if you get lost. . . .”

“You’re so right! I’m always getting lost—and like you say, nobody ever comes to help.”

She took off her glasses and looked at me sadly with her faraway eyes. Maybe this smart lady felt like me sometimes. Turning to stone. Getting catapulted into space alone.

"You should pray. Just pray, and you'll be saved. That's what the priest always says."

"Uh, thanks . . ."

Why was she tearing up? It's not easy for Adam when Eve starts crying. Maybe she was just sad because she couldn't afford a phone with GPS. I had to beg my mother for five years before she agreed to get me one. And now Mother was dying. That's why I was here at the hotel. She wanted Kyu-chan to take care of me after she was gone.

"Tell me. What's Mr. Kutani like as a person?"

"He's very smart. And a very good man. If you put us together and divided us in two, you'd have just enough to make two normal people. He's a man of faith. No saint, but good."

"Yes?"

"He used to say he became a politician to do God's will. To be a good Thomas—whatever that means."

"Maybe he meant he wanted to do the kind of work that'd be worthy of the name he'd been given."

"Is it true what they say—that Kyu-chan is going to be arrested?"

"So you know about that?"

"They say he hired his girlfriend as his secretary. It's all over the papers and TV. It was on the news, that he'd done something wrong. They say all politicians are *corrupt*. Is Kyu-chan *corrupt*, too? I don't really understand."

"I think what he did was more or less standard practice back then, but it still doesn't look good . . . Especially not if there was that kind of relationship . . ."

"Was she really his *mistress*?"

"Apparently."

"Which means loving somebody who's not your wife?"

"It's not a very nice way to behave, is it? There's no excusing it really." She looked quite upset, biting her lip, as if she were the one married to Kyu-chan.

"No excusing what . . . the mistress?"

"The man. Really, men sometimes . . ."

"I wish it was me. I'm jealous."

She wiped her eyes with a finger and smiled.

"Something must have happened between them," I said.

"What do you mean?"

"I don't know. Things happen when you're grown-up."

I had loved Kumi so much I couldn't help myself. She was cuter than a porpoise and always used to smile and say hello. When she pushed down on the pedals of her bike, a sweet smell like osmanthus flowers came from the crotch of her skirt. The smell was so nice that I started chasing after her as hard as I could, running behind her bike all the way down the street shouting, "I love you, Kumi-chan! Marry me!"

It was the morning of July 12, 1978. Kumi got scared and ran into a convenience store. A man who worked there—he wore a pointed hat—grabbed hold of me and took me to the police. My mother cried and cried that day. "You're a grown-up now," she said. "You can't go running after people just because you like them." And she went on crying. I don't understand all the fuss about being a grown-up. Just for trying to make friends with someone, they'll arrest you and accuse you of being a stalker if you're not careful.

"But you don't believe Mr. Kutani is a bad person, do you, Adam?"

"On December 11, 1972, he stood up for me against Saeki and Kanazawa. They were the class bullies. He got really beaten up for it."

"Beaten up? Why?"

"He saw them picking on me and tried to protect me. Saeki and Kanazawa started hitting him and screeching like Bruce Lee. Kyu-chan is a good person, that's why they made him class president, but he's no use in a fight. My mother says the strongest people are the ones who don't fight, but I'm not so sure."

Shirotani-san was listening carefully. Her ears peeped out from her long brown hair. I wanted to take them in my mouth and chew them like chewing gum. But I resisted. You mustn't give in to temptation.

"They beat him and beat him, but he just stood there with his arms open wide. He really did turn the other cheek—just like the priest told us to do. Blood was pouring from his nose. He had his arms spread wide like Jesus on the cross. I put my arms around him and said, 'That's enough, Kyu-chan. Let's go,' but he wouldn't give up. The bullies probably just wanted to tease me and push me around a bit—but Kyu-chan was so stubborn. It made them mad, and they really laid into him."

"Was he badly hurt?"

"His nose was all bloody. Some of it went on my hand. It was warm. I'd gone stiff as a board by then, but the warm feeling softened me up."

"You seem to remember it very well."

"It was a clear winter's day. Not a single cloud. The blue of the sky was like water from a spring. You could smell the sunlight in the air. We put our arms around each other and cried."

Shirotani-san was carrying a shoulder bag, with a neat little buckle shaped like a heart. It was quite a big bag for a woman to be carrying around.

"So Mr. Kutani's really a good person, then?"

"That's what I'm trying to tell you. Even if they burned him at the stake, he would never lose faith. He's weak—but in other ways, I think maybe he's really strong. I don't really know."

For a while she sat tapping the bottom of her ballpoint pen against her cheek, then started twirling it around her fingers like a baton.

"I could write it up. There's perhaps not quite enough for a whole article in it. It's an interesting story, though. Right now, everyone's all fired up about Prince Charming turning out to be just another grubby middle-aged politician."

She was still twirling the thing around her pretty little fingers. It flashed and shone every time it turned. I felt myself falling deeper under her spell. I would happily have married her. Maybe she would let me have *sex* with her. I was fired up, too. This hotel lobby was a nice place to be in.

"What's wrong? Are you upset about something? You've turned bright red."

I couldn't have said why, but I felt myself stiffening all over. I liked her. I felt so embarrassed and shy. But if I came on to her, they'd arrest me and tell me I was a grown-up now and ought to know better. I didn't know what to do. Maybe I'd just turn into a big stone, right here in the lobby. And stay here quietly till the end of time, till the whole world was destroyed by atomic bombs.

The sparkling chandeliers looked like Christmas, and the ceiling of the lobby reminded me of a church. A church of love. The piano could have been an altar. I could see the white body of Jesus above it and Shirotani-san standing next to me in a white wedding dress. We would make a promise of everlasting love in front of Him.

Her phone was ringing. She flipped up the silver lid with a pale finger, tossed her hair back, and pressed the phone to her ear.

"Hello? Yes, it's me. No, not yet. Yes. Tomorrow. What, after I get back to Tokyo?"

She kept pushing back her hair with her fingers as she talked, nodding all the time. She looked so sexy. The way she kept twisting her pen around the fingers of her right hand was bewitching. There was a whiff of peppermint on her breath when she sighed. Who was she talking to? Her boyfriend? What if she was making arrangements to have *sex* with him after she got back to Tokyo tomorrow? That would be hard to take.

"I really don't think that's going to be possible," she was saying—turning him down loud and clear. What kind of person would keep insisting after a refusal like that?

"After the party, he's meeting with supporters, as far as I know."

Maybe the man on the other end of the line had a wife, too. There's no excuse for someone to have more than one woman for himself. If one person takes more than his share, someone else gets left out—and that someone always seems to be me. It's not fair. That's why the Bible says adultery is a sin.

"All right. I'll see what I can do. But I'm telling you, I don't think it's very likely."

She snapped her phone shut with a click.

"Who was it?"

"So you're not upset anymore?" she said with a twinkle in her eyes.

"If you make fun of me, I'll go all stiff again."

I wanted her to take me seriously. I didn't mind listening if she was having love problems. I may not be like other people—but even so, I don't like being treated like an idiot.

"I'm sorry, it's just . . . my brother—well, he's like you. But his case is much more serious. He can hardly speak. He has to live in a special home. He still comes back for the holidays, though. Whenever he gets annoyed, he sits down on the floor and refuses to budge. And he weighs nearly two hundred pounds, so it really is like trying to shift a boulder to move him."

“I get like that, too, sometimes—so heavy I don’t know what to do. Sometimes I start beating myself around the head with my hands. But maybe it’s all part of God’s plan.” I know what it’s like. You’re a stone, with no way to defend yourself except by keeping still and ignoring everything around you.

I couldn’t help wondering about the person on the other end of the line. “Was that your brother on the phone just now?”

“He can’t use the phone. He can hardly talk.”

“Who was it then?”

“The desk.”

“The desk? What, like furniture?”

“Ha! Might as well be—my boss. Sits there like a piece of furniture and expects me to run around dealing with all his impossible requests. Wants me to get an interview. Whatever it takes, he says . . .”

“An interview?”

“They want me to talk to Mr. Kutani and get his side of the story.”

“So why don’t you just talk to him?”

“Don’t think I haven’t tried. I keep applying for an interview, but he won’t see me. Besides, he won’t say a word to anyone about the scandal. No comment.”

“Maybe he turns to stone, too, sometimes?”

“I’m sure he wishes he could when he’s being hounded like this.”

On the banks of the Urakami River is a place strewn with large stones. But these are no ordinary ones. They’re the remains of people who just couldn’t take it anymore. People who came in search of water when the atom bomb fell. This is where the faithful were burned at the stake. They turned to stone, and have stayed like that ever since.

Her soft eyes looked inquiringly into mine. Was this it? Had the moment arrived at last for Adam to be *seduced* by Eve? Had Adam finally found the piece of his rib he’d been looking for all this time? Maybe, just maybe, these forty-five years of loneliness were at an end. If my mother found out, she’d probably come rushing along to see it for herself, even with the tubes stuck up her nose.

“If I hand this note to his secretary, Adam, and he passes on your message, do you really think Mr. Kutani will see you?”

“No doubt about it. He’ll come and find me. We connected with our eyes when he came in.”

There are a few people I can do that with: the teachers in the Sunshine Group at school, the people in the volunteer care group. My mother says God sends these people to watch over us and make sure we're not alone in the world.

"It looks as if the allegations are going to hold up. There will probably be a hearing as soon as he gets back to Tokyo tomorrow. They're saying he might be arrested there and then. So tonight is my only chance. Do you think you could introduce me?"

I would have done anything for her. I nodded proudly and told her to leave it to me. Our team leader at work told me off once for boasting about being close friends with Kyu-chan when he was on TV.

"Right, then. I'll just pop over and pass this on to his secretary. And then, if you don't mind, I'll come back and wait here with you."

She stood up. In her hand she was holding the piece of paper with my name and phone number on it. She walked up to a man who was standing by the door to the room where the party was being held. When she handed him the note, he glanced suspiciously in my direction. I don't like people in suits and ties. At work, we all wear sweaters and tracksuits. All the people at work have friendly smiling faces, like porpoises. Soon there'll be no porpoises left in Omura Bay, they say.

"I got it to him," she said with a grin when she came back. The smell of roses wafted up from the pleat in her skirt.

"What else do you remember about Mr. Kutani?"

"On December 29, 1972, we ate some sweet bean porridge with sticky rice together. That was after the neighborhood *mochi* party, where we pounded the rice with mallets . . ."

"I'm amazed how well you can remember the dates. That's more than thirty years ago."

"It was my job to tear the date off the calendar pad every day. I always remember numbers. Even the numbers on cars."

"How do you remember them?"

"I don't really know. My mother says God flicks through a calendar in my brain till it gets to the right date, but . . . When I think of something that happened a long time ago, the date just pops into my head. Probably there's something weird about my brain."

"It's not weird, it's a real talent. To be able to remember the exact dates of everything like that . . . I keep getting more forgetful all the time."

She stared off vaguely into the distance again. "It's a special gift from God." She said this with some feeling.

"I don't want any kind of special gift. I'd rather be a normal person—like half of Kyu-chan."

"Do you have any family?"

"Only my mother."

"What about brothers and sisters?"

"No."

"And your father?"

"I never had a father. My mother says the Holy Ghost appeared to her one day."

"Wow! An Annunciation? Maybe you're the Second Coming!"

"I think she was joking. A baby can only be born if the parents have *sex*. I wonder who she did it with, though."

Shirotani-san rolled her eyes and was silent. There was something innocent and childlike about her. She looked more like a porpoise than anyone else I knew. I wanted to marry her, and have *sex* with her, and have three children. I'm sure our kids would be supersmart. We would go to church together as a family and eventually have grandchildren. Then, at long last, when we reached the kingdom of peace and love, we could all just give thanks and praise to God.

"Have you seen Mr. Kutani recently?"

"He gave a talk at our church on December 23, 1995."

"Hmm, that's quite a while ago. Not long after he was elected to the Diet, I think. What did he talk about?"

"I'm not really sure. I think he said he was going to work hard for world peace and get rid of nuclear weapons. He was wearing a suit with a bean-colored scarf around his neck. Like in *The Godfather*."

"Do the people at your church still support him? I asked for an interview with local support groups, but they wouldn't see me."

"They won't speak to anyone from the TV, either. My mother says it can't be true. Kyu-chan is a fine man, she says. She says there must be some kind of misunderstanding."

"But I think that's part of the reason people are so suspicious—because he refuses to say anything. I thought he might take the opportunity to explain himself while he was back in his home city, but apparently not. He may feel this is a purely private matter—but as a politician he owes the public more information."

"Why has he come home this time?"

"He was invited to give a speech by the local business community. It's been scheduled for a while now. Apparently there was some talk about canceling, but thanks to the scandal, the place was packed. That's what happens when you're in the news. Did you get a chance to talk the last time you saw him?"

"We shook hands as he was getting in his car to leave, at the bottom of the slope in front of the church. He said: 'It's been a long time.' And he told me to get in touch if ever I needed his help. That's why I came to see him today."

"But that was nearly ten years ago. Do you think he remembers?"

"Kyu-chan wouldn't tell a lie."

"Is there something wrong? Something you need help with?"

"My mother is dying. She says she can't let go until her mind's at ease about what will happen to me. But I don't know how I'll manage after she's gone. I don't want to go into a home. The people at the association say I should try living in a community house, but Mother kept saying she wanted to discuss things with Kyu-chan first. So I've come in her place."

My mother can't get up on her own anymore. She's hooked up to a ventilator machine, and her shoulders heave when she breathes. Her breath smells bad. She's asleep most of the time. Every now and then, she opens her eyes to look at me, and a sticky goo leaks out of her wrinkly eyes. "Maybe I should take you with me," she says. "Bring you with me to God." She's always crying these days. When I wipe her eyes with a tissue, she says, "You're a good, kind child," and then starts crying again.

I don't think God would allow us to die together. But I know I'll be lost without her. And the thought of living in a home with a bunch of strangers is scary. I've never lived with anyone except my mother.

She scolds and nags me a lot of the time. But I'm sure I'd be lonely on my own. A helper might come and see me sometimes—but no wife. There'd be nobody to talk to at night. I'd be free to drink as much beer as I wanted, but who would wake me up when I fell asleep in my underpants, getting bitten by mosquitoes on my roly-poly tummy?

"But I wonder if he'll have time to help you, though, Adam. He's got his hands full with his own problems. They're going to arrest him tomorrow."

Why did she have to be so mean? I felt my body starting to stiffen again. I might really set hard before too long, stuck like that in silence for millions of years.

"I'm sorry. I didn't want to upset you."

I was beginning to get quite annoyed. Why didn't she notice how I was feeling? It was so mean. I didn't care what other people did—but I didn't want her, of all people, to say nasty things.

"Have you got a job, Adam?"

"I used to work in a pickles factory. Now I fold boxes at the community workshop. Sets of noodles they sell as souvenirs. They put me in charge. I'm a veteran."

"You fold boxes?"

"We fold along the lines, then put them together. I've been doing it for fifteen years now. I can fold a box in five seconds flat, with my eyes closed. I'm an expert."

If only I could show her how good I was at it. It would bowl her over if she saw how quick and neat my technique is. Even our team leader says he can't keep up with me. Anything to do with folding boxes, just leave it to me. I get paid sixty thousand yen as wages—that's six times more than other people. Part of my job is to teach the new people when they join.

"You're a master of your trade, Adam."

It's true. The youngsters look up to me. It's time I got married and settled down.

Her cell phone was ringing again. She frowned and answered the thing impatiently. The ballpoint pen was twirling around her fingers faster than ever now. I could tell that I was in danger of falling completely under her spell if I wasn't careful. I might start stalking her and get arrested. I would end up all alone in a cell, pulling at my winkie and crying myself to sleep.

Why does the pain get worse the deeper you love someone? They said I have the mind of a junior high school student. But I've got the body of a middle-aged man. I'm forty-five now, going thin on top. The thick hair that grows out of my nose is shot through with gray. Even my mother sighs sometimes when she looks at me now. "Your hair used to be so soft and fluffy," she says. "Like cotton candy. How did you grow up into such a scruffy old man?"

I deliberately looked away from the pen spinning around her fingertips. There's no place in my life for romance. It's not right for me to love anyone.

I looked at the points of twinkling light on the chandeliers. They were so pretty. If they put up a big crucifix on the second-floor level, the whole lobby would be like a church. I felt like praying. I wanted to ask Him to show me a woman's body. Lord, please let me have *sex*, I wanted to say. But you're not allowed to pray for things like that.

I did once—on Sunday, July 8, 1996. During Mass, I started to have dirty thoughts that made me blush to my collar. When we got home, my mother wouldn't stop nagging me till I told her what I'd been praying for. After I finally confessed the truth, she beat me hard with a ladle.

"How *could* you? How *could* you think such filthy thoughts? After our ancestors went to the stake with pure thoughts and prayers on their lips!" She was furious and said I had to learn to pray for more appropriate things. I wasn't allowed any supper for a week. "I'm not eating either," she said. "We'll go and pray for forgiveness instead." So we prayed together every evening, apologizing to God for what I'd done.

"Give us the strength to stand firm in the face of trials and temptations. Amen." Now *that* is a suitable prayer, she said. She told me I had a dirty mind. She said I should scoop my brains out of my head and wash them clean with cold water. When I asked her how I was supposed to do that, she started beating me again with the ladle.

The lobby was full of people talking on their phones. More people had arrived with big black cameras over their shoulders. Some of them were sitting down working with small computers balanced on their knees.

I spaced out for a while and lost track of time. Suddenly the door to the room where Kyu-chan was having his reception swung open, and the corridor was humming with activity.

"Looks like they've finished," Shirotani-san said. She picked up her camera. "Look after my bag for me, will you?" she said, tossing it down on the sofa and hurrying off toward the reception room without waiting for a reply.

The big bag with its wide bottom toppled over. The silver lid of a computer poked out, along with something else made of soft pink stuff. I caught the sweet-sour scent of a woman. Maybe it was her panties. Bad thoughts welled up inside me. I considered stuffing them in my pocket and running away.

If she wouldn't marry me, at least I could carry her smell around with me. I would bury my face in her panties and inhale her woman's smell to my heart's content. And then cry lonely tears. My mother used to say God is always watching when you're thinking bad thoughts. Maybe I'll be punished for them one day.

Camera bulbs flashed white-and-blue as a wall of people with Kyu-chan at its center moved quickly toward the elevator. Shirotani-san returned to where I was sitting. "They're going to hold a press conference. In the Diamond Room, on the second floor." She pushed the computer back inside the bag and put the pink thing into her coat pocket. It wasn't her panties at all, but a handkerchief.

"Thanks," she said. "It doesn't look like I'll need to wait here with you anymore. Maybe we'll meet again someday. Bye." She slung the bag over her shoulder and ran up the escalator. The bottom of her skirt rose up as she ran, exposing her long white legs all the way to her thighs.

My mind was blank with shock, and I hurried up the escalator after her. People were spilling into the room at the end of the corridor. There were lights everywhere. The whole area glowed with a holy light. It was as though Jesus Himself were sitting in glory there. Narrowing my eyes, I edged forward with my hands held in front of me, but a man blocked my way and refused to let me inside. "You're not Press," he said.

"Excuse me, is this the Diamond Room?" I asked a young man holding a camera the size of a bazooka. "Yeah, I think so," he said before disappearing inside with a woman in jeans carrying a long cable. The door shut behind them.

Shirotani-san was somewhere in that bright-lit room, no doubt about it. It didn't matter if they wouldn't let me in. I was bound to find her eventually if I kept a close eye on the door. There was a pay phone near the entrance, and I decided to wait there for her to come out. I didn't mind waiting for hours if I had to.

I had been there ten minutes or so when several men suddenly ran out shouting, "He's resigned! He's resigned!" Then the doors swung open, and a crowd of people surged out.

I looked around desperately for Shirotani-san, but I couldn't see her anywhere. I kept bumping into people, bouncing around like something in a pinball machine. I was swept out into the middle of the corridor, only to find Kyu-chan standing there in front of me in a smart suit, a look of surprise on his face.

He looked as though he had something he wanted to say, but he was swallowed up again into the crowd of journalists before he could speak. In the babble around me, I kept hearing the word "resignation." They were ganging up on him, nagging at him to give a "full account."

Hit him on the right cheek, and he would offer you the left. Kyu-chan hadn't changed. He always was the kind of person who would take a beating in silence. He took what was coming to him patiently, without tears. The world is a cruel place. Things would be a lot happier if more people would just turn to stone.

I waited until there was no one left in the corridor or the Diamond Room. I still hadn't found Shirotani-san, so I took the escalator back down to the lobby. I still thought I would bump into her again if I waited there. "Please let me find her," I prayed to the bright light of the chandeliers.

Every now and then, people walked past. I must have been looking at them oddly, because someone from reception came over and made some comment. I went stiff, and this time I was really determined. This time I really *will* turn to stone, I thought. I'm not budging till I see her again. But even stony me still gets hungry. I could hear my tummy rumbling loudly for attention.

How much time passed after that, I couldn't say. I might have been as old as the hills. I watched the faithful pass by in procession, their hands bound with rope. I saw the weeping, wailing children who were burned alive when the atom bomb fell and they turned to stone. I watched them quietly out of the corner of my eye.

My watch said 9:21. It's a radio watch, the kind that never loses a second. And it's solar powered, so it will keep going forever. Life was much easier after my mother bought it for me. The one I had before was always losing time. Just a few seconds here and there, but whenever it happened, I felt I was trapped in a different time zone, losing a bit of weight with each second lost until I disappeared completely. It made me feel nervous the whole time.

I yawned and a tear dribbled from the corner of my eye. Then my phone rang. Probably Mother, wondering where I was. But the number on the screen wasn't hers; it wasn't the hospital number either. Maybe it was Shirotani-san. My stony heart started pounding in my chest, and I let out a loud "Yeeaah!" The person at the reception desk gave me a funny look.

"Hello. Is that Adam's phone?" A man's voice. Too bad.

"Kyu-chan?"

"Hello. I thought it must be you, Shu-chan."

I was slightly disappointed that it wasn't her. But it was Kyu-chan I had come to see. Besides, I thought maybe he would be able to tell me something about her. My mind was really firing today. I felt quite proud of myself.

"Where are you now, Shu-chan?"

"At the hotel."

"You're not still in the lobby?"

"I am."

"Waiting for me?"

"Yes."

"Come up to my room. I'll send my secretary. The lobby on the first floor, right?"

Soon afterward, the elevator doors opened and a young man in a suit came over to where I was standing.

"Mr. Yamamori?" he asked me.

"The name's Adam," I said.

"Mr. Kutani is waiting. If you'd like to come with me."

The man was as silent as a monk, and even after we got out of the elevator, he said nothing as he led me to Kyu-chan's room and knocked on the door. Kyu-chan opened it and waved us inside. He looked tired and wasn't wearing a tie anymore.

It was a beautiful room, with huge windows at the front and side. I once stayed in a fancy hotel in Oita for the annual meeting of our Youth Division, on the night of March 7, 2001. This room, though, was even bigger and more spick-and-span than the one we had then. But it was too big for one person.

It felt silent and empty. It was the kind of room where a person might go to Confession.

"You've had a lot of calls, sir, asking you to get in touch," his secretary said from by the door.

"I don't want to talk to anyone else apart from my friend here this evening. I'm sorry, but I'm afraid you'll have to refuse all calls."

"Things have been crazy since the story broke on the evening news."

"I phoned the secretary-general earlier this evening to let him know. I left a message for the head of the support group as well. I'm sure everyone will be relieved to get it over with."

"But people are desperate to talk to you. What do you want me to say?"

"Tell them I'll see them when I get back to Tokyo tomorrow. To be honest, I'm not sure there'll be time for this kind of thing anymore."

"Are you sure you're doing the right thing?"

"What else can I do? I'm sorry to let everyone down, but I don't have any choice. So for tonight, no more messages please. You should try to get some rest."

"I don't think there's much chance of that." The secretary then snapped to attention and gave a formal bow. "I want you to know how much I appreciate everything you've done, sir," he said. He sounded as if he were trying not to cry. Then he turned and left the room. As soon as he was gone, Kyu-chan's expression relaxed, and he held out his hand to me. His sleeves were rolled up to his elbows.

"Good to see you again. It's been a long time. I knew it was you when I saw you in the lobby."

"So you did recognize me."

"How could I miss a tie like that? It looks like a red bandanna. It suits you."

"My mother gave me a hard time about it. She says my taste is terrible."

"How is she?"

Suddenly *I* wanted to cry. "She's dying," I said quietly.

"Is it an illness?"

"Her lungs are weak. She's hooked up to an oxygen machine in the hospital, and she wheezes when she breathes. Her eyes are gummed up. She's old now and getting weaker all the time. Her face looks like a chicken."

"I'm very sorry to hear that. Unfortunately, I won't be able visit her on this trip. Please give her my best wishes when you see her."

"She told me I had to remember to say thank you when I saw you. So: thank you very much."

"What for?"

"For all you did for us."

"But that must be thirty years ago now."

Everything in the room was bright and shiny. It was like being in a showcase. I walked over to the window by the big sofa. When I parted the lace curtains, I could just about make out the flickering lights of the docks across the dark sea.

"The view's better on this side," he said. "More neon." I went over and looked out the other window. The main road ran directly in front of the hotel; there were neon lights blazing everywhere.

"Look—over there you can see the spire of the Nakamachi church."

Straining my eyes, I could just about see the white cross of the church in the darkness. It's a beautiful building. It looks like it's made out of cream.

"I had a bit of time to myself after I checked in this afternoon, so I stood here looking out at that cross on top of the steeple. Pure white against the blue sky . . . I don't get to church much in Tokyo."

"I haven't been going either since my mother went into the hospital."

"It's important to find time to talk to God."

"Do you talk to Him, Kyu-chan? I try my best. But He never talks back."

"Most of the time, that's how it is. God doesn't answer. For hundreds of years, the faithful here must have whispered the same questions and answered them themselves. Forgotten by the Church, in hiding, in secret . . . It's the same for me, too, most of the time. But I think, just once, something special occurred."

"Really?"

"Do you remember in junior high when the two bullies beat me up that day?"

"Saeki and Kanazawa? December 11, 1972."

"That's right. Blood was pouring out of my nose, and I hardly knew where I was. And still I let them hit me."

"You were my savior that day, Kyu-chan."

"My head felt woozy from the first blow. I was scared, and I wanted to run away. But my feet seemed to have a mind of their own. Without knowing why, there I was standing bravely in front of them. Go on, hit me. Hit me all you like, you jerks . . . For a moment, I felt a voice from outside whispering in my heart. I often think maybe it was the voice of God I heard that day."

He closed his eyes and seemed to be thinking back on what had happened. I always knew he had a deep faith.

"Maybe that's what we'll hear in our hearts at the Last Judgment . . . Anyway, I was thinking about these things earlier as I looked out at the cross on the church, when suddenly I heard a voice say: enough. It was just me talking to myself, of course—but it reminded me of that time in school. It made up my mind."

I couldn't really follow what he was saying, and I wasn't sure how to respond. Instead, my tummy started rumbling.

"What did you do about dinner?"

"I haven't eaten yet."

"You mean you waited all that time without eating anything?"

"Yes."

He sighed. "I'm sorry," he said, patting me on the back. When we were at school, he used to pat me like that whenever I was teased and went stiff. His hand felt as warm as ever. He could make even stone feel soft with his hands. I was certain that everything the television and newspapers were saying was just lies. Kyu-chan was one of the good guys, just as he always had been.

"There are some sandwiches left if you like. I had some cold noodles at the party, but I was still hungry so I ordered room service. There's coffee, too."

On a table next to the bed was a plate covered with a silver lid shaped like an egg cut in half. Kyu-chan sat me down in a chair and lifted the lid. Underneath was an assortment of pork cutlet, egg, and vegetable sandwiches.

"I'm hungry. You sure you don't mind?"

"Help yourself. Finish it off. I'll order some more later."

"In that case, I'll have the lot. Amen."

After this quick prayer, I reached out for the pork sandwich. Kyu-chan smiled and poured some coffee. When I bit into it, the juice oozed out from between the batter and the meat and soaked into the bread. It was enough to satisfy even a picky eater like me.

"Just before the last election," I told him, "I bought twenty *katsu* sandwiches at the convenience store and handed them around to everyone in the place I work at. They say *katsu* sandwiches are good luck, since it sounds like the word for 'winning.'"

"Why did you do that?"

"I asked everyone to vote for you. But they said it wasn't fair to ask for favors without giving anything in return. Then after I produced the sandwiches, they all voted for you."

"Oh dear. I shouldn't be hearing this," he said with a laugh, holding his hand to his head in embarrassment. "That's a resigning offense in itself."

"Is it true they're going to arrest you?"

"There'll be a hearing at the public prosecutors when I get back to Tokyo tomorrow. Word came through before I got on the plane this morning. Probably they'll arrest me as soon as the hearing is over."

"And then will you have to go to prison?"

"Probably."

"What did you do?"

He reached down and scratched his ankle. With his socks off, he had a poor man's feet. His socks were over on the bed where he'd tossed them. With my doglike sense of smell, I could pick up the sour whiff of his feet.

"I did something wrong. I'm prepared to take full responsibility for what I did."

"Is it true you gave your girlfriend a job?"

He looked uncomfortable for a moment. "I can't lie to you, can I, Shu-chan?" he said in a whisper. I thought he might start crying. "I'll tell you what happened, if you don't mind listening." I nodded, then polished off the second pork sandwich and moved on to the egg.

"It started a while back, just after I was elected. A woman came to see me. The person who introduced her said she had some problems she wanted to discuss."

"Everyone comes to you with their problems, Kyu-chan."

"She was in her early thirties then. She had a baby who was severely handicapped, and her husband's family had been very cold toward her since the baby was born. They'd basically forced her to separate from her husband. The way they treated her was awful. She was struggling to get by—she couldn't very well go to work with a newborn baby in her arms. But she was determined to raise her child on her own. And that's when she came to ask for my help in finding a job."

Kyu-chan *is* one of the good guys. If he hears that someone's in trouble, he won't rest till he's done something to help.

"Was she pretty?"

"I suppose so, yes."

"Well, you *had* to do something to help, then."

He laughed. "A politician has to help people who come to him with their problems, Shu-chan—whether they're attractive young women or not! But it wasn't that simple. She had no real prospects, and there were various factors that made it difficult for her to find a job. She's a very proud person and didn't want to depend on benefits, so she was struggling to get by. I didn't know what to do. It was another member of the Diet—someone who'd been there much longer than I had—who advised me to give the woman a job as my secretary for a while. So I decided to pay her a salary for three months, just until she found another job. It was a routine thing at the time. Lots of other members were doing the same thing. I didn't really give it much thought. I began to realize what I'd done a few years ago, when several people were arrested on similar charges. I wanted to come clean, but people always stopped me."

"Is she the one they say was your mistress?"

"Mistress? There was a relationship for a while. But it lasted less than two months."

"Did you have *sex* with her?"

Kyu-chan leaned his head to one side, looking a bit like a praying mantis. "You don't beat about the bush, do you, Shu-chan? But you can understand—you're a romantic, too. You know what it's like when two people's hearts connect—as if you're sinking into each other."

"I wouldn't know," I said. "I'm not a big hit with the girls like you."

I was starting to feel a bit resentful. I imagined the woman he was with was Shirotani-san, and it gave me a sharp pain inside. I banged myself on the head, just once, with my hand.

"It started not long after I hired her as my secretary. I had a meeting of some kind, and after it finished, I was talking to her in the lobby. She was feeling down about things, left alone to look after a child who couldn't even feed itself; forced into a divorce without alimony or any kind of support. It was a miserable story. I remember her asking, Is it really such a crime to give birth to a handicapped child? I felt really sorry for her, and before I knew what I was doing, I was stroking her on the back and praying, asking God to have mercy on her."

"You always used to pat people on the back when you felt sorry for them."

"It happened very naturally. Suddenly, I had my arms around her. Her back was so tense it felt as though she had a pair of wings tucked away there. I could sense something welling up inside her. I think we both felt something. It's at moments like that that two hearts can really respond to each other. We took a hotel room and held each other as if nothing else in the world mattered. I felt as if I'd caught hold of an angel that had fallen to earth. You know what I mean when I say we embraced?"

"It means you had *sex*."

He went red. I suppose he was embarrassed.

"For two months, I thought of nothing but the next time I could see her. She was constantly on my mind. I must have been in love."

"But you were married, Kyu-chan."

He hung his head and sighed. He made me think of someone condemned to be nailed to the cross or burned at the stake.

"I feel terrible for my wife and children. We have two daughters—one in high school, one in junior high. They haven't spoken to me for two months now. At home, they turn and look the other way whenever we meet. They look so upset and depressed the whole time. I'm sure they're suffering more from all this than I am. The media can be so unforgiving. I don't mind them attacking me, but not my family . . ."

"Does this mean you've given up on world peace and banning nuclear weapons?"

I was getting upset, too. I couldn't stop thinking of Shirotani-san as his mistress. It was because people like Kyu-chan took two women for himself that I was left with none at all.

"For those two months, I hardly thought of anything else," he admitted. He didn't look very happy about it.

"As long as I had her in my arms, nothing else mattered. Even if war had broken out and nuclear bombs were exploding all over the world, I probably wouldn't have cared. I had forgotten everything—politics, faith, God. I thought of her all the time. There was no room for anything else. She was like a sunburst—so bright I was blinded to everything else. Have you ever been in love like that, Shu-chan?"

On December 20, 1989, an older guy from work took me to a sex place in Nakasu where I was allowed to touch a woman down there. There was a ball on the ceiling they called a "mirror ball." It kept turning round and round like a frozen moon, throwing a dim light. It was like being at the bottom of the sea. I paid ten thousand yen for the thirty-minute service, and a woman came and plopped herself down in my lap. She was wearing a short skirt as if she was on her way to play tennis, with no panties over her silky smooth bottom.

Between her legs was what looked like a hairy sea cucumber. It was too dark for me to see clearly what was going on down there. All I knew was that it was something fuzzy and damp. Her fingernails smelled like vanilla ice cream.

I couldn't make out her face very well. "My name's Miyo," she said. She didn't treat me like an idiot at all. She unzipped my pants and put her hand on me. "Who's a big boy, then?" she said, stroking my winkie and balls with her fingers. So this is what it's like to have *sex*, I thought, raising my eyes to God in thanks. "Where do I stick it in?" I asked, but she just shook her head. "That's not allowed," she said.

But I didn't really mind. It felt nice cuddling in the dark, watching the mirror ball go round and round. But when my thirty minutes were up, Miyo went off to her next customer and I was left alone.

I stood outside under a cheap plastic umbrella and waited for her to come out. "Come on, let's go. It's freezing," the guy with me started grumbling. Eventually he pushed off, too. I remember there were two cars parked in the alley outside the club. Their registration numbers were 7670 and 8231. In a restaurant window nearby was the number 1970.

Late in the night, the rain turned to sleet. I kept count as it fell on my umbrella, so I would know how much had fallen. The numbers got bigger and bigger until they started to spill out of my head.

This was in the days when my watch was always off by a few minutes, and I felt I was trapped in a separate time zone from Miyo. I began to worry that I might never see her again. It was nearly morning when she finally came out. She was with a scary-looking man in a white suit with sharp, pointy lapels. I plucked up my courage and called out to her: "Hey, can we do it some more?"

She looked over at me. "Have you really been waiting out here all this time?" she said. "In the cold? I'm sorry. It's not that I don't like you—I quite like nice and simple people. But I can't play with you if you don't pay for it. It's my job." Then the man in the white suit put her in a car, and they drove off. She turned around to look at me several times as they disappeared.

I thought of nothing else for the next six months. I saved and saved, till eventually I had fifty thousand yen. I even gave up *pachinko*. But when I went back to Nakasu again that summer, Miyo had already left the club, and I had no way of finding out where she'd gone. The other people who worked there were suspicious and refused to give me her address or phone number. In the end, they grabbed me and threw me out of the place. Miyo, woman number 729 in my life, had vanished. I kept on looking for another six months. That was real, grown-up love, which I'll never forget for as long as I live.

"Shirotani-san is number 927."

"Shirotani-san?"

"Yeah. You must know her. She writes for a newspaper. Long hair, carries a big bag, always twirling a pen around her fingers."

"Never heard of her."

"No? I met her while I was waiting in the lobby and fell in love with her right away."

"Still the same old Shu-chan. You always were a romantic. All it took was for someone to say hello, and you were head over heels."

Not one of the 926 women I've been in love with has ever returned my feelings. Shirotani-san was number 927.

"I wonder what paper she works for," I said.

"She must be new. I don't recognize the name."

"You and I have known each other for a long time, right?—ever since we were kids. So I don't have to hide anything from you. I really want to have *sex* with her. I can't help thinking about it. I want to have children who'll live on after I'm gone. Once, a long time ago, I said a dirty prayer to God and made my mother really angry. But I can't help it—I really want to have *sex* at least once. Does that make me a bad person? Will God punish me for being a dirty old man?"

Kyu-chan smiled and shook his head.

"I don't think that's a sin. I don't think it's even anything bad. If it were, then I'm deep in sin, too. Every man on earth would be a sinner. And probably all the women too. Even love itself would be a sin. It would mean that God made a mistake when he created Eve out of Adam's rib. But . . ."

"What?"

"You need to consider the other person's feelings."

"I know. Otherwise they can arrest you for stalking. Maybe we could start as friends?"

"Why are you asking me? I don't even know her."

"But you could look her up."

"Look her up?"

"You're a member of the Diet. You could ask your secretary to find out, if you wanted to."

He heaved a sigh and flopped back in his chair. I could see his bare feet poking out from the bottom of his trousers. Bits of hair sprouted from his shins.

"I've resigned. I made an announcement at the press conference just now. I'm not a Diet member anymore."

He looked a bit weepy. Maybe he was just tired. But I had no choice. There was no one else I could turn to.

"My mother is dying. She told me to come and ask you for advice. She said you wouldn't want to see me left on my own. If I got married, she could probably rest easy."

"Listen, Shu-chan. Don't you understand what I've been saying? I can't do anything for you now. I'll probably be arrested tomorrow and locked away. I'm sorry to let your mother down, but there's nothing I can do."

His face was pale and heavy, his eyes sunken like one of those statues on Easter Island.

He must have been tense from all the stress. But my mind was fixed on seeing Shirotani-san again, and that made me blind to how tired and grouchy he was feeling.

"You *have* to take care of me, Kyu-chan. I'm only half what I should be. All the things God should have given to me went to you instead. You took them all for yourself; that's why I'm so stupid. Don't you think you owe it to me to help me out?"

"That's enough, Shu-chan!"

He refused to look at me, covering his face with his hands. I got to my feet and tugged at his arms, trying to pull them away from his face.

“Stop ignoring me. Talk to me properly! I know why you won’t look me in the eye! Shirotani-san was your mistress, and now you’re feeling guilty!”

I tugged at his shirtsleeves. “Talk to me, Kyu-chan! Talk to me!”

“Stop it!” he said. He was really getting angry now.

“Why are you trying to duck out of it?”

At this, he suddenly pushed my hands away from his shirt. He picked up the plate of sandwiches and banged it down hard on the table like a monkey in the zoo. The two vegetable sandwiches that had been left there went flying through the air. I felt something cold hit me on my cheek. A wet tomato seed.

He looked at me with a cold glint in his eyes. Suddenly, I understood. He wasn’t one of the good guys anymore. He wasn’t someone who managed to be weak and strong at the same time. He had a look in his eyes just like those bullies, Saeki and Kanazawa.

“Go home, Shu-chan. I want to be alone tonight. Go on, go home. I’m sick of being criticized. Why can’t people take care of their own problems? It’s not a politician’s job to be a nanny to the whole world.”

I felt a wave of anger wash over me as I got to my feet. Kyu-chan wasn’t my old childhood friend anymore. This is what happens when two people grow up: they’re not children any longer—and not friends either.

“Go on, go home. Why should I have to take shit from you, of all people?” He muttered something under his breath. As I touched my hand to the doorknob, I heard him suddenly shout out from behind me: “Wait!” I shuddered with fright.

He strode over to the door, his spindly ankles and bare feet sticking out from his trousers. He took a piece of paper from his shirt pocket and put it into the breast pocket of my jacket.

“I’m sorry I kept you so long. It’s late. Use this ticket for a taxi home.”

Nervously, I opened the door without a word.

“Good night.”

I heard his voice behind me and then the sound of the door clicking shut.

I had turned to stone. I couldn’t even move my head to look behind me. By the time I got into the elevator, I could feel myself getting heavier. It was as if I was sinking fast to the bottom of the sea or a lake. I had no one left to depend on now except Shirotani-san. What would I do if she vanished too, just like

Miyo? What would happen to me when my mother died and I was completely on my own?

I waited for her in the first floor lobby, with its high ceiling like a cathedral and its glittering chandeliers. I didn't know where she was, but somehow I felt I would see her again if I waited here. I thought of the pure white figure of Christ on the altar of the Urakami church and pictured it on the wall of the lobby under the high ceiling. It was a long time since I'd said any prayers before a crucifix.

I yawned. It was 10:46. There was still no sign of Shirotani-san, and the man behind the desk was giving me funny looks. I decided to call it a day. But then, just as I was leaving the hotel, I suddenly caught a glimpse of her in the distance, going up the steps to the elevated walkway in front of the station. She had that bag slung across her shoulders as she took the steps two at a time. She was wearing a white coat. There was no doubt about it: it was her.

I took off after her as quickly as my tubby body would go. In spite of the cold, I broke into a sweat almost immediately. Soon I was gasping for breath, but I didn't give up. I kept on running as fast as I could, desperate to catch up. She went along the walkway and headed down the steps to the streetcar stop.

There was the screech of iron wheels and a gust of air at my shoulder as a tram came to a halt. The automatic doors opened. As she stepped inside, I grabbed her by the wrist and called out her name. But the face I saw when she wheeled around looked nothing like Shirotani-san. It was long, like a cucumber, or one of those pug-faced festival masks. I let go of her hand with a gasp, and she glared at me. The doors closed, and the tram began to move. She kept her eyes fixed on me as it pulled away.

It turned out to be the last tram of the night. I heaved myself back up the stairs to the station and got into a taxi.

"Uramon," I said. "Back of the university."

I felt exhausted. I leaned back in the seat and stretched. Neon signs streaked past outside. They looked so pretty. I took off my shoes and turned right around to look out of the rear window. Shirotani-san had vanished into the city. Tomorrow she would get on a plane and fly back to Tokyo—a whole city of dazzling light. I had no idea how I would look for her there.

"Listen, have you got the money to pay for this?" the driver asked suddenly.

He must have been watching me in his rearview mirror. My mother had told me off for sitting like that in taxis: "Sit properly; you're not a child anymore." I'd forgotten.

"D'you have any money?" he asked again.

I took the ticket that Kyu-chan had stuck in my breast pocket and plunked it down on the little tray next to the driver's seat. "All right," he said. I didn't bother to reply.

I could tell he was still keeping an eye on me in his mirror. People's eyes can stab like thorns. Sometimes the world feels like a hellhole of strangers' eyes. My mother and I have crawled our way through it together all these years. On June 12, 1968, she got into a fight on the train with two high school students who were looking at me with smirks on their faces. When they refused to apologize, she laid into them with her umbrella, but they shrugged it off and laughed in her face, which was streaming with tears. "Hey! So the dummy's mom is a dummy too!"

She was so angry that I felt frightened when we got off the train. I knew I was different from other children. "I'm sorry for being what they called me," I told her. I wanted to make her feel better. She put her arms around me as we stood in the middle of the road and squeezed me so tight I thought my backbone was going to break. "There's nothing wrong with you, Shu," she said. "You're my sweet, precious Adam, a gift from God." And she started sobbing again.

We were locked in a bear hug like two wrestlers. I had to lean back and gasp for breath. But my mother's a Mary, and I knew she would always look after me just like the Holy Mother. She would never tease me. The thought made me happy. And that's the way it has been—she really has taken care of me, for more than forty years now. Of course, there have been times when she's shouted and scolded and smacked me. But I knew I was safe as long as I was with my Mary.

And now she was all shriveled and old, with oxygen tubes up her nose and crusty yellow goop in her eyes. The flame of her life has almost burned itself out. And her baby boy, once soft and white like cotton candy, was a middle-aged man with thinning hair and a flabby belly and a face red from gulping down beer like a fish. Who would want to take care of a shabby old thing like me when she was gone? Please God, I want a wife. I want a family. Where had Shirotani-san disappeared to?

"Here you are: Uramon."

The driver obviously wanted to get rid of me. He had opened the automatic door and was scowling from the rearview mirror. Really, I'd wanted him to pull over on the other side of the road, but I decided to say nothing. I got out. The temperature had dropped, and without a coat I felt quite cold.

I was so worked up now that I started beating myself about the head as I walked along the bank of the Urakami River. Both my hands and my head were hurting. But my hands were beyond my control. I begged them to be friendly, but they wouldn't listen and kept on pummeling me. Bang, bang, bang.

Why was the night so dark? The only light came from the occasional bits of brightness that escaped from the windows of apartment buildings along the river.

The wind whistled as it blew; otherwise, I could hear and see almost nothing. There was no one around. I thought of home. It would be just as cold and dark there. My body started to feel heavier again. I came to a wide dry stretch by a bend in the river. I caught a faint sound coming from somewhere. My hands stopped hitting me. It was a delicate sound like the chirping of a bell cricket. But it couldn't be a cricket at this time of year. I looked around me. The only things I could make out were the large stones that had been washed onto the side of the river.

I heard the voices of men and women crying out.

Water, someone give me water! I'm burning! Somebody, please, water!

The heat, the heat! Kill me quick! Let me die and go to God! Run me through with your spear!

I'm always muttering to myself, but these weren't my own words I was hearing. I was not the one screaming and weeping and crying out in pain. These were the voices of the stones. The stones were crying.

Terrified, I held my breath and ran straight across the dry riverbed as fast as I could.

I came out onto a brightly lit road and started up the hill toward the place with the cross. Not a single car passed. There was no one else out on the streets at this hour. My heart was still pounding, and I could feel myself getting heavier and heavier with every step I took.

I climbed the footpath lined with Chinese tallows and streetlamps until I emerged at the park in front of the Motohara intersection. I slumped down on a bench. The cold seeped into my backside, but there was no way I could stand up again. My body was too heavy. A small bulldozer stood abandoned in a corner of the park, with its clawlike shovel raised in the air.

Maybe I'll turn to stone here too, I thought. Maybe I'll become like those people by the riverside, left to weep and cry for tens, hundreds, thousands of years. Why has God abandoned them? Why doesn't He do anything to help? Maybe God isn't there anymore. Maybe He's not anywhere. Maybe Heaven is empty, with no one at home.

Maybe they all knew it. My mother, the priest, even the pope in Rome. Maybe the faithful everywhere knew that Heaven was empty, but they kept praying anyway. But what would that mean? It was all too hard for a dummy like me to figure out.

Can you hear me, God? Are you out there somewhere? Don't leave me all alone. Even if I turn to stone, I still want a family. I want a wife. I want children. I don't want to go back to an empty house. The tips of my toes get cold when I sleep alone. At night, even the stones on the riverbank long to be warmed by the touch of someone's skin.

Please Lord, let me have *sex* . . .

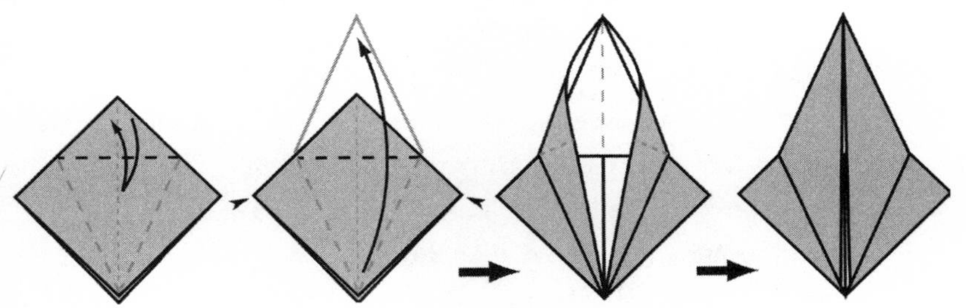

INSECTS

The bright green insect comes crawling up my bloodstained leg, its square jaws munching at the skin that flaps like a leaf from my calf. It turns its long narrow face toward me and examines me with its expressionless compound eyes. "Are you still alive?" it asks. I wake up screaming.

From the silence around me, I realize it must still be the middle of the night. I want to throw myself into somebody's arms. I shut my eyes but it's no use—I'm awake. A surge of images from the past comes back to life, vivid and unstoppable.

What a miserable business it is, getting old!

"Are you still alive?" Sixty years have passed since I was asked that question. At the time, I had no idea who was talking. I couldn't even tell whether the voice was a man's or a woman's. It sounded more like the trilling of a cricket, the buzzing of a fly, or one of the other noises made by the creatures that crawl upon the earth. I can still hear it calling to me, even now: "Are you still alive?" There's no sense of desperation or panic in the question. It isn't saying, "Stay alive! Don't die!" The tone is more like someone asking, "Are you still awake?" There's something dopey and amiable about it.

I had just paused to rest after crawling out of the rubble on my hands and knees when I saw the cricket flitting, apparently unscathed, among the ruins. It must have been carried here by the blast of the explosion. This must be the thing that was speaking to me, I thought: a crackbrained thought that would never have occurred to me normally. I think I may even have replied to it. "Yes, thanks, I'm still alive."

After that, I lost consciousness again. I have no idea how much time passed. My next memory is of being picked up in someone's arms and then moving as if swept downstream, past the brick walls that had escaped destruction.

I don't recall much else about that day. One thing I do remember is ants—swarms of black ants scurrying back and forth between pools of blood scattered among the rubble and glass. It occurred to me that it was this great army of ants that had picked me off the ground and was carrying me along.

I saw a body that had split open at the abdomen. I didn't know who it was. I was too scared to look at the face. Gooey white intestines spilled out like noodles. A knot of what might have been a tapeworm squirmed around the open wound.

I was fifteen years old and training to be a nurse. Trembling, I saw with my own eyes the reality that insects are everywhere around us: in the trees and bushes, under the eaves of houses, in the earth beneath our feet—and even inside our bodies.

All around me were the faces of people crushed in the rubble. But my first emotion wasn't exactly sadness. The human world was over, I thought, and the world of insects was about to take its place.

It was the arrival of another postcard from Reiko that had made me dream of the green insect. I reached out and felt for the light switch by the pillow. The sleeve of my nightgown fell back to my shoulder, and a whiff of body odor rose from my armpit. I remembered the faint smell of mildew my grandmother used to give off long ago.

If I rub at the back of my hand, I can feel a hard strand of narrow sinewy bone. The skeleton is beginning to emerge from beneath my skin, and the blotches and blemishes are spreading. I am an old woman now, and I don't have much time left. But death, I feel, is still some distance away. My periods came to an end long ago, but a warm-blooded woman still lurks inside this decrepit body, threatening to come crawling to the surface.

I switched on the light and picked up Reiko's postcard from the tatami where I had left it the night before.

Dear Michiko,

I hope this finds you well. Last month I spent another enjoyable week at the hot spring in Kannawa. It's been fifteen years since I moved here, and I know a lot of the people at the resort by now. We sit and soak for hours, chatting away and quite forgetting the time.

There's nothing quite like a long refreshing soak on a hot day—and that first sip of beer after a long bath! It's heaven when the evening sun glints on the surface of the water.

Why don't you come out and stay? We could have a good soak together and talk about the past. It's fifteen years now since he died, and there aren't many friends left with whom I can share memories of the good old times. Maybe you could tell me about a side of him I never knew?

Best wishes,
Reiko

What a peaceful old age she's having! How can she be so relaxed and cheerful?

Anger welled up inside me. I poured some water from the jug and gulped it down, still lying on my stomach. The timer had switched off the air conditioner, and the house felt hot and humid. The blood had rushed to my head. I threw the thin blanket off the futon and sat up in bed. "Leave me alone!" I shouted, brushing my gray hair from my cheeks with my fingers.

Things are not over between him and me. There is such a thing as never-ending love. Even fifteen years after his death, the longing for him still burns inside me. Most of the time it's a small flickering light, like the dying embers in the ruins of a burned-out city. But sometimes, late at night, it still bursts into flame and scorches my heart.

Tell me, Holy Mother: why was I the only one who didn't die that day, buried under the rubble? Of the five trainee nurses in the hospital, why was I the only one to survive? Why did my parents and my four brothers and sisters have to die? Did no one ask them the same question I was asked: "Are you still alive?" If only a cricket or an ant or a tapeworm had been on hand to speak to them, maybe they, too, would have made it out from under the debris.

I heard the low whine of a mosquito by my ear, drawn by the sweat that coated my skin. Although I'll brush them off if they're buzzing about my cheek, I can't bring myself to swat them or kill them with coils.

Every living thing on this earth—however insignificant—has had to struggle to survive. I find it moving, to think of all they've endured to get this far. Sometimes I even feel like saying a little prayer for them, though it's unlikely Our Lady or Jesus would care much about a lowly mosquito.

I was wide awake now, with a dull headache somewhere deep inside my skull. I turned on the air-conditioning and sat with my hands in my lap and my eyes closed, arching my back like a cat and letting the cool air blow into my face. It was no good—sleep was out of the question. I got up and went to sit in front of my little altar to the Virgin Mary.

No light came in through the curtains. Morning was still some time off. I struck a match and lit the two large candles on the altar.

I love the soft light of the candles, warmer than a lightbulb but not as bright as sunlight. It's a mellow kind of light—like a small beacon between this world and the next. In candlelight, sharp edges are soothed, softened. Mary's round cheeks and the veil of blue fabric that covered her hair stood out in the subtle light.

Our Father, who art in Heaven . . . calm this anger in my heart! Take away the jealous thoughts that make me hate Reiko.

I put my hands together and prayed. I felt the darkness wash over me—the same darkness in which our ancestors spent their lives for so many generations. It brought me a little peace of mind.

Tell me, Holy Mother: Did they struggle like this against hatred and anger when they prayed to you in secret? Did they, too, suffer from the sin of envy?

A chain of prayers joins me to those people. We are linked together like the beads on a rosary. It won't be long now before I take my place on the chain.

I moved my face closer and saw what looked like some lint under Mary's lower eyelid. My eyesight has never really recovered from the operation I had for cataracts. Without my glasses, everything is blurred as if I'm underwater. Most of the time, it doesn't bother me; I have already seen enough of this world. I rarely watch TV and don't read the papers either. Often I don't even use my glasses when I'm at home. But I needed them now.

I took a pair out of the drawer of the simple desk I use as an altar. When I looked again with them on, I could see a mosquito perched quite still under one of Mary's eyes. Despite the slippery surface of the porcelain, it seemed to have no trouble staying put. It was probably the same mosquito I'd heard buzzing in the dark a few minutes earlier. I watched it stretching out its hindmost legs—first the left, then the right—as if trying to shake the numbness out of them. Its belly was red and swollen.

Suddenly, it fell from there onto the white cloth that covered the altar. Maybe it had sucked out too much blood and couldn't support its own weight. Or it had been stunned by the thin smoke from the candles. The mosquito lay on its back for a moment, then kicked its legs and flew off.

I crossed myself and said my prayers to Our Lady. I felt a slight sting and looked down to find a red bump on my right arm. I pressed down on it with a fingernail and made the sign of the cross over it.

If I had remained buried under the debris like Noshita and Kino and all the others, I would have been spared things like this sixty years later: being roused in the middle of the night and battling mosquitoes. But then I would never have met him either. I would never have experienced that moment of sinfulness when I blazed up, briefly but brilliantly, as a woman. Am I glad I survived, or would it have been better to have perished along with everyone else? I honestly can't say.

I remember crawling out of the rubble and losing consciousness. When I came to, I was in a clearing of bamboo that, by some accident of geography, had escaped the heat rays and the blast of the atomic bomb. Green bamboo sighed in the breeze, and a spider with vivid yellow and black stripes waited patiently in an unbroken web. I must have spent two days and nights there.

The wounded lay on their sides in the clearing. Most of them died during the first night. The stench of death was heavy in the air. I lay half-covered by withered bamboo leaves, staring into the blurry bright light.

I felt no sadness. I was exhausted. My body weighed a ton. Everything seemed to fall apart in the summer sunlight. The line between life and death was gone. Apart from lethargy, I felt nothing at all.

On the morning of the second day, I watched a fly crawl across the cheek of the woman lying next to me. It moved across her high cheekbones and temple, rubbing its front legs as though performing some kind of ritual.

A jagged tear ran down the dark blue work trousers she was wearing, but the flesh of her white calf was without a scratch. The woman lay quite still.

Probably dead, I assumed. After a while, the fly got onto her eyelid. Suddenly, there was a flash of movement as she swatted it away. There was still a clear light in her eyes.

I wonder if anyone remembers the flypapers that used to hang over the counters in fish shops. Sometimes they would get so thick with flies they looked like solid black sticks. We may owe our lives to insects, yet we hardly ever stop to consider their little lives at all. I can't help feeling we're unforgivable in some ways.

One time, I saw a fly crawling across the pale bony chest of Jesus in the cathedral. Maybe a fly was there with Him at Golgotha. Maybe it asked Him: "Are you still alive?" And Our Lord opened His blackened eyelids and raised His feeble head to look down at the people gathered at His feet.

Ever since I was a little girl, I've been fascinated by the idea of Noah's Ark. It can't have been just horses and oxen, cats and dogs on board. All kinds of other castaways must have been on the ark, too: fleas and lice sheltering in the coats and manes of the animals, beautiful green grasshoppers crouching among the grass and reeds.

Flies must have laid their eggs in the dung of the cattle, and the seeds of flowers and grasses would have been carried in the mud that caked the animals' hooves. The ark must have been full of life—and dirt, and smells! And all these creatures had a part to play in bringing the world back to life after the waters receded. I read somewhere that it takes hundreds of millions of microbes to support the life of one human being.

Only once have I mentioned my belief in the importance of insects to someone else. To him. Sasaki-san was a devout Christian, from a family of secret Christians who had fled from Sotome to the Goto Islands during the years when the faith was outlawed.

"You're a sweet girl," he said when I told him. "But the thing you're suggesting . . . I don't know: I'm not sure it could really be considered Christian actually."

It was an ambiguous response. He hadn't really agreed or disagreed. After the war, he went back to the Goto Islands for a while but reappeared in Nagasaki soon after. He was working in a printing company while he finished his teacher training. I was in my early twenties then—just one year younger than he was.

The neat arrangement of his features was enough to make you wonder if he had the blood of foreign missionaries in his veins. It may have been this neatness that made it so difficult to bring his face to mind when I tried to remember him later on. In those early days, he struck me as almost too perfect—depersonalized.

I had heard bits and pieces about Sasaki's experience during the war. I knew that he had been with the Special Attack Forces in Chiran and had received his orders for a final mission. But engine trouble grounded his plane, and the war ended with him still waiting for an opportunity to attack.

I asked him once if he had really been ready to be enshrined with all the other war dead at Yasukuni, but he didn't reply. After that, we never spoke again about what had happened.

Maybe it was these experiences that had trimmed the flab from his faith and concentrated his mind on God. I was young and naive and respected him for what he'd gone through. Love was already beginning to stir in my heart. When I first met him, of course, Reiko wasn't yet on the scene.

Sasaki used to carry batches of printed paper from the warehouse to the truck outside. I limped behind him with a stub of pencil, totting up the number of hymnbooks and Bibles and making sure they tallied with what I had on the form in front of me. Again and again we did it, back and forth between the warehouse and the truck. The low-grade pulp we used was beginning to improve in quality around that time. The difference wasn't that obvious if you had only ten or a hundred volumes. But when you were dealing with thousands at once, the batches were quite heavy, and shifting them was serious work. I remember how he used to gulp water from the faucet next to the warehouse during his breaks, dripping with sweat.

Please don't be angry with me, Holy Mother. I'm merely telling you what happened.

I was already starting to feel the ache of physical desire. Never have I been so struck by the sheer attractiveness of a man as I was then. I remember the way the water splashed from his bared gums, the shining drops that ran down his Adam's apple and chin. I longed to throw my arms around him, to embrace the sweat-soaked muscles on his neck as he toweled himself dry around the open collar of his shirt. The bomb had made me ugly, and I had spent most of my later teenage years indoors—but even an unlovely specimen like me wasn't immune to the flood of emotions that comes sweeping over you.

I couldn't help the way my voice rose in pitch whenever I spoke to him. Ozaki was always giving us dirty looks.

Ozaki was the same age as Sasaki, but his face had been shattered by metal fragments in the atomic blast. Far from having a chiseled jawline for water to drip from, in Ozaki's case the neck seemed to start immediately below his lips.

He was a man of very few words, and I can hardly remember the sound of his voice. But I haven't forgotten the things he said. Like me, he lost his parents and all five siblings in the blast. Once in a while, he would talk to me tearfully about what had happened.

"The bones came jumbled together from the kitchen . . . there was no way of telling my parents from my brothers and sisters. I put them all in the same urn. Sometimes, late at night, I hold them in my hands and cry."

Ozaki looked deliberately at my leg, as if appealing to me for sympathy. After all, hadn't we both been scarred by the same thing? I knew exactly what he was trying to say. There were two types of people now: those whose lives had been affected by the bomb and those who hadn't suffered.

There was no denying the mark on my cheek—you know all about it, Holy Mother. I used to try to hide it under heavy makeup, but even then it would show up blue under the glare of a lightbulb. And I still drag my left leg behind me when I walk. So I, too, have every reason to feel ashamed of my body and the traces on it of that day.

And yet here I was, infatuated with beautiful, healthy Sasaki. Was that wrong of me, Mother Mary? I don't think any woman could have resisted him as he was then—with his faith, his strength, and his idealism.

Ozaki got on my nerves, and I tried to brush him off. He had three operations to fix his jaw while he was still in his twenties and eventually hanged himself in the forests of Mount Konpira after the miseries of radiation sickness on top of everything else became more than he could bear.

Tell me, Mary, how can such terrible things happen? Wasn't it possible to save him? Or was he being released and called home to God?

Sometimes I can feel him staring at me even now—his eyes crawling across my breasts, down my back, and across my cheeks. My scar tingles as I imagine them on my skin.

His desire was so obvious that it frightened me. They were like an insect's eyes. Even beetles and cicadas and snails become lecherous when summer arrives and males and females reach out to satisfy themselves. Even the smallest insects feel the insistent hum of desire thrumming inside them.

Why didn't I just give him my body to do with as he wished? The thought makes me feel tearful now. If he and I had lived our lives together, leaning on each other for support and nursing one another's spiritual and physical scars . . . Who knows, I might have enjoyed a peaceful old age and never had sleepless nights like this, kept awake by anger and jealousy.

How soft and soothing candlelight can be for the soul, Mother Mary.

The night deepens, and the insects fall silent until there's no sound at all. A small stabbing pain runs down my left leg. Ever since that day, I have had to keep the leg stretched out in front of me when I sit on the floor. The pain comes most often in winter, but even in the summer, I feel it in the morning or when there's a chill in the air, as though there was a sliver of ice on my leg. I imagine the shards of glass still inside me grating against the nerves there.

I hitch up the bottom of my pajamas and look at the discolored thing that has been part of my life since I was fifteen. The leg can't support my weight, and the muscles atrophied long ago, leaving a thin wizened husk like a piece of wood. All that remains of the surface wound is a reddish brown discoloration on the skin.

I can still remember the shock I felt when I saw the leg for the first time in that clearing sixty years ago. My left leg was completely covered in sharp fragments of glass. It was as if they had been sucked in by a magnet. A distant relative from Mitsuyama who had come looking for her daughter stumbled on me lying there.

We barely knew each other, but she took me home, disinfected my cuts with iodine, and used a pair of chopsticks to pick out the glass from my legs.

Toward evening that day, an eight-year-old girl was brought to the house on a wooden screen door used as a stretcher. It was my relative's granddaughter. She was wrapped up like a mummy, with just a few sprigs of hair sprouting from her head, and two holes cut into the cloth for her eyes and another for her mouth. They set her down next to me. From time to time, she stirred and let out a low moan that disturbed my sleep.

I awoke to the sound of a man's voice during the night.

"It's no good. Her breathing's getting weaker."

"Maybe we should have her baptized," I heard my relative say.

"There's no priest," another man's voice replied.

"In an emergency, anyone can do it. That's how they used to do it in the old days. Fetch some fresh water. I'll baptize her."

There was the sound of a whispered prayer and a faint splashing of water as the man wet his fingers to make the sign of the cross on the girl's forehead. A feeling of calm came over me. It was as though our ancestors were in the room beside us.

"I baptize you in the name of the Father, and of the Son, and of the Holy Ghost."

After a while, I felt that something had come to an end, and I heard my relative's tearful voice. "It's all right, Michiyo. You can go to heaven now." No sound came from the girl. To this day, I can't say for sure whether any of this really happened. Was it just another of my feverish dreams?

It was around noon the next day when my grandfather came to collect me, wheeling a pushcart behind him.

"You're alive!"

He knelt down by my side and wept, rocking back and forth as his cracked voice honked like a sea lion. The body of the young girl still lay beside me. My grandfather made the sign of the cross and hung his head.

"Come on, let's get you home. Your grandmother's waiting. If you don't get better, I don't know what we'll do."

My grandparents lived in an old house that backed onto the mountains upriver, close to the source of the Urakami, an area where the faith had been kept alive for generations.

"What about Mommy and Daddy?"

There was no reply.

"And Toki? And Shin'ichiro? And Fuji-chan and Sanae-chan?"

Again, nothing.

"We'll look after you and make you better. No point taking you to the hospital. There's no medicine anyway. Let's go home," he said, lifting my light body easily in his arms.

The skin on my left leg was peeling. I moaned in pain. I didn't ask again about the rest of the family. His silence told me all I needed to know.

Not a trace was left of the house in Matsuyama. My parents and my four brothers and sisters must all have been home at the time, but we never even found their bones. We ended up just putting white ash in their graves.

My grandfather loaded me onto the pushcart and wrapped me in a blanket, then bowed his head repeatedly in thanks to our relative.

"You get better, now, you hear?" she said to me. "You have to live for Michiyo too now." She was crying. I lay on my side in the pushcart and watched as her silhouette got smaller and smaller and faded into the distance. I remember watching the wheels of the pushcart as they turned. The pushcart's handle was red with rust and smelled of iron. Slowly and carefully, my grandfather made his way down the long winding slope from Mitsuyama. Occasionally he would stop and look back to check on me.

"You all right back there, Mitsuko?"

All along the way, we passed people heading into the mountains. They were like soot-black shadows. Almost no one was dressed in normal clothes.

At the top of a small hill, my grandfather stopped to rest in the shade of a tree.

He wheeled the pushcart around so that I could see the scorched earth where Urakami used to be.

"Look at that," he whispered, wiping his forehead with a cloth he wore at his waist. "Even the church is gone."

For the first time, tears welled up in my eyes. There was nothing left. Everything was gone. Our house, the iron foundry, the tofu shop . . .

Of the church that had stood on the hill, only the foundation and a few fragments of the walls remained. It looked like a mouth ravaged by tooth decay. The houses in Matsuyama had been completely destroyed. Trails of smoke rose from the blasted landscape. The rubble stretched on without end.

The next instant, a green cricket flitted up from a clump of grass and settled on my bloodstained big toe. Once I got over my surprise, I realized somehow that I wasn't going to die. The insect was my guardian angel.

We used to see them in the fields all the time back then. They made a distinctive sound. As summer drew to a close, you would hear them singing in the grass: su-wee chon, su-wee chon, su-wee chon. It could get quite loud at times. My sister always used to make the same joke whenever she heard it. "The cricket's in love," she would say. "Why's that?" I would ask—even though

I already knew the answer. "Because he's always singing about his sweet-one, sweet-one, sweet-one!" she said with a laugh.

Slowly and silently, the insect crawled up my damaged leg. It was quite unharmed. It seemed so pure and clean. Never have I felt the beauty of insects as powerfully as at that moment.

Then it spread its thin brown inner wings and flew off toward the wasteland.

"Why did this have to happen?" my grandfather kept saying. Bloodied bodies lay in the shade of the tree. "Water. Please, give me some water," they cried out to no one in particular. Their voices were like sighs. Occasionally one of them would raise a thin black arm into the air. After a while I couldn't bear to look and kept my eyes tight shut.

My grandfather spat into his palms and roused himself with a grunt. We started downhill again. Eventually, back on level ground, we reached the ruins of the cathedral, where a number of people had gathered. Their bodies were charred black, so that it was impossible to tell the men from the women. The skin had started to fester and crawled with flies. I was struck by the thought that the flies stood in the way of their slipping away, that they were holding them back, asking, "Are you still alive?" In my heart I told them to leave the people alone. "Let them be. Let them sleep."

A few of the wooden houses behind the cathedral had survived the blaze. My grandfather trundled the pushcart down the deserted alleys through the heat. We met no one.

My younger brothers and sisters had spent most of that summer with our grandparents, away from the city with its hunger and air raids. But on August 8, they traveled home to be with our father, who was on furlough from his posting in Moji. At our first family meal in months, we had white rice—a rare treat in those days—along with some dried fish he'd brought back with him from the Inland Sea.

Our father had a beaky nose and big eyes. When he glared at us with those big eyes, it scared us stiff. But that night we all were delighted to be together again, and it was a relaxed, happy summer evening.

The river ran in front of the house. Through the gaps in the trees, you could make out the red brick walls of a small prison. Today, it's part of the Peace Park—the small hill with the big peace statue. On the adjacent hill was Urakami Cathedral. We used to be able to hear the bells.

That evening, we were able to forget the misery of the war for a moment and enjoy the cool breeze on our sweaty skin. It was the last meal we ever ate together.

"What happened to the house?" I couldn't help asking, even though I could see with my own eyes that most of the area around the church was nothing but scorched earth.

"Everything burned down," my grandfather said in a whisper. Stooping forward, he somehow managed to pull the pushcart forward one step at a time. I still feel a pang when I remember my question. It must have taken all his reserves of strength not to break down and sob as he tugged me through the ruins.

Once we escaped the blackened remains of the city and moved upstream, the greenery around us grew richer, and I heard the sound of running water. The unspoiled scenery had a calming effect on me, and I fell into a deep sleep. Even now, I sometimes feel as if I'm still slumbering on the back of that pushcart, adrift in dreams as my grandfather pulls me along behind him.

"Easy does it . . ." Supporting my bad leg with my hands, I shuffled over to the cushion in front of the desk by the window. I switched on the fluorescent light and read through the postcard again. "Tell me about a side of him I never knew. . . ." All right, I thought. If that's what you really want, I'll tell you. You know what I mean, don't you, Mary? We saw a side of him that Reiko knows nothing about . . . But forgive me, Mary! Help me control this anger that rolls in like a tide and blurs the world in front of my eyes.

Reiko came to work in the printing firm about two years after I joined. Everyone still bore the scars of the war in those days. Even he wasn't unaffected. He was studying to become a teacher, and a look of exhaustion would sometimes cloud his symmetrical features like a reminder that the shadow of the war still hung over us. It was probably my first glimpse of the emptiness he carried inside.

But Reiko was seven years younger and had grown up in the countryside. She had hardly known real hunger. This, along with the fact that none of her family had even been wounded in the war, probably explained why she was so untouched by the deprivation and depression that weighed so heavily on the rest of us. Maybe it was simply that she had been a little girl during the war years and didn't remember much about them. Or she just had a naturally cheerful, confident personality. Perhaps it was a combination of these things. She was one of those happy-go-lucky young women who started to crop up everywhere in the years that followed.

I remember clearly the moment when she and Sasaki were introduced for the first time. She bowed formally and flashed her sweetest smile. "Pleased to meet you," she said in a sweet, slightly nasal voice. Something responded in his eyes, and I felt a rush of anxiety and jealousy.

As I feared, they soon were close friends. In no time at all, she had his heart right where she wanted it, pliable as putty in those soft hands of hers. All I could do was look on in silence.

One day, I was watching them eating lunch together under a pink-flowering chestnut tree in the courtyard of the company building, when Ozaki suddenly turned to me as if he had finally figured something out. I suppose the resentment on my face was plain to see.

"Jealous?" he said.

Hopelessly, I tried to laugh it off. "Not at all. Two good-looking people like that . . . they make a lovely couple."

"Out of your league," he said.

I was so upset that I let fly at him. I can still remember the way he bit down on his malformed lip. He seemed to wilt. How could I have said such awful things? But I wasn't myself in those days, Mary.

Not long after that, Sasaki had an offer from his old junior high school, and left to return to the Goto Islands. Reiko followed two months later. They were engaged to be married.

I was tormented by jealousy, day and night. Why had he chosen her over me? Now I realize that it was only natural, but at the time it felt like the cruelest, most unfair thing in the world. How I used to bother you, Mary—nagging away with the same questions every night in my prayers.

Show me a side of him I never knew. What could I possibly say in my reply? How could she be so naive? A side of him she never knew! Would she be able to face the truth?

Unlike Reiko, I can't dash off a letter just like that, and I hated the idea that anyone but her might read what I was about to write—so a postcard was out of the question. I spread out a sheet of writing paper, but the pen stopped in my hand as soon as I put down the standard greeting. My mind churned with things I wanted to say but couldn't find the words to express. More than half a century had passed, yet in my heart I was still a jealous young woman.

Reiko sends me one of her chatty postcards about once a month, keeping me abreast of her life, apparently oblivious to my real feelings. Probably she's just not very sensitive to these things. At times, though, it occurs to me that she might be playing a tricky kind of game. Maybe forcing me to write an inoffensive reply every month is her way of rubbing my nose in it.

My feelings didn't change even after they were married. I have never known anyone else in my life who seemed as decent and attractive as he was then. I simply refused to believe that he could live happily with anyone but me. Even when they'd been married for ten years and had three children, my love didn't fade.

I grew older. He did too, of course—but age never seemed to spoil him. If anything, he only grew even better looking and more impressive, like a tree reaching maturity. His back was as straight as ever, while his hair acquired a touch of silver and the lines on his face were more sharply defined. But his eyes remained soft and clear—until the day he was suddenly brought down, like an old tree felled by lightning. A cluster of wire-thin blood vessels in his brain abruptly burst, and he died of a hemorrhage. The fifteen years since then have passed in the blink of an eye. He still lives on inside me.

How ashamed I would feel if he could see me now that I have passed him in years. My fingernails have yellowed, and there are dark blotches on my skin. White hairs sprout from my nose and arms. My body is practically ash already. But when I close my eyes and remember him, my skin seems to regain the bloom and softness it once had. My hair becomes long and black, and I feel the dying embers inside me begin to spark and flare.

My hatred and jealousy haven't faded, either. I can't help it. I still resent Reiko for taking him away from me. The way she basks in her memories makes me want to scream. What a mean-spirited person I am. Forgive me, Holy Mother. But I can't stand the way she has consigned everything to the past. In my heart, he's still alive.

If they had vanished completely from my life after they moved to the Goto Islands, things might have been different. But no, they refused to disappear.

They always got in touch when they returned to Nagasaki and asked me to dinner. After the children were born, I was invited to join them for family meals.

The three children came to accept me as part of the extended family. They called me their "Nagasaki auntie," and sometimes when I joined in the fun, I found a kind of consolation in it, as though these moments were an extension of the times I'd spent with my own family before I lost everything when the bomb fell.

Reiko and I were almost like sisters. I think she must have been at least dimly aware of my feelings for her husband. Sometimes I feel the kindness she showed me stemmed from pity. She must have sensed how lonely I was without a family of my own. Or perhaps, it occurs to me now, letting me see her happy family life was a way of warning me to stay in line. But if that was her intention, it failed. My love for him didn't die away. I ached with envy, and my feelings grew stronger than ever.

And then, almost unavoidably, an indiscretion took place.

He had turned forty; I was nearing the end of my thirties. He was back in Nagasaki on his own for the first time in years, on a summer training program. He asked me out, and we had dinner in Chinatown.

I was a little tipsy from the Chinese wine we had, drunk sweetened with lumps of rock sugar. Noticing that I was a little unsteady on my feet, he offered to see me home.

You saw it all, Holy Mother. In the flickering light of the candles, you witnessed everything.

The first thing I do when I get home is to light the candles on the altar to thank Our Lady for seeing me safely through the day. But he tried to stop me.

"Better not light them now—not after you've been drinking," he said.

"I don't sleep properly unless I do it."

"So pious. I'm impressed," he said. "But be careful you don't knock them over." As he spoke, he reached out from behind and cupped his soft hands around my neck. I twisted my body and tried to wriggle free.

"No. Don't. Our Lady will . . ."

"That? It's just a doll. Hollow. There's nothing inside," he said quietly, his voice slurring slightly. I could hardly believe what I was hearing. I had always thought of him as devout.

"God is watching."

"No he isn't."

"Sasaki-san! How can you say that?"

"Anyone who lived through the war knows it. You too—you survived the atomic bomb, didn't you?"

"By the grace of God."

"By the grace of pure luck, more like."

"Luck?"

"We're like your insects. Eat, mate, reproduce. Who lives, who dies? It's just luck, and that's all there is to it."

"It was part of God's plan, I think, that I was the only one to survive in my family. He must have had something in mind."

"God doesn't spend his time watching over every little person in the world. He doesn't remember our faces and names. There are too many of us. We cover the land everywhere you look. Like insects. God doesn't keep an eye out for every insect that's born or dies. They don't even have names. Their faces are all the same. And they don't give a damn about him, either. What makes you think people are so different?"

He held me quite firmly in his arms. I couldn't have put up much resistance anyway.

Holy Mother, you saw everything. He tore off my blouse and grabbed my trembling breasts in his sweaty palms. Then we coupled in front of you, as though you weren't even there. It was my first time—but I was longing for it. I burned with passion, panting and moaning shamelessly, not caring where I was.

The candlelight must have cast our shadows on the walls, our long thin arms entwined, like a pair of huge insects locked together.

When the moment was over, we simply returned to the same relationship we'd had before. From the way he looked at me when we met, you would never have suspected a thing. And I continued to have dinner with them.

But after hearing the things he told me that night, I couldn't understand how he could go on working at a Christian school. What did the Bible mean to him? How was he able to pass on the message of the Gospels to the young people he taught? He seemed so empty, so unreadable! I don't think I ever met anyone as hard to understand. Was it just a sense of duty, or respect for tradition, that made him join in their prayers day after day?

We never spoke a word of what had happened until his dying day some twenty years later, just before his sixtieth birthday. He kept the secret locked inside him. Never was there a hint that we might sin again in the same way.

Reiko is always eager to talk about him whenever we meet. She still sees him not just as a man with film-star looks but as a devout and hardworking husband. She's so shallow, she just projects herself onto the unknown part of him. She doesn't understand him at all, does she, Mary?

Who knows what lay at the bottom of his heart . . . what feelings he had as a survivor of the Special Attack Forces. Perhaps he wasn't quite human, but a beautiful, faithless insect, spreading its wings in a clear blue sky. When the bomb was dropped and people rejected God, they all became insects of a sort. I, too, have lived in confusion and fear for sixty years now. My life has been a blank, unthinking stretch of time. I regret the sin I committed with him—truly I do. But I savor the memory of the pleasure that surged through my body that night.

I still sometimes imagine myself lying on the pushcart behind my grandfather, daydreaming as I'm shunted gently from side to side.

After crossing the wasteland, we headed upstream. When we came close to the head of the river, my grandmother came out to meet us, her hair bound in a white kerchief, her mouth open wide so that I could see her teeth as she wept and wailed. Sometimes that open mouth of hers appears in my dreams, like a gateway to another world.

She carried me, wrapped in my blanket, into the tatami room at the back of the house. For a while she just wept. Then, still sobbing, she said the same thing my grandfather had said: "We'll look after you. We'll make sure you get better." Using some of her precious stock of white rice and eggs, she made a warm congee for me, but I was overcome with nausea and couldn't swallow. The white gruel was dyed with the blood that oozed from my gums, as though mixed with red perilla. I felt as if the red ash of the flattened city was spreading through me, like a disease I'd caught from what I'd seen there.

"You have to eat. Think of it as medicine." With my grandmother's encouragement, I eventually managed to swallow some of the food—but all I got was a taste of iron, and I threw up again almost immediately. My body seemed to be on fire, and the thirst was unbearable and unrelenting. For several days I lived on water alone, dozing and waking, sinking repeatedly and floating to the surface again.

At one stage, she brought in a small watermelon—heaven only knows where she'd found such a thing in those days. "This should be easier to get down. Plenty of water in this. You must try to eat something. Your body needs the fuel. I'll leave it here for you."

I have a vague memory of her voice as I floated in and out of consciousness. When the body is weak, one's sight and hearing grow faint as well, though the other senses, smell and touch, can become sharper than usual.

What I do remember is how the sweet, gentle scent of its juice intensified a thirst that was almost molten, making me lift myself up, still barely conscious, and suck the watermelon down, all but burying my face in the fruit by my pillow.

I suppose it was a simple will to live, an instinct that made me cling to a life that hung in the balance. I don't retain many memories of those days, but the sense of rapture as the sweet juice trickled down my throat has remained with me to this day.

"She looks like a little cricket," my grandmother apparently whispered when she saw me. A cricket, of all things! I don't know what strange coincidence made her compare me to a cricket rather than another kind of creature, but perhaps there always was something insectlike about me even from those early days.

She was still sniffling when she called in my grandfather. "Look at her. Just like a little cricket," she said, tearful and smiling at the same time.

I often woke up in the middle of the night convinced that I had heard voices asking, "Are you still alive?" In my dreams, I saw severed hands and feet and heads on the ground. Eyeballs torn from their sockets grew legs and gaping mouths. They spread their wings and flew away. The voices would continue to sound in my sleepy ears after I awoke—but whether they were human voices or merely the babble of river and mountain spirits, I was never sure.

There was a military supplies factory and some houses on the middle reaches of the Urakami River, but almost no one lived this far upstream. At night, the area was as quiet and dark as the bottom of a well. A small mountain stream ran close by the house, and there were rice paddies where frogs and toads came to mate in the summer. They laid their spawn like transparent pellets in the puddles on the ridges and paths between the fields.

It was the frogs that woke me late at night—countless frogs calling out to one another in the darkness. The noise would build to a crescendo, like monks chanting in a temple, and then abruptly stop as if on cue. When the frogs fell silent, another voice would make itself heard. Su-wee chon, su-wee chon, su-wee chon. "Who is your sweet-one? Who do you love?" I answered back, with tears in my eyes. Then one or two frogs would begin croaking, and soon the whole chorus would start up again, drowning out the insects' song.

My hair began to fall out. It came out in clumps when I combed my hair, and before long I was totally bald from my forehead to the back of my scalp. I looked like a backwoods samurai whose topknot had come undone. My grandmother hid the mirrors, but feeling with my fingers gave me a clear enough idea of how I must look. I didn't want to live my life like this. Sometimes I wished I could turn into a toad or a lizard or some other faithless insect.

Physically, my condition was wretched. I still couldn't hold down any solid food. The only thing that kept me alive was the watermelon my grandmother somehow managed to get her hands on.

It must have been in late September that my grandfather came to tell me about the Kunchi festival. We'd assumed there would be no festival this year, but it was going on after all, he said, and the young boys were running in the streets again just like every other year. I was surprised to see him so happy about a pagan celebration.

Little by little, I clawed my way back to normal life. Slowly, my appetite improved, and eventually I was just about strong enough to walk. The wounds on my leg healed over, although smooth bits of glass still emerged from time to time, coated in blood and fat. I began to spend whole days out on the cool veranda, idling my time away. Sometimes I felt that my heart would burst with sadness. Shadowy memories of my parents, or of Toki, Shinichiro, Fuji, and Sanae, would press against my chest until I thought I'd suffocate.

Sanae had just turned five at the time and referred to me in her childish lisp as her "big fifter." When she saw me coming home at the end of the day, she would run out of the house calling my name. She used to jump into my arms and rub her plump red cheeks against mine. It was as though I were raising her myself. Without ever becoming a mother, I knew the anguish of losing a child—just as you did, Holy Mother.

When autumn arrived, a few friends who had survived the bomb came to visit, but my grandmother just thanked them politely at the door and wouldn't let them in to see me.

As winter approached, the loneliness seeped deep into my bones. I found it hard to sleep and often lay listening to the moaning and creaking of the oak trees on the hills behind the house as they bent under the force of the north wind. Alone in my room, I often woke up screaming. After a while, my grandparents took to sleeping near me.

One cold night, I awoke to hear my grandmother talking in a small trembly voice.

"We should never have let the children go that day."

"There's no sense in thinking like that. They were happy to go. They were excited to see their parents again."

I heard her tearful whisper again, and the sound of sniffling.

"Why did it happen?"

"What?"

"Why did such a terrible thing have to happen? They were just innocent children. They had no idea."

"I don't know. How should I know?"

There was a catch in my grandfather's voice, too.

"It must all be part of God's plan."

"What could He have been thinking?"

"No one can know that."

"But I want Him to explain Himself. The whole family was wiped out, Hiromitsu. I can't understand it. How could Our Lady have allowed this to happen to us?"

"The family wasn't completely destroyed. There's still Mitsuko . . ."

"She'll never have any children. No one will marry her the way she looks now. She'll be the last of the family line. And our faith will die out with her, too."

"All right, that's enough. You'll wake her up," my grandfather said in a whisper. For a while her voice fell silent. I could feel her looking at me in the darkness.

"Can you hear the sound of water?"

It was the middle of the night, in deep midwinter. The frogs had long since fallen silent. When the groaning of the trees on the hillsides stopped, there was a moment of silence, in which the gurgling of one of the small streams that flowed into the Urakami River could be heard.

"You can always hear water wherever you are in this house," my grandfather said.

"The people before us must have lived their whole lives with that sound in their ears, day in, day out, year after year . . ."

"What about it?"

"The way we believe in God hasn't changed at all. Our faith is as pure as ever. It's been handed down through generations. We haven't done anything wrong. No matter how hard things got, even when we were persecuted, our faith kept running like a clear stream. It never stopped once. Think of that magnificent church we built here."

"What are you trying to say?"

"Maybe we did something to make God angry with us?"

"Don't be so stupid. It wasn't our fault the country went to war."

"Are we being tested again? Does God still not trust us, even after all this time? Even though our ancestors were burned at the stake for their faith? Why was the whole family destroyed like this? Why can't He believe in us, the way we believe in Him?"

"I don't know. All we can do is pray," my grandfather said brusquely. But she wouldn't let it rest.

"We were at war. America and England were the enemy. So there were air raids . . . maybe that couldn't be helped. But the people in those countries have the same religion as us. How could they do such a thing? They even destroyed the church. Why did God allow His people in Urakami to be killed by their fellow Christians?"

"Look. God's intentions are too deep for us to understand. I've made up my mind not to think about it. The world's full of things we'll never understand. All we can do is to trust Him and pray."

"I just want someone to tell me why."

"Come on, now go to sleep. You'll wake her up."

There was a rustling as he turned over to sleep. I shut my eyes and pulled the covers over my face to stifle my sobs. Everything fell silent, and before long

I heard them snoring, occasionally grinding their teeth. Left alone in the darkness, I prayed to Our Lady with all my heart.

Despite everything, spring eventually arrived as it always does. With the change of season, I could feel rough bristles when I rubbed the palm of my hand across my scalp. At last, my hair had started to grow back. I wasn't going to spend my life as bald as an egg after all.

"Granny! Grandpa! My hair's growing back!"

They both were stirred by the news. "What a relief! We thought you might not pull through," they said. People still didn't understand what was causing the hair loss at that stage. All we knew was that in many cases, people who suddenly lost their hair died soon afterward. My grandparents had heard the rumors and feared the worst.

Gradually, day by day, my scalp darkened in color and eventually was covered in thick black hair. It was almost the first time I had felt any happiness since the bomb. A couple of months later, no hint of my baldness remained, and a little light began to shine into my life again. I was walking by then, too, albeit with a limp in my left leg.

One day that spring, as I walked toward the hospital through a still mostly derelict part of the city, I came to a place where a confusion of shepherd's purse and speedwell was in bloom by the river. The embankments had not been repaired yet, and the air was heavy with the smell of the earth. Along the banks, scattered with rubble, grew lush green grass, and there were white and yellow and purple flowers everywhere.

A wooden cart had sunk in the middle of the river. The water was clear, and a school of killifish darted in and out of the wheels. Most of the city was still a wasteland, but here and there shacks and temporary housing stood out against the desolation, and people's laundry fluttered in the breeze. I stood and hummed the "Apple Song," a popular tune that played constantly on the radio just after the war. I stared up into a clear blue sky, just as the words of the song suggested.

Under my grandparents' care, I was recuperating. I began to help with the housework. When harvest time arrived, I tried to help in the fields, too. My body began to regain its strength, and there was talk of my going back to nursing school. But after everything that had happened, the prospect of coping with other people's wounds was terrifying. Splintered fingertips, perforated skulls, festering skin—I had seen enough of these things.

I hardly ever went out, but people from our church started to make suggestions. It wasn't good for me to be cooped up indoors all the time, they said. On top of that, it wasn't easy for two old people to keep the household going on what they made from the farm alone. So, shortly after my nineteenth birthday, I started work at a printing company that dealt mainly with religious materials.

Sasaki and Ozaki were my co-workers. Of the six employees, five were atomic bomb survivors. He was the only exception. We all had injuries or disfigurements of one kind or another, and I found it easy to relax when I was around them. It did us good to share our troubles. He alone stood out; he alone bore no scars from the bomb.

All of us felt uneasy and resentful around him, me included. But in retrospect, it occurs to me that Ozaki's presence around us may have helped allay these feelings somewhat. His injuries were much worse than anyone else's. I think the horrendous condition of his jaw brought the rest of us a cruel kind of comfort. It's an awful thing to admit, but somewhere inside me lurked the hard-hearted thought that, compared with him, I wasn't so badly off.

Maybe . . . A chill passed through me, and the candles on the altar guttered suddenly. The Virgin's smile seemed to freeze. Maybe that's why Reiko was so keen to have me correspond with her. Maybe a glimpse of my miserable old age would make her feel better about the way her own life had turned out. "Compared with her," she might think, "I should consider myself lucky." Perhaps that's what all those postcards were about—part of a cruel game she was playing with me.

Maybe that innocent, sunny manner of hers was just a front. Deep down inside her was something else, faceless and horrible, some parasite like a tapeworm coiled white in her black guts.

> Why don't you come out and stay? We could have a good soak together and talk about the past. It's fifteen years now since he died, and there aren't many friends left with whom I can share memories of the good old times. Maybe you could tell me about a side of him I never knew? . . .

I ran my eyes over Reiko's brisk, flowing handwriting again. I had to tell her the truth. I couldn't keep up this pretense of friendliness anymore. I had to confess the truth about what he and I had done together.

I wrote a greeting on a fresh sheet of paper. My pen felt a little unsteady as I pressed down on the smooth surface of the paper. My revenge. I was going to have my revenge at last on this thieving creature.

If you really want to hear about the past, there is one thing that remains especially clear in my memory. Once—just once—he and I slept together. We betrayed you, one summer's night thirty-five years ago.

I always meant to take the secret with me to the grave. But I decided that after all the time you two spent together, you had the right to know about this other side of him.

What we did was a sin, something shameful. But perhaps sin and shame don't really exist if they aren't exposed. I've always believed that God knows everything. But if—just if—He doesn't exist, then who would retain any memory of what happened between us?

I breathed out softly and touched the tip of the pen to my cheek, a habit that had been with me since I was a schoolgirl. I heaved a heavy sigh. Sensations I'd had with him that night revived in me now with sudden force. His lips brushing the mark on my cheek, his hot hands grabbing at my blackened leg, the strength with which he pried my knees apart . . . How could I forget? My cheek and my bad leg were the parts of my body that shamed me most. I tried to twist away, tried to resist . . . But it was useless. He pressed too hard. He was too insistent. I was powerless to resist. And above all, I welcomed it.

Holy Mother: you saw everything, you watched unblinking through the flames of the candles.

He pressed his lips to my ugly leg. I told him to stop. "Our Lady . . . ," I'd said, but he had cackled in my ear and said, "That's just a hollow doll." He told me we were just like insects, that God had no special interest in us. The insects had no God. They didn't care.

And I became like an insect, too. An insect that mates with the wet tip of its body.

You speak so blithely, so innocently of the past, Reiko, that I'm forced to assume your memories of him are fading. It's only when a person is truly present to us that we feel the whole range of emotions. Hatred. Resentment.

Irritation . . . To you, perhaps, he feels far away. But not to me. He still lives on inside me. I've never forgotten the weight of him, the feel of him against me.

I'm old now, and my body is like cold ash. But when I think of him, my heart warms and sparks into flame. Even now, I love him very much.

But I hate him, too—that man who toyed with me and used me for his pleasure for that one single night. He branded me with his hands, his lips, his skin.

Maybe when you read these words, you'll find him coming to life again too. In fact, maybe you're seething with anger and hatred at this very moment. You may feel like killing me. And you'll want to pay him back for what he did—even though he is already dead.

I imagine after you read this you won't find it quite so easy to soak happily in your precious hot-spring bath again. But that's what happens when people reminisce. Things come crawling out from under the rubble inside them . . . resurrected, if that's the right word.

So here it is, Reiko: the side of him you never knew. Tell me—can you still live with him happily after all these years?

Before I knew what I was doing, my blue ink had filled the page. So I signed off, squeezing in my name at the bottom of the page. I then read over what I had written. It was too much. I couldn't send this. The only thing to do was tear the letter up and toss it away. But I couldn't bring myself to do that either.

I took another sheet of paper and started to write a routine letter—seasonal greeting, recent news, all the usual stuff . . . But suddenly my pen stopped still. I couldn't go on.

I've never forgotten his dismissive laugh. "That's just a hollow doll," he said. But you saw everything, Holy Mother, didn't you?

Why does that episode still shine so vividly in my memory? If the moment when I regained consciousness under the rubble ("Are you still alive?") was the low point of my life, the brief time I spent with him was the peak. Sometimes I feel as though I crawled out of the rubble simply for that moment of pleasure in his embrace.

I wrote a postscript on a separate sheet of paper.

P.S. Reiko: Let me tell you about another side of him you never knew. You can't possibly imagine what he really was, but I know. He was an insect. A cricket that landed close to the epicenter after the bomb fell. A godless insect.

When summer comes, that area is filled with the sound of insects: cicadas, ants, flies, and crickets in the grass. Here and there, an occasional lizard flits between the shadows. These creatures hid away on Noah's Ark and have survived through all the disruption the world has seen ever since. When autumn comes, their front legs twitch together as if in prayer, and they wither and die. Maybe they also long for faith, like us.

That's what he was, Reiko—one of those insects.

She probably wouldn't understand a word of what I'd written, but I licked the envelope shut and stuck on a stamp. Then I put it safely away in the drawer of the altar, with its carved roses.

Why are you always smiling, Holy Mother? I blew out the candles and crawled back under the futon. Pale hints of light floated up to meet my eyes, now grown used to the dark. Daylight was starting to come in through the curtains. The night was nearly over. I would have a doze, then go out while it was still cool and post the letter in the old red mailbox near the epicenter.

Soon the brown cicada larvae would come crawling up from under the magnolia trees in the garden, twitching and squirming as they emerged and spread their wings. The first sloughed-off husks must be accumulating under the trees already. Insects were stirring deep within the earth, hidden under the grass, or lying in wait in the hollows of ancient tree trunks. Soon, from all directions, it would be time for them to emerge.

Summer was here again.

I'm lying on my side in the pushcart pulled by my grandfather, watching the wheels turn and breathing in the smell of iron. I'm wrapped in a rough blanket, and I can feel a burning in my legs.

Out of the sky above the wasteland, a huge green cricket lands on my damaged leg and crawls toward my buttocks. With a laugh, it asks: "Are you still alive?" Then it thrusts the moistened tip of its tail into me and shoots its seed, thick with the smell of green grass. It explodes inside me like a million shards of broken glass.

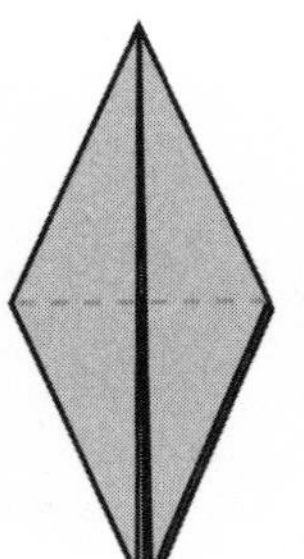
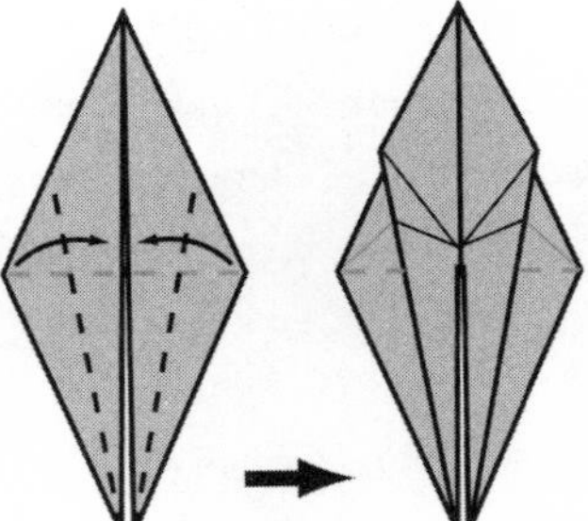
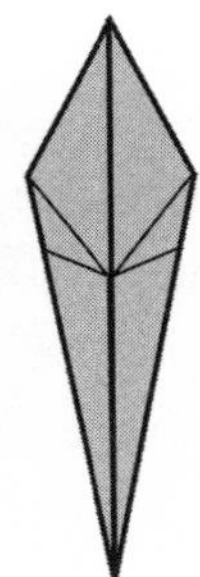

HONEY

Thanks to the metallic screech of my rusty brakes, the youth sitting on his haunches at the back of the shop has already turned to look in my direction before I get off my bike. It's dark inside, and my eyes are still dazzled by the summer sun. I can hardly make out his face. But I can feel his eyes on me.

Sunlight streams through the thin clusters of leaves on the tallow trees as I stand on tiptoe, straddling the saddle. I wipe the sweat from my forehead, fully aware of the impression that a mature woman in a sleeveless dress must be having on him.

The shop deals mainly in secondhand motorbikes. It's an old, run-down kind of place, with no air-conditioning. The metal sign outside is faded. The whole building looks off balance, as though it might topple over if the newspaper store next door weren't there to support it. It doesn't seem like a workplace at all. It's like somewhere left over from the past, with a thick sediment of oil from engines and chains and other bits and pieces they've repaired covering everything.

And I know he's been waiting for me. Waiting for the brakes on my bicycle to get loose, for the screeching to start, and for me to come in to get it fixed.

And me? I'm here to seduce him. How did it start? Accidentally enough—a random flash of pale skin; I caught him staring at my thighs. But the next time it was no accident. I looked him in the eye as I gave him another glimpse. Yes, I've teased him and led him on. And now I can't stop.

He looks me up and down as he ambles over from the back of the shop. His white overalls are stained with oil, but with his clean-cut features, he never really looks dirty. How can he stare at me so calmly? He doesn't seem embarrassed at all. There's a smirk on his face, but his look is steady. Maybe he's out to seduce me, a married woman. Like most teenagers, he's probably cocky as anything.

"Looks like the brakes have come loose again," I say, slipping down from the saddle. The hem of my dress hitches up as I raise my leg. I still feel his eyes on me, but I'm not bothered by that now. I enjoy it, like being tickled. He doesn't try to hide the lust in his eyes. I can feel his gaze licking at my skin.

"That could be dangerous," he says. His voice is almost a whisper.

Checking to make sure the manager isn't there, I step into the eerily quiet interior, taking off my broad-brimmed hat and the long black gloves I'm wearing over the elbow to protect me from the sun.

"What's the good of wearing those if you're going round with bare legs?"

I can tell from the way he's talking that he's on his own. I allow myself to become more daring.

"I took off my panty hose before I left the house."

"That sounds like a come-on, that does."

He wipes the black oil off his fingers with a towel and wheels my bike with one hand toward the back of the shop. I follow him as he pushes his way through the jungle of handlebars. Of course he could check the brakes just as well by the entrance—but we both know why he's trundling the bike to the back where no one can see.

He crouches down and takes hold of a pedal with one hand, then gives the wheel a gentle spin and squeezes the brakes. There's a loud squawking like the sound of some exotic bird being wrung by the neck, but he doesn't even flinch.

"Brake connector's rusty. That's why it keeps getting loose. And it's catching here. That's where the noise is coming from."

He points to the rim of the wheel, but I'm not really interested. I've heard it all before.

"Can you fix it?"

"It's covered in rust. And it's old. You can't get these parts anymore. You'd be better off buying a new one, really. These brakes will just snap off one day."

"Wow. That sounds dangerous."

“Yeah, it is. I’ll tighten them again for now, but really . . .”

“Where’s the boss?”

“He went to the bank. He should be back any minute.”

“OK . . .” I crouch down opposite him, with the bike between us. The usual routine. I relax my knees and open my legs a fraction. His eyes brighten. I can feel them crawling up my skirt. I give in to the ravishing feeling of being exposed like this. I hardly know what I’m doing. Something is surging up inside me. I can’t resist.

“. . . lady . . .”

The desire in his eyes is almost innocent in its nakedness. He looks adorable. I have to fight against the urge to give him everything right here and now. Hurriedly, I get to my feet.

“No.”

“What’s wrong?”

“Not here.”

Next to the shopping in the basket on my handlebars is a single unripe kiwi fruit I picked up in the garden last night. I’d forgotten all about it. Actually it’s still too early for them to fall off the branches. And kiwis don’t often fall anyway—unlike persimmons. It was odd, finding this one on the ground.

“What’s that? A baby kiwi?”

He picks it up curiously, his attention diverted. I can’t help laughing.

“What’s so funny?”

“You. ‘Baby kiwi’! It sounds so cute. They flower in June. The fruit starts after that. Grows really slowly, though. They’re all about that size now. By next month, they should be big enough to eat.”

“You grow them at home?”

“In the garden.”

“In a greenhouse?”

“No. Just normally, in the garden.”

“I thought they were tropical. D’you live near here?”

“In one of the houses at the top of the hill. Come up and see it sometime. You go up past the medical school, then follow the bus lane left at the top. It’s the old house with a brick wall, one block in. You can’t miss it.”

Cradled in his grubby hands, the kiwi with its hard coating of golden hairs reminds me of the forbidden fruit—as if there’s some secret meaning to it. I imagine the little thing ripening and swelling in the warmth of his hands. He's still staring at it, a look of wonder on his face. "It's so hairy," he laughs. "It's kind of disgusting, really."

"I'll leave the bike here. You can bring it up when you've fixed it. How about 10:30 tomorrow? I'll show you the house."

Even after this, he gives me the usual business patter. "I can fix it for you right now if you don't mind waiting. The shop rule is that customers come to collect their bikes." He doesn't get it.

"There'll be no one else at home," I say. Suddenly, his eyes flash with understanding. "Ten-thirty, on the dot. All right?"

I hand him a piece of paper with the address. He looks it over, and a boyish smile crosses his face.

"Here, let me take another look just to be sure," he says. He leers at me and gets back down on his haunches. I'm about to do the same when his face freezes. The manager! I turn to face the entrance, where a dark, rotund figure is silhouetted against the sunlight.

"Have you had time to fix that scooter yet?"

An elderly nun in a pale beige summer habit is standing smiling by the door. I feel a surge of shame. What if she saw what was on our minds?

It's not far to the house from the shop. You follow the gentle curve of the bus lane uphill under the shade of some big camphor trees, keeping the dry stone wall of the university medical department on your right. At the top you turn into a back street and step into a quiet residential area that stretches out over the slopes of the hill.

In the afternoon, there are so few people about you'd think no one lived there at all. Our place is a big house on the corner, surrounded by a red brick wall and a thick stand of trees.

The long black gloves don't really go with my sleeveless white dress. I'm carrying a parasol as well. It's the height of summer, and the air is practically burning. A ten-minute walk is enough to leave you drenched.

My sweat has quite a sweet smell, apparently. When I still lived in Tokyo, I had an affair with one of my superiors at work that lasted nearly three years. He called it the "smell of honey." Used to say he could never bear to let his Honey Girl go.

I open the arched metal door to find my husband's parents sitting under the trellis in the garden where the small dark kiwi fruit are ripening.

"Been doing some weeding?"

They look like caddies on a golf course in their broad-brimmed hats, green-and-yellow striped gardening gloves, and long white sleeves.

"How about some lunch?" I say.

They both flap their hands at me. "Thank you for asking, Mihoko," my mother-in-law calls out. "But you don't have to worry about us."

"What do you want to do about tonight? For Father's birthday? How about sushi?"

Birthdays in this house are a low-key affair. Usually they don't do anything beyond a simple "Happy Birthday." They don't even bother with presents. But I've been looking for a way to thank them for the travel vouchers they gave us last Christmas so that Shinji and I could go to Hawaii, and for once we've agreed to have presents today.

"Don't worry, Mihoko. I'll make something. You come over to us. Shinji's home early tonight, isn't he?"

So that lets me off the hook. I rejoice quietly to myself. Shinji's mother always cooks the most amazing meals. I pretty much hate any kind of housework, and I'm certainly not what you'd call a natural in the kitchen.

"Great. I'll bring the presents with us when we come."

My father-in-law is eighty this year, but he's still full of beans. In fact, he's amazingly fit for his age. His skin is still smooth and hasn't lost its luster, and his hair is a nice, elegant gray. My parents look far more decrepit than he does, and they're twenty years younger.

"It was somewhere around here, I think," I can hear them say.

"Right on this spot."

"Why were they all together here?"

"And what were they talking about?"

They patted the ground where they sat. The sunlight shone in bright streaks on their backs.

When the house was rebuilt, they put up a trellis made of wood and steel to replace the one where wisteria had grown. But the wisteria refused to take. It's more than a decade now since my father-in-law planted a couple of kiwi saplings instead. They shot up, covering the trellis in no time with a cross-stitch pattern of vines that produce white flowers every year, from May to June. The fruit gradually turns golden and ripens in the autumn. And the harvest gets bigger every year. When we counted them in early autumn when I married into the family three years ago, there were 227 on the vines. They're much smaller than the ones you see in the shops, though.

"They wouldn't have had time to take cover or run away."

"It was all over in a flash."

The door facing the kiwi trellis gives on to a corridor that connects his parents' side to the part of the house where Shinji and I live. A shrine room is just off the corridor. On the other side of the netted screen door, a white statue of Our Lady stands with her arms open wide, gazing out into the garden.

From the cherry and plum trees, I can hear the steady din of cicadas, mingled with the pleasant humming of the wings of insects that gather on the trellis. Even when the flowering season is over, the roof of the trellis, tangled with vines and leaves and fruit, is constantly abuzz with the bees, gold bugs, potato beetles, and ladybugs that make their homes there.

It was from my father-in-law, who's an amateur entomologist on top of everything else, that I learned that the little black-and-yellow striped insect I'd assumed was some kind of wasp is actually a beetle called a "tiger longhorn."

No one bothers to pick the fruit, so even when it's ripe it's not good enough to give to the neighbors. The birds and ants end up eating most of it. But my parents-in-law obviously enjoy watching it all change over the course of the year—the bright greenery in the spring and summer, the growing autumn fruit, and the way everything withers and dies when the chill sets in. I've even seen my father-in-law on his knees with his digital camera, taking close-ups of a kiwi split open on the ground, the green, half-rotten flesh pushing through the broken skin. He kept saying to himself how beautiful it was. They really love this miniature world, even its death and decay.

"He planted the vines out of respect for Mr. Lange. From New Zealand," my mother-in-law tells me.

It must be obvious from the look on my face that the name means nothing. She looks up and closes her eyes. Evidently she's decided not to bother explaining. "Listen to the wind," she says. "The rustling of the leaves, the whirring of the insects' wings, the smell of the sunlight, the hint of honey in the air . . ." I sometimes haven't a clue what's on these people's minds.

It's my father-in-law who comes to the rescue. "Lange was the prime minister of New Zealand. A wonderful man. Refused to allow nuclear weapons into his country. And he took a leading role during the talks to ban them altogether." OK, but what does that have to do with kiwi vines?

"Father thinks New Zealand is like a modern Garden of Eden. Bursting with golden kiwi fruit."

The words "Garden of Eden" bring me to my senses. I've told the boy from the motorbike shop to come to the house tomorrow. What is going to happen? Are we going to be expelled from Paradise?

"Here, try one," she says. "This one looks about ready. They're supposed to be a good source of iron," she adds, plucking one of the larger fruit from its hiding place under the round leaves.

"The ones that get direct sunlight ripen faster," she mentions as they both drift toward the faucet under the eaves, where they take off their gardening gloves and wash their hands.

The house is more than twenty years old now and starting to show its age. But I like it here. They had the bathroom and plumbing redone specially before I moved in. I had my reservations at first about sharing a house with them, but in fact everything has been pretty laid back. The place was designed with two separate households in mind, linked by a corridor, the original idea being for Shinji's elder brother and his wife to use half of it. Even though the two living areas are connected, it's not like we're constantly traipsing back and forth on visits. Apart from special occasions like birthdays and Christmas, we don't even eat together most of the time.

I do worry about the future sometimes—about Shinji's parents needing to be looked after at some stage. That wouldn't suit me at all. Luckily, both of them are still in good shape, so there's no immediate danger. On the whole, life here is pretty comfortable.

Of course, there are inconveniences. One day not long after we got married, I'd just had a bath and was pottering around the kitchen in a towel when I bumped into my father-in-law, who'd come over to our side of the house for some reason. He blushed bright red, and my mother-in-law had a few quiet words with me about it afterward. Back when I was single, working in Tokyo and living on my own in an apartment in Hachioji, I often used to loll about watching videos in my underwear. I suppose I should have realized that it wasn't really an appropriate way to behave now that I was married. Still, minor adjustments like that are easy enough.

It was the other stuff that took me by surprise. The family traditions, for one thing. They're totally different from what I grew up with. The biggest shock was how often they pray—not just Shinji and his parents, but the whole family. It isn't just grace at mealtimes, either; they're always at it. My own family is Christian, too—nominally. But we hardly ever go to church except at Christmas. My parents do occasionally give money to the church, but they do it grudgingly, as though paying some kind of local tax. With us, our faith is a pretty superficial thing.

Here, though, they have a shrine room in the middle of the house and a statue of Our Lady the size of a little girl. It was all quite unfamiliar to me at first. I remember saying to Shinji once: "So you really believe in God then?" He looked shocked. "But you're a Christian too, surely. You're not saying you've lost your faith, are you?"

My husband is a cardiologist. He says he can sense the presence of God when he's operating on a patient and sees how perfectly all the tiny blood vessels, valves, and organs are arranged inside the body. Being face to face with His Creation is how he describes it. Sometimes, apparently, when he is massaging the heart of a patient he knows is beyond help, he asks God to tell him when to stop and let go.

"Do you never have moments like that?" he asked me. I pretended to be thinking it over, but he just laughed. "You never take anything seriously, Mihoko. People your age are all so empty-headed nowadays." Yes, we are empty-headed, at least to start with. Sometimes I think it wouldn't be so bad to live without ever feeling guilty. Though I realize how wrong that would be, too.

On the other side of the kiwi trellis is an old plum tree. Its soft pink flowers are the first signs of spring every year. The trunk is thick, with a green-and-white mold on the bark that looks like the blotches on an old person's skin. It's not really something you want to look at too closely. One day in January, I noticed a few new branches poking out of the mottled trunk like skewers, with small, bright flowers on them. Even though much of the tree is old and decrepit, its upper body is still bursting with vitality.

There is a hollow in the trunk that looks a bit like the face in Munch's painting of the scream that was in a textbook at school. Apparently, starlings used to nest there, but even they moved out in the end. Now, the hollow is rotten and clogged with rubbish. Early this summer, I was helping to tidy the garden when I reached all the way inside it, despite thinking how nasty it looked. There was a sour whiff of rotting vegetation, from dead leaves and stagnant water. I was scooping it out when a large black snake suddenly emerged from deep inside, arching its dark sickle head and glaring at me with its yellow eyes. I watched as the whole length of the snake uncoiled and slid down the tree, then slithered with surprising speed along the brick wall and disappeared into a damp bush of fatsia.

Where did the snake go after that? Sometimes I wonder if somehow it might be hiding in a hollow inside me. I mean, look at me: a thirty-three-year-old married woman, proposing to take a boy just out of high school to bed. Why on earth? There must be something wrong with me—there's no other explanation—something bad inside. Otherwise, how could I keep flashing my thighs at him without feeling a twinge of guilt? Like the snake that was sleeping peacefully under the dead leaves until I prodded it and drove it out of its refuge, it seems only a matter of time before I get chased out of Paradise, too.

For lunch, I decide to cook some pasta: pepperoncino with garlic, oil, and red chilies. All I have to do is keep an eye on the time as the thin Buitoni pasta boils to al dente firmness. For the sauce, I just cut open the packet and dribble it out of the foil onto the plate. It's almost no effort at all.

But even though it's more or less an instant meal, there's a rich taste of garlic and a sharp bite of chili when I lick the pale yellow olive oil off my fingertips.. Add a few slices of Parma ham and the salad left over from breakfast, along with a kiwi from the garden, halved with the tip of a kitchen knife, and it's a pretty respectable lunch. The kiwi is still slightly hard and sour, but as I sip my coffee at the end of the meal, I feel quite satisfied.

On Mondays and Thursdays, I go swimming at a sports club in the city center, so after putting the plates and bowls in the dishwasher, I toss my swimsuit into a bag and leave. If I don't swim, I get out of shape in no time. The boy at the bike shop told me I should trade in my bicycle for a scooter or a motorbike. "It must be tough getting up those hills on a bike," he said. But I don't want to give it up. When I'm running errands in the neighborhood, I try to walk as much as possible. If I need to go farther afield, I take the bike, making sure to pedal up all the hills. The car is a last resort. For me cycling, like swimming, is an important part of my regime.

Mine is an old-fashioned bike with a basket on the handlebars, which I've had since I was in high school—fifteen years ago. It was in storage at my parents' place for a while after I left school, but I started using it again when I moved back to Nagasaki. It's been with me for so long that I'm quite attached to it now; it reminds me of the days when I used to pedal to school and back under the willows along the river.

But the sports club is too far to go by bike. I have a new red Beetle Salsa that I use for running around town. There's also a Mercedes in the garage, which Shinji shares with his father. As I take the car out of the garage, I catch a glimpse in the mirror of the twisted vines and leaves on the kiwi trellis, and my mind turns again to thoughts of what might happen here tomorrow.

I'm only playing, really. But a strange thrill runs through me when I imagine taking things further. Even so, I'm not sure whether I really will go through with it.

The car is like an oven after being in the garage so long. The air-conditioning doesn't seem to make any difference at all. Through the windshield, I can see fat summer clouds stretching out across the sky. The roads are unusually crowded, probably because of the peace ceremony tomorrow. Lots of the cars have out-of-town plates. I realize I've come out without my gloves. The sun beats straight down on the back of my hands.

The sports club has a twenty-five-meter pool downstairs, with a gym on the second floor and a coffee shop and sauna on the third. Even though the five-lane pool is a bit on the small side, it's hardly ever crowded, probably because the club is so expensive. Most of the people there are like me, housewives from well-heeled families. They sit in the coffee shop after their workout and gossip over iced coffees about what a hunk such-and-such an instructor is and the appeal of a well-shaped set of pecs.

Occasionally there are rumors that something's going on between a member and one of the instructors. But I'm not interested in any of that. I just want to empty my mind and tire myself out so I can get a good night's sleep.

After a quick shower, I push my long hair under my swimming cap and head for the pool. Apart from three other women in the water and a lifeguard looking languidly on, the place is empty, just as I expected.

If I had children, I would probably be splashing around with the crowds in a public pool right now and worrying about getting sunburned. Maybe it's a blessing not to have any.

I'm standing with the water up to my waist when I recognize the woman in the lane next to me. It's Kei—a classmate from high school—swimming with an unflattering splashy stroke like a wounded frog. She seems to notice me, and I can see the indecision on her face through the splashing. I pretend I haven't seen her, pull my goggles over my head, and set off at a gentle crawl in the opposite direction.

The ripples cast undulating shadows on the blue-painted bottom of the pool. Silver bubbles form as I breathe out through my mouth and nose, skimming the plastic surface of my goggles as they rush to the surface. As I swim, my mind a blank, I feel myself become one with the water and light. Bliss. When I reach the far end, I perform a rolling turn that maybe isn't as technically correct as it used to be and head back again. Kei is standing in the next lane watching me, leaning forward in the water.

She says something as I reach her, but I can't make out what it is with the water in my ears. I hop up and down and tap my right hand against the side of my head. Warm water trickles out of my left ear, and Kei's voice clicks into focus.

"Wow! I wish I could swim like that."

"I really pile on the weight if I don't exercise."

She obviously wants to talk, but I pretend not to notice and start on another lap.

When I climb out of the water for a break, Kei is beckoning me over. There's no escape. Toweling my hair, I sit down on a plastic chair next to her.

Kei has the typical flabby physique of a middle-aged mother of two. But it's not just her age—she was always a bit on the dumpy side, even at school.

"Sorry I kept you out late the other night," she says.

"I'm the one who kept you. Did your husband give you a hard time about it?"

"I don't think he even noticed," she says with a laugh. "He never gets home till late anyway."

I think it was the first weekend in July when a bunch of us from school got together for a mini reunion at an *izakaya* pub in Dōza—me, Kei, Nagasawa, and Yamaguchi. We must have had a fair bit to drink. At the karaoke place we went to next, we hardly sang at all; instead, we sat around taking it in turns to confess our romantic indiscretions.

Nagasawa and Yamaguchi talked about old boyfriends from before they were married, then I admitted to the affair I had with my superior at the stationery company where I used to work in Tokyo. We kept it secret for three years until I tried to break it off when I realized his wife was onto us. At that point, things got a bit messy for a while; he turned into a bit of a weirdo and started stalking me.

It was partly to get away from him that I agreed to meet Shinji. I figured maybe it was time to settle down and move back to Nagasaki. Hearing that Nagasawa and Yamaguchi had had similar affairs in the past was a relief. Maybe everyone goes through something like that when they're still single, I thought. But Kei said nothing. She just sat there listening and, when it was her turn, said she had nothing to confess. "That's what happens when you get married young," she told us.

Kei got married immediately after graduating from the two-year junior college she went to after school. The first baby arrived soon afterward. She'd never had a real job, and I suppose the rest of us tended to look down on her a bit as a result.

It was past midnight when Nagasawa and Yamaguchi went home, leaving Kei and me alone. Since we live in the same general direction, one of us suggested grabbing a coffee somewhere before sharing a taxi home. We ended up in a late-night jazz café.

Our coffees were down to just ice melting in the bottom of the glass by the time she opened up.

"To tell you the truth," she said, "I had one, too. And after I got married."

"Had what?"

"An affair."

"You? You must be kidding. I don't believe it."

"Why not?"

"You've always seemed so happy at home."

"I am happy at home. But that doesn't mean I don't want the experience of being in love."

Kei's husband is five years older than her, a chef with his own late-night restaurant. He's a good looker—way out of her league, I'd have thought. Of course I would never say that to her face. So it was incredible to think she could have cheated. The other way around, sure—but Kei cheating on him? Never.

"Who with?"

"A college student nine years younger than me. He used to come to the house to teach the boys."

I couldn't believe what I was hearing. It seemed amazing that a nondescript person like her had such a scandalous secret in her past. And with a student nearly ten years younger? Sounded unlikely to me.

"I'm not making it up. How long is it now since you got married?"

"Three years."

"It's been thirteen for me. Ten when it happened. After all that time, you stop thinking about your husband in that way—romance, passion, whatever. But you're still young. And you're still a woman."

Once she started, there was no stopping her, and I lapped up the details. There was a touch of boastfulness in her voice, but that didn't put me off. I was excited by what she was saying. Something seemed to catch fire inside me. I felt my legs trembling as I listened. So things like this really did happen after all.

"But how did it happen?" I asked admiringly. Maybe there was a twinge of jealousy in my voice as well.

"He was from Sasebo originally. He'd come to Nagasaki for his studies. He used to give my boys their lessons, and then quite often I let him stay for dinner. At first I treated him like a younger brother. After dinner he'd sit watching TV and chatting with me and the kids. Sometimes after they went to bed, we'd stay up late talking, and since my husband never gets home till the morning . . . well, we had plenty of time to ourselves."

"And then? How did it start?"

"I suppose you could say I seduced him."

"How?"

"I was wearing a tank top with nothing underneath. You could see everything."

"Wow, Kei. Talk about still waters . . ."

I felt a charge of erotic excitement run though me. I folded my legs and squeezed them tight.

"OK, so I know I'm not slim. But some guys prefer a woman with a few curves, right? Anyway, he couldn't take his eyes off me. I could feel him staring the whole time. You know what they're like at that age. It just mounts and mounts till they grab anything they can get their hands on."

Again, it was like an electric shock. Until now, I'd always thought I preferred a man I could depend on. I'd never thought of younger men in that way.

"So—what then?"

"We were watching TV. Suddenly he reached out and started feeling me up through my top."

"And?"

"We kissed."

"Wow."

"We'd had grapes for dessert. The second time we kissed I put a grape in my mouth and pushed it in under his tongue."

I seemed to hear a voice shrieking inside my head. I could picture it perfectly—the pale, almost transparent green fruit rolling back and forth between their tongues. I could see it as clearly as on an endoscope in a doctor's office.

I felt my nipples harden under my blouse. My thighs were sticky with perspiration.

We'd gone into the café intending to have nothing more than one iced coffee each, but by now we'd moved onto Cutty Sark with lots of ice and water. Our glasses glinted under the orange lamps. I remember the sound of a trumpet in the background.

Kei's sudden confession had made my heart pound. I was a little breathless.

"It lasted for three months. I used to go over to his little one-room apartment. I was crazy about him. Sometimes I thought I wouldn't mind leaving my family if it meant I could live with him for the rest of my life."

"What about now? Did you stop seeing him?"

"He began making outrageous demands. Telling me I'd better come running whenever he sent me a text. Asking me to do all kinds of pervy things while he watched."

"Pervy?"

"I can't talk about it. Not here. It's too embarrassing." She looked around at the other customers, sunk in the dim orange light. Cigarette smoke eddied under the lampshades.

"Once, I remember crying my eyes out after he told me I smelled like an old woman. But in spite of the way it ended, I don't regret it. No one will ever love me like that again."

Her plump face looked tired.

"Maybe we should think about getting home," I said. It was past three in the morning.

No doubt about it: Kei's story that night awoke something inside me. By coincidence, it was around this time that the brakes on my bike stopped working properly, making that awful noise.

I began to notice younger men—I'd hardly given them a second look before. I suddenly saw high school students in a new light. I watched them when they took off the jackets of their uniforms, the boyish innocence on their faces belying the surprisingly muscular bodies beneath their open-neck shirts.

And I could sense them looking back at me too, feel their eyes stroking my breasts and thighs as I made my way through a crowd of boys waiting at the bus stop, the brakes on my bike squealing as I passed.

Before long, I was deliberately unbuttoning my shirt to show my cleavage, relishing their attention. I seemed to hear them groaning with desire, like bees buzzing at nectar.

It was as if a switch had been flipped inside me. I no longer wanted only to be led; I wanted to lead the way. I had a new band of followers. I enjoyed the thrill of discovery.

It was around then that I dropped in at the secondhand motorbike shop to get my brakes repaired—and met him for the first time.

"You won't say anything, will you? About what I told you that night?" Kei lies back on the reclining chair like some marine animal, her flabby belly hidden under a towel.

"About what?" I say, as if I've forgotten all about it. She is obviously feeling embarrassed. I'm not surprised; it was embarrassing enough just listening to it.

I lie there with an innocent look on my face. The reflections from the pool flicker on the ceiling, tracing faint patterns. A whiff of chlorine floats in the air.

"Don't pretend. I could tell you were hanging on every word."

"Oh—you mean you and your boy toy?"

"You're only jealous. Or maybe you still don't believe me. You think something like that could never happen to me."

"That's not true."

"Do you want to know what happened next?"

"I thought you said you split up?"

"Well . . ."

"Don't tell me if you don't want to . . ." Really, of course, I'm dying to know. She'd described how the affair started. I want to hear how it ended, too. The bike shop boy and I are still feeling each other out. Nothing has really happened yet. But I'm sure it will flare up soon enough when the time is right. I want Kei to tell me what the future holds, after that first burst of flame. Will it just turn to ashes? Or will it linger on painfully till I'm old?

"It's two years now since the last time I saw him."

"How did you split up?"

"After he graduated, he just kind of disappeared. He got a job with a trading company—he lives in Kobe now."

"Just kind of disappeared," I sigh, remembering all the fights I had in the dying days of my relationship in Tokyo.

Kei holds a hand over her mouth apparently to cover a giggle.

"What's so funny?"

"He sent a New Year's card—addressed to the boys."

"What's so funny about that?"

"When I saw his childish handwriting, I burst into tears."

"Why?"

"I can't forget him. Even now I think I might go to him if he asked me to."

"What, and leave your husband and children?"

"Isn't it awful? Sometimes I think there must be something wrong with me."

Seen in profile, Kei looks like someone I don't know at all. She falls silent, and after a while, I can tell she's dozed off. I drape my towel over the chair and walk toward the diving board. I glide into the water without a splash. The bottom of the pool looms up in front of my eyes before buoyancy brings me to the surface. I kick out and work my arms.

I've always been a strong swimmer. I was on the team in junior high. If I increase my speed, I know that I can cover twenty-five meters in next to no time. But I move my arms slowly. I want to enjoy being held by the water.

I swim on slowly, looking for a glimpse of his face in the clear blue water. I feel something about to rush over me, but for the life of me I can't tell what it is.

When I take off my goggles after my third set of fifty meters and look up at the poolside, Kei has gone.

Recently, I find myself thinking about the boy from the bike shop all the time. I sometimes feel as though I've spent my whole life thinking about people who aren't there. It's as if absent people are more attractive to me than those I'm actually with.

It was the same when I worked in Tokyo. Alone in my apartment in Hachioji, I used to enjoy daydreaming about my lover, wondering what he was up to. Right now, he'll be with his family, I'd think. I would picture him bathing his little girl, splashing water over her with gentle hands that weren't at all gentle when he handled me. Thinking of these things made me upset, but there was something good about it, too—as though the pain was somehow grown-up.

On nights when he was coming over, I would take my time preparing a meal, even though I'm not normally much of a cook, and buy a bottle of the expensive red wine he liked. I'd greet him with a big smile and then, later on, do anything he asked me to in bed. I sometimes find myself looking back on it fondly now, even though the sadness when he left me there was often so bad I used to cry myself to sleep.

Over and over, we went through the same routine. Three years passed before I knew it. Other men used to ask me out from time to time, but I stayed faithful to him. I liked him the way he was—aloof and mean. He used to treat me roughly, like a plaything. Once he was done, he would turn his back and lie smoking a cigarette, indifferent to me. Not once did he stroke my hair or hold me in his arms. He left as soon as he got what he came for, with barely a word of goodbye. But in a way, it was good that he was so unromantic.

It was when I tried to break it off, worried that his wife was getting suspicious, that he abruptly changed. He'd always ignored me except when he wanted me, but now he started phoning constantly and coming over to the apartment two or three times a week instead of just on Friday nights. He lost all his attraction for me. I tried to get away, but he started bugging me at the office, asking me to take him back. "I don't want to lose you. I can't bear to let you go . . ." Over and over, with tears in his eyes. Then there were threats, and the stalking began . . . That soon brought me to my senses.

It was during this rough patch that my mother called from Nagasaki to tell me about the possibility of a formally arranged introduction to someone she'd heard about through the church. "He's a little older than you, but it's a good family: they're all doctors and professors. He's the youngest. A cardiologist. Very nice, very polite. And a good steady income. At least say you'll come and meet him."

My brother had recently qualified as a pediatrician. It was this unprecedented event that gave my mother the confidence to even consider an introduction to someone with such an impressive background. "Our family's just as good as anyone else's," she liked to say proudly. But there's a big difference between one that has produced doctors and scholars for generations and a down-to-earth family like ours. Until my brother, our lot had produced nothing but a long succession of factory workers, city hall officials, and department store clerks. The undercurrent of a family's traditions—people's ways of thinking, their intelligence, their hobbies and interests—doesn't change overnight just because one of them has become a doctor.

Take Shinji's father, for example—a man who listens to Mahler symphonies with his after-dinner coffee. My dad still collects CDs of sentimental old Japanese *enka* ballads, and my mother is hooked on the young actors in her favorite Korean TV dramas. It's like two different worlds.

Shinji was fifteen years older than me, quite plump, with glasses. At least he still had his own hair. Maybe that was what allowed him to squeeze into the "just passable" category. But getting married and sharing the next few decades with him? Let's just say I had my doubts.

We met every day for the next three days. It was at the end of our third date that he took me to the house for the first time. When I saw the garden and the kiwi vines in fruit, I remember thinking: I've had enough of Tokyo, this is where I want to live. It came as a relief more than anything else.

We sat on a bench under the trellis, with sunlight drifting through the canopy. The kiwis were ripe and golden, and we talked easily as we sipped from glasses of lemonade. "Do you know what a kiwi is really?" he asked. I guess he must have begun to notice already how little I knew.

"It was just a bird, originally," he said. "The national bird of New Zealand. An endangered species. For a while it looked as though they might become extinct. They're protected now, but they're still not easy to see. It's small, and flightless—it lost the use of its wings a long time ago. Small, round, and brown . . . quite like this fruit, in fact, if you stuck legs and a beak on it. The name comes from its call. I like to think that when people bite into the fruit they think of this funny little bird skulking away in the depths of the forest."

The soft light of late summer lay in golden patches on the ground, and a faint breeze stirred the leaves. I could sense time flowing gently by.

The prospect of enjoying this slower pace of life suddenly appealed to me. It was like a lungful of fresh air. I think that was when I decided to say yes—not so much to Shinji himself, but to the entire way of life I'm living now, of which he is just one part.

I went back to Tokyo to sort things out. I told the head of the department and my co-workers that I was leaving to get married and then finally spoke to—him. He didn't take it at all well.

"You've just been blinded by money," he said. I could tell he was losing control.

"As if you can talk—you're just blinded by sex," I spat back.

He flinched, then started making wild threats. "I'll kill him. I'll stop the fucking wedding!" He was yelling now and picked up a kitchen knife.

I reached for the phone to call the police. He must have realized I wasn't kidding; it seemed to bring him to his senses.

"OK, OK," he said eventually, "I'm going." And he slunk off, leaving a cloud of dejection and resentment behind him.

For a while after I moved back to Nagasaki, he kept bothering me with text messages until I changed my addresses. Since then, I haven't heard a thing. I was worried that he might turn up at the wedding, but everything went without a hitch.

Sometimes I wonder what I ever saw in him. But now and then, I feel a pang of nostalgia for the nights when I sat waiting for him to call—for the times when he'd turn up at my apartment and use me to satisfy himself. Of course I'm quite happy with the life I have here in my little Garden of Eden. But if I'm honest, I think I might be getting a bit bored.

There's never any problem with money. There's no need for me to work even part-time. Shinji treats me well, and his parents never interfere in our lives. I know how lucky I am. Yet sometimes I can't help feeling a little . . . bored by it all. I can't help longing for a bit of adventure.

And just at this stage in my life, along comes Kei, with perfect timing, to whisper in my ear and tempt me to taste the forbidden fruit. It's as if she disturbed a snake lying curled in some hollow inside me. Startled it and sent it slithering out of its hiding place.

Two laps of the pool: fifty meters. Twenty sets makes one kilometer. My target is to swim this distance twice a week. When I was on the school team, we used to do far more than that every day, but I'm not swimming competitively anymore. My main aim is to keep my weight down. Also, I love the sense of accomplishment and the pleasant exhaustion after finishing my laps. The water washes me clean right to the tips of my fingernails.

I take a shower and call Shinji while I towel my hair.

"We're having a little celebration at home tonight. It's your father's birthday."

"August 8, of course. I'd forgotten."

"I was thinking of getting him a watch."

"Sure. Sounds good to me."

"Oh, and your mother is giving us dinner. So try to get home early if you can."

Shinji often eats out, so I'm used to having meals on my own. But I want to make sure he's there tonight. It's always a bit awkward when it's just me and his parents. Even when he's there, the three of them are always talking about highbrow stuff. I wind up sitting there bored out of my mind, pronging olives with my fork like a child left out of the grown-ups' conversation.

"Don't worry," he says. "I haven't any operations scheduled for this evening." He often tells me how happy his parents are that I joined the family. The truth is they probably think of me more as a granddaughter than a daughter-in-law. They both were in their thirties when Shinji was born. There are eight years between Shinji and his eldest brother, and fifteen between Shinji and me. So it's only natural that they might see me as a member of their grandchildren's generation—especially since Shinji treats me more like a daughter than a wife these days.

Maybe that's part of the reason why he doesn't make love to me much anymore. Not that I exactly want to be touched by a short, fat man like him—however brilliant he may be intellectually. A man's libido starts to fade when he reaches forty-eight, according to him. But I know otherwise. Once, he came home around three in the morning, and while he was taking a shower, the green light on his phone kept flashing to indicate a new message. I couldn't help it, even though I felt a bit guilty as I picked up the thing to look. The message was from a number saved under the name of "Momo." "Thanks for tonight," it said. "I had a great time. Can't wait to see you again soon."

That's the way it is with men. The desire builds and builds until they're nearly bursting. Once they've shot it out, they're like empty bottles. Then, clear as glass, they turn away and hurry home in the early morning.

But I wasn't jealous. I felt more impressed than anything: I didn't think he had it in him. I pretended not to notice and haven't bothered to find out anything more since then. Maybe he's keeping some big secret from me—but I'm not going to start probing and risk waking up the big black snake that might be inside him.

"Try not to be late."

"All right. See you later."

My hair's still wet. I apply some mousse and give my head a shake. Wet hair gives me an untamed look, as if I've had a frizzy perm. I leave the club and head down to the parking lot in the basement.

I want to stop by the supermarket near the station to pick up supplies for breakfast, but the roads are jammed, the traffic at a standstill. I sit staring at the sunlight on my wrists, the hoods of the cars glinting in the opposite lane, the deep green of the tallow trees. Again, there are cars with out-of-town plates everywhere.

I think ahead to the ceremony tomorrow. What a day to have chosen for him to come to the house! But it couldn't be helped.

I want to feel his hands on me, those work-stained fingers with dirt under the nails. I want him to treat me roughly, like a plaything.

What's wrong with me? Somewhere deep inside, my yellow-eyed serpent is flicking out its tongue.

I've been reading the Old Testament in the Bible Shinji's mother gave me. I think she was shocked by how little I knew. It was her idea to start with the Old Testament. "The New Testament might be a bit difficult at first. The other part's full of interesting stories." But I can't get past the bit in Genesis about Adam and Eve and the Fall.

I suppose it's not surprising, given my situation. All kinds of thoughts come into my head when I read it. Personally, I think it was unfair of God. He must have known that his two newly created people would sin—and still he let the snake wander around the garden. He could have dealt with the thing before the trouble started.

Maybe the Fall was part of his plan all along. Maybe God had already reckoned on all the sins that would be committed by all the men and women in history. Probably he's known from the start what was going happen. Which would mean he's always known that one day I would make a pass at the boy from the bike shop and invite him up to the house.

Tell me, Lord—if you really are up there in heaven. Where does this twisted heart of mine come from? Why is this descendant of your Eve about to commit a mortal sin without so much as a twinge of guilt?

When I finally make it to the station building, I pick out a pair of matching his-and-hers watches at the jeweler's on the second floor. Nothing formal, but a neat design, with a black pearl face and alligator skin straps.

They're the latest model—solar-powered, and connected by radio waves to one of those superaccurate atomic clocks: 186,000 yen for the pair. Before I got married, this would have been an unthinkable amount of money to spend. But now I just slap it on the credit card with barely a thought.

Once that's out of the way, I go down to the supermarket on the first floor to pick up some bread for the morning, along with bacon, peppers, and some lemons to put in my tea, and some hand cream. I pack everything into a cheap shopping bag.

Back in the parking lot, I put the paper bag with the watches on the passenger seat. As I dump the groceries in the back, the top of the bag rips open and a lemon rolls out, coming to rest in the hollow of the ivory-colored seat. A funny premonition takes hold of me. Maybe this is God's answer to my question.

Anyway, something has happened. I don't know what it is, but it's as if everything has fallen silent—over the rows of parked cars, the dark stains on the concrete floor, the walls, even the lemon on the back seat, glinting in the light from the rear window. It's the kind of silence that sometimes hangs in the air just before someone starts to speak.

I've had other odd moments like this since I moved in with Shinji and his parents. Their faith must be having an influence on me. Even a lapsed believer like me isn't immune.

I steer the car back onto the clogged highway. It's now late afternoon, and the sunlight isn't so fierce. I sit at the wheel as the car crawls forward, brooding about the boy and the reckless game we're playing.

Maybe it will come to nothing. Maybe I'll invite him into the house and lead him on for a bit, and that will be that.

There is a gap of fifteen years between us, after all—he's barely half my age. Obviously we could never have any kind of future together. I'd be an old crone when he was still in his prime. He'd soon get tired of me and run off with a younger woman. It's too bad we couldn't have met when we both were teenagers. Maybe I should just swallow my regrets and leave it at that.

I pull off the highway just past the Takaramachi intersection. Before long, the place where he works comes into view. A couple of weeks ago, I beeped the car horn at him when I saw him working outside. He saw me coming and gave me a wave. It wasn't much, but it put me in a good mood for the rest of the day.

There's a group of young people standing in front of the shop, taking no notice of anyone else. Probably his friends. Suddenly, I know he's there with them. My heart jumps.

The lights change to red at the crossing by the shop, and I look over and try to pick him out of the crowd.

There . . . the tallest one, with the spiky hair like a hedgehog . . . yes, no doubt about it. It's him. I'm getting ready to signal excitedly with a blast of the horn when I feel his eyes on me. He's seen me. He's definitely seen me. But what happens next makes my hand freeze in midair before it reaches the horn.

He is leaning against a moped parked under the tallow trees in front of the shop. Next to him is a young woman with a moped of her own. As I watch, he slips his arm around her waist, pulls her close, and kisses her in front of everyone. And I'm sure he's looking my way as he does it.

The girl dodges out of reach with a laugh and pushes his hand away. But it's obvious she doesn't really mind. She's wearing one of those tank tops that leave the midriff exposed and a pair of bright blue, well-washed jeans. For all her curvy bust and hips, she still has the face of a young girl. But she's interested. She's definitely interested. In the sunlight coming through the trees, the group laughs and jeers at the couple, egging them on.

The lights change to green, and I put my foot down on the accelerator. I forget all about sounding the horn. My eyes are misting over. I feel a tightening in my chest. Why this anguish and frustration? And why the tears filling my eyes? I remember the bright yellow lemon on the back seat. It was an omen. I knew something bad was going to happen.

As soon as I get home, I go to my bedroom and bury my head under the bedclothes. He definitely saw me. He must have known I was watching from the car. That's why he grabbed hold of her. Probably she's not his girlfriend at all. The whole thing was an act, put on for my benefit. I feel my anger and sadness start to fade slightly.

Early in the evening, before Shinji gets home, I wash my face and sit down in front of the mirror to put on my makeup again. By the time I sit down to dinner, it's as if nothing ever happened.

After grace, I sheepishly sing "Happy Birthday," and Shinji's father blows out the candles. He's grinning from ear to ear. Someone opens a bottle of good Burgundy, and we all drink a toast.

Then, with the cake back in the fridge, we start on the meal that Shinji's mother has prepared from scratch. Almost as soon as she sits down, she's back on her feet again, bustling in and out of the kitchen to check on the pasta and some smoked things she's made.

The phone rings soon after we've begun. It's their eldest son, calling to say happy birthday. Shinji's mother answers it and, after a brief chat, hands it over to her husband. "It's Shinichiro. He's got Shinzen and little Ma-kun there with him."

My brother-in-law is a doctor in Tomachi, now fifty-six. His own son is already the father of a three-month-old baby boy, even though Shinzen himself is still in medical school.

The old man takes the phone and starts cooing happily at his great-grandson. Of course the baby can't talk, but apparently someone is holding the phone in front of him. Shinji's father keeps saying the child's name, his eyes wrinkling with affection.

"It doesn't matter how many times you say it. He doesn't know what you're talking about."

My mother-in-law puts a bowl down in the middle of the table: cold pasta topped with okra and salmon, all drizzled with fresh pesto and lemon juice. This is one of my favorites, so even though I had pasta for lunch, I greet its arrival by clapping my hands and saying how delicious it looks.

"You're always a pleasure to cook for, Mihoko," she says. "You think everything tastes good." But I can tell she's pleased.

The birthday boy is still gurgling into the telephone. "It's me, Ma-kun. Grandpa. You remember Grandpa, don't you?"

Eventually, my mother-in-law has had enough. "Come on," she says. "You're going to go gaga over that child."

He hangs up with a grin and comes back to the table. After helping himself to a generous amount of pasta, he twirls it thickly around his fork and tucks in. He certainly doesn't eat like an old man.

"You'll choke on that if you're not careful."

With everybody in a good mood, I decide to hand over my presents. They undo the ribbons and put the watches on right there.

"Thank you."

"I'm so glad you came to live with us, Mihoko. Everyone else in the family married young except Shinji. I was starting to worry."

"Here we go again. I told you, I was always too busy to think of getting married."

I just smile and nod my head. The people in this family are like a different species.

It's only been a few hours, but that girl I saw him with this afternoon has already taken on a new appearance in my imagination. She's much better looking, with pearly skin. She needs to be a beauty to deserve him. They make a nice couple. I start to worry.

Maybe there won't be any room for me to squeeze in between them. But at the same time, I'm more convinced than ever that it's me he really wants.

I swing back and forth between these opposite opinions. I can't confirm it either way. After a while, I lose track of who is trying to seduce whom.

"I never thought sixty years ago when we stood here in the ruins that I would live to see my great-grandson's face."

"Everyone was just bones—I thought we were the last of the line. Do you remember what you said to comfort me? We're not the last, you said, we're the first." The old couple clink their glasses again.

"You did well to keep going that day," my father-in-law tells her. Gray haired and elderly, they look more like brother and sister than husband and wife.

The exact blood relationship between them is a bit complicated, and I'm not sure of all the details, but Shinji's parents come from distantly related families. They used to live next door to each other on this plot of land. Apparently when they still were small, their parents made arrangements for them to get married one day. Instead of rebelling against this plan, the two young people seemed to grow fond of each other quite naturally when the time came, as if it had been waiting to happen.

"There was no fence between the houses. We had that wisteria trellis instead. We often used to sit and talk there before the war. When it was blooming, it was better even than the cherry blossoms."

"It was quite a sight, wasn't it?—all those lavender flowers hanging down in big, long bunches."

Inevitably, we all turn to look at the trellis outside, now laced with kiwi vines. A soft orange light is shining through the leaves.

"To tell the truth, I never really felt comfortable under the wisteria when it was out. I was worried about creepy-crawlies."

"Do you remember that bench made out of a log?"

"Yes. Who was it put it there?"

"It came from a tree that Kiyoshi cut down on Mount Konpira. He dragged it all the way to the city on horseback."

"He was surprisingly tough for such a bookworm."

I'm amazed how clearly they can remember things that happened more than sixty years earlier. I can't even remember what I had for lunch a few days ago. For me, time is not something that builds up like snow, gradually becoming "the past"; it just seeps away into a hole somewhere.

Right now, that empty heart of mine is seething. I am not going to let some nobody like her get her hands on him. I repeat it to myself like a curse.

Physically I'm still sitting at the table, smiling and nodding. But in reality I'm somewhere far away; already driven out of Paradise, wandering in a wilderness . . .

"I wonder if they had a premonition that something was going to happen. Do you remember how they teased us the night before, when we all were cooling off under the wisteria after supper? They kept saying, 'You two had better hurry up and get married.' Remember?"

"They'd been saying it for a while by then—ever since I got my call-up papers. I was due to join the regiment in November. 'You never know what might happen,' they said. 'At least get married before you go.'"

"They sent us up to Mitsuyama to attend a ground-breaking ceremony for the house they were planning to evacuate to . . . We were the only ones to survive."

"I remember my father had a fever that morning. Normally, education came before everything else, but that day he made an exception and asked me, as the eldest son, to represent the family. He didn't want to bother any of the other relatives. He sounded oddly emotional . . . That's how I wound up skipping the lectures that day."

"My parents told me to go on ahead—they were going to follow later that morning. Afterward, the air raid sirens sounded. They must have been late leaving the house. It was a beautiful clear day. I remember taking some eggplants as a present."

"That's right—we used to grow eggplants and pumpkins behind the trellis. I was wearing some new gaiters my father had given me."

"It was in the papers that a new type of bomb had been dropped on Hiroshima, but we never imagined . . ."

"'This good, strong country of yours will become a wasteland in July and August.'"

"What's that?"

"Something a classmate showed me. His name was Furukawa. We roomed together. He showed me one of the leaflets the Americans were dropping from their planes. He was a bright, quick-thinking guy from Saga—cheerful, and popular with children. It must have been just a few days before it happened . . . The print looked like matchsticks, on yellow paper. I told him, they'll string you up if they find you with this. He just sighed and said, 'You know, I think we're going to lose this war.' He was killed along with everyone else, listening to some lecture."

"A wasteland? Is that what it said?"

"God wasn't up there above us when it happened. Not up in the skies where the B-29 bombers flew. It was out of His control."

"He wasn't present . . ."

"That's the only way I can make sense of it. I simply can't understand it otherwise."

Shinji, who has been listening quietly to his parents until now, suddenly speaks up. "What's got into that cat?" We all turn to look out into the garden.

A black cat is rubbing itself against the bark of the two things supporting the fabric of the trellis: originally a couple of small saplings, one male and one female, planted slightly apart. Around knee height, these merged into a kind of double spiral as they grew. Down at the base the stems are quite thick and from a distance they bulge like warts.

With its front paws on the warts, the cat has wrapped its body around the intertwined trunks, stretching out its neck and moving its head from side to side as though sniffing the scent of the leaves bobbing in the breeze. It looks a bit like a bottle partly buried in the sand, swaying gently as the waves wash in and out again. As I watch the cat's face, its eyes shut tight, the image of a woman in ecstasy sneaks into my mind . . . this restless mind, which won't leave me in peace these days.

By a natural association, I assume the cat is in heat. When I was a girl, I had a brown tabby called Mii-chan. I remember how Mii-chan used to come and curl herself around people's legs at certain times of the year.

"*Oni matatabi*," my father-in-law is muttering. "Devil's silver vine. Where's that digital camera?" he asks.

"Where you left it." She hands it to him from the magazine rack.

He always keeps one in the living room so that he can photograph whatever birds and insects come into the garden.

"Is it something unusual?"

“Another name for the kiwi is *oni matatabi*—devil’s silver vine. It’s a kind of catnip. That cat is high on catnip. I’ve heard about this, but I’ve never actually seen it before . . .”

The cat doesn’t pay us any attention even when we move over to the window. It keeps pressing itself against the vines, as though an invisible person is stroking its neck. Eventually, the sudden flash of the camera startles it, and after a glance in our direction, it slinks off into the azaleas.

Night comes. The heat is stifling, and it’s hard to sleep. I toss and turn, switching the air-conditioning on and off. I try to keep my agitation under control, but it’s no good.

I want him for myself. I’m not going to share him with anyone. But how do I know if he’s even interested? Doubts and angry thoughts keep sweeping over me. It’s enough to make me feel like crying.

In the middle of the night, I hear what sounds like the wind. It gets louder, and then I realize it’s Shinji snoring in the next bed. I’m wide awake now and too irritated to get to sleep again.

I can’t bear to stay and creep downstairs to sit at the kitchen table. I pour myself some mineral water and drain half the glass. Already I can feel the vexation beginning to subside. With my head in my hands, I stare at the silvery water in the glass. “What should I do?” I ask the night.

It’s nearly daybreak by the time I fall asleep, but I’m awake again at six. Immediately, one question dominates my thoughts: Will he come? I’m beginning to worry a bit about Shinji’s parents, too. What if they don’t go out? At their age, their plans could easily change at the last minute if they’re not feeling up to it.

The soft light of early morning comes in through the curtains. For a while, I lie in bed with my eyes wide open. What should I do? Shinji is quiet now, lost in a deep sleep, a still, shadowy mound wrapped in a thin blanket.

The digital clock by the bedside is showing 6:30 when I get up and go back to the kitchen. The unfinished glass of water is still on the table where I left it.

I toss the water in the sink and open the shutters. This is Shinji’s job really, but I don’t feel like sitting here in semidarkness waiting for him to get up. It’s already light outside. Our neighborhood is one of the last to get the light. But the clean glow of morning is all around us now.

On the parents' side of the house, everything is still closed up. Evidently, they're still asleep. The shutters between our living area and theirs tend to stick. I use this as an excuse to make an extraloud clatter as I open them. The window faces the trellis, where sunlight is already spilling through the gaps in the foliage. Dark fruit hang from the vines like misshapen Ping-Pong balls.

After the shutters, I push back the screen door to let in the morning air. A halo of sunlight surrounds the statue of Our Lady.

I turn away from her smiling face to look out at the trellis. It was here that the bones of the family dead were found—on this very spot, sixty years ago.

Both the statue and the crucifix next to it point toward where the bones were collected. It's like a grave site.

Shinji's parents always take care to keep the area free of weeds and clutter. It's as if they've been living here as grave keepers all these years.

It's funny how you always find a graveyard wherever a hillside gets plenty of sun, as though the best spots are set aside for people who can't enjoy them. Where I grew up is the same: a cemetery stretches out directly behind the house, and we walked past tombstones more or less every day. In an area where so many people died when the atom bomb fell, it would be silly to be afraid of the dead or spooked by their graves.

Over by the matted branches of the trellis are small translucent insects with a rainbow-colored sheen. I can already hear the pleasant buzzing of their wings.

On the screen door is what looks like a little row of black dots. When I take a closer look, I realize that it's two ladybugs with tiny red blobs on their black backs. They are mating, their backsides joined together. It doesn't look like much of a sin. Certainly it doesn't seem to merit a fall from grace.

I try to think of a way of seducing him: something daring that he won't be able to resist.

I remember Kei's story of how she let her bare nipples show through her tank top . I can smell a bit of sweet sweat prickling under my arms. I'm turning myself on.

And then it comes to me: something I *know* will work.

Shinji's mother is sitting in a black dress looking out into the garden, waiting for her husband.

"It's already quite hot," I say. "I hope you'll be all right at the ceremony."

She's dabbing at her eyes. The wrinkles around them are wet. I pretend not to notice.

"What plans do you have for the afternoon?"

"Oh, we'll have lunch somewhere and then go to church."

"Are you sure you won't get tired in this heat?"

"If we do, we'll just come home."

"What, during the ceremony?"

This is the one outcome I want to avoid at all costs: it would be a total disaster if they suddenly came back while I'm alone with him.

"I expect we'll stay till the end of that, whatever happens. You never know if we'll still be here next year."

She takes a lace handkerchief out of her bag and dabs at the perspiration that's started to appear through her makeup.

"Should I close the door and turn on the air-conditioning?" I say, but she waves the suggestion aside. "It's all right. We'll be leaving in a minute."

Out in the direct sunlight, a heat haze is rising from the lawn.

"Were you thinking about your relatives?" I ask. "The ones who died?" I feel I should at least make an effort. Today of all days it seems odd to be avoiding the subject. She's still patting her forehead and neck with her handkerchief. She sighs.

"I often think how lucky we've been—to live together for all these years like this . . . We stayed up in Mitsuyama at first. It wasn't till two days later that we came back. We tried and tried to get back to the house, but there was rubble everywhere, and everything was on fire. Even the cathedral was destroyed, except for part of the walls."

"Yes. This area was so close to the epicenter . . ."

A wasteland. The word comes to mind again. My eyes drift up toward the actual center of the explosion, 165 feet up in the blue sky. Here on the hill-side, we are probably about the same distance from the center of the blast as ground zero down below.

"There weren't many houses here then. The area was still covered in trees. They were all stripped bare. The atomic wind and the heat rays wiped out everything. We found glass and tiles that had bubbled in the heat. But there was practically nothing left of the wooden parts of the house. The ground was still hot and smoking."

"Was it easy to find the bones?"

"He worked out where the house used to be by following the lines of a ditch that was buried under the rubble. We found the remains all together where the wisteria trellis used to be. I wept. Why were we left behind? Why did we have to be the last of the line? That's when he said it. He was bending down to pick up the bones. When he heard me, he raised his head and said: 'We're not the last. We're the first.'"

What can I say? My mind is a blank, and any words that come to me turn to ash before I can speak.

"All right, let's go. I'll call a taxi," Shinji's father shouts.

My mother-in-law slips her handkerchief into her bag and gets to her feet. "Look after things while we're out," she says.

The roads must be clogged with traffic; the taxi seems to take forever to come. I watch the clock anxiously. They have just started to discuss whether it would be quicker to walk when the car finally arrives. "We're going to be late, thanks to you," I hear her complaining as they get in. I wave them off with a smile and finally relax as the car pulls away. But my heart begins pounding again when I step back inside.

Absentmindedly, I go about my usual routine, stripping the bed and putting on new sheets. It gives me a start when I realize what I'm doing. Right: this is it. I take off my sweaty polo shirt and skirt and pull a black sleeveless dress over my head.

It's a simple outfit that ends above the knee. I used to wear it all the time before I got married. I run downstairs and throw my dirty clothes into the machine. After a moment's hesitation, I decide not to press the switch just yet. I go and sit in the living room.

It's already 10:30, but still the doorbell hasn't rung. The sound of the clock on the wall is making me frantic. I try to block it out, but I can't ignore it. I'm supertense. I can make out sounds with amazing clarity—a dripping tap, voices echoing through loudspeakers somewhere in the distance, the noise of cars' mufflers passing outside—everything.

Every second seems to last an eternity. When I next look up at the clock, it's 10:50. Sadness floods over me. He's forgotten. There's no doubt about it now. He's probably riding his motorbike along the coast road, with the girl behind him squeezing her breasts against his back, clutching him like a pair of mating insects. I feel myself losing control, and can't hold the tears in any longer.

Suddenly, the sound of the bell breaks the silence, ringing twice and echoing through the house. The whole building seems to flinch. I check the cherry blossom–pink varnish on my nails as I press the button on the machine. "Hello? Who is it?"

His voice is almost a whisper: "I've brought your bike."

"Wait a minute." Flustered, I wipe my tears with a handkerchief and take a deep breath. After a quick glance around, I hitch up my dress, then peel off my blue panties. Curls of pubic hair lick at my skin like black flames.

I scrunch up my underwear, throw it into the washing machine, and flick the switch. The water starts to cascade down the glass window. I fold my hands in front of my chest. Standing by the washing machine without any underwear, I look up to heaven and whisper a prayer. "Forgive me."

He's waiting with the bike on the other side of the green iron gate. There's an odd look on his face.

"You came," I say. I'm so happy for a moment I feel as though I'm going to start crying again. But as I open the gate, I still have the presence of mind to make sure that no one's watching from the upstairs window of the house across the road. There doesn't seem to be anyone around.

He pushes the bike inside and stops before the front entrance.

"You took your time."

"The old man gave me a hard time about it. Said there was no need to bring the bike. He wanted me to have you come and pick it up."

"Did you manage to sort things out?"

"I told him he should try thinking about the customer's convenience for a change. He gave me a look like his eyes were going to pop. But he didn't say anything else, so I just left."

"You'd better hurry right back, then." I'm trying to sound him out, but he just smiles such an open smile you'd think it would melt in the sunlight.

"I'll tell him I bumped into a friend and we got talking."

"Not just a friend—a girlfriend, right?"

I can't help it. The jealousy flares up again, and the remark just slips out. I want to know whether yesterday was deliberate. Did he realize I was watching? The look of surprise on his face makes it clear he hasn't a clue what I'm talking about.

It's a side of him I don't know. A handsome young boy like him must have plenty of girls to play around with. Why should he bother with an older woman? I feel a stab of loneliness. I can't bear the thought of giving him up.

"Do you want to try the brakes?" he says, starting to crouch down beside the bike.

"Not here. It's too hot. Let's go into the garden. I'll show you the kiwis." I lead the way.

"You're going to show me your hairy kiwis?"

"Don't push your luck."

"You're the one pushing your luck. One of these days, the brakes will pack up, and it'll be too late. Too late for you, for me, the bike . . ."

He keeps up his suggestive remarks as he follows behind me with the bike. I can feel his desire against my back, as hot as the summer sun. Everything is silent except for the clicking of the bike's axles. The heat rises from the ground to touch my buttocks and thighs. I start to sweat. I feel a squirm of embarrassment at the thought of what I am about to do.

He props the bike on its stand under the trellis. It's almost as hot in the shade as it is out in the open. My skin, damp with perspiration, starts to give off a sweet smell that only makes me feel more uncomfortable.

"Wow, you weren't kidding about the fruit. There's loads of it," he says, looking up at the trellis like a child. He reaches out to touch one of them. "They really are kind of obscene, though. Hairy," he says, and laughs.

To my surprise, he looks at his hands. He turns them over and shows me both sides.

"These stains are hell to clean off. The oil gets right in under the nails." A strangely serious look comes over his face. For a moment, I have the absurd feeling that he might start crying.

A siren sounds and the bells in the church begin to peal. "11:02," I say. I feel panicky.

"What's it matter?" he shrugs. He sits down next to the bike and says something, but I can't make it out over the sound of the siren.

Look at me, standing here with no underwear on, observing the minute of silence and murmuring a prayer for the dead. It's blasphemous. I gaze up through the trees. The siren and the church bells toll their rebuke.

Finally, the sound fades, and something wings away into the echoing sky. The boy turns the pedals slowly with his right hand. It's as if he's been waiting for the bells to finish. The wheel starts to turn faster, until he pulls sharply with his left hand on the handlebar brake. The wheel stops without a sound. I stand across from him on the other side of the bike, staring at the whorl in his short spiky hair.

"Let's try it again. Here, crouch down."

He grins at me with his big white teeth, like a horse. His eyes are flushed with excitement.

In the shade of the vines, the hum of the turning wheel mingles with the sound of beating insect wings.

The countless tiny hairs on the unripe fruit are golden. Shards of blue sky show between the leaves. The fine hair on my skin shines in the light.

The sun is reaching its zenith. Everything around us is giving off light and heat.

I crouch down opposite him, the bicycle between us. He lets his gaze move to the area around my knees, exposed as my skirt rises up my legs. With one hand holding the pedal, the other on the handlebars, he turns the wheel, unable to look away.

At first, the pedal is slow and heavy. But the wheel soon picks up speed, and as the bike begins to shake with the force of the rotation, I loosen the grip on my knees and my damp thighs slide apart until I am totally exposed.

I watch the rapt look in his eyes. His mouth hangs open.

Something slimy wriggles inside me. I feel a quiver of pleasure, and my knees start to tremble. What would happen if he reached deep inside me now? Even as I shudder at the thought, I long for it to happen.

The semicrouching position is too uncomfortable to hold for long. I adjust the position of my heels and settle into an easier pose. I open my legs wider to give him a better view. Then I hitch up my skirt. My soft thighs and buttocks stand out stark white in the sunlight. It feels like squatting to pee in the woods. My body is wet with sweat, and a honeyed smell oozes from every pore.

Over his shoulders, I can make out the corridor inside the house, but my eyes are dazzled by the light and the interior of the space behind the screen door is just a hollow. Beyond the silhouette of Our Lady with her arms outstretched, I can see nothing.

I feel misgiving for a moment. But the brakes are long past working now, and when the boy's oil-stained fingers reach out to touch me, there is not so much as a screech.

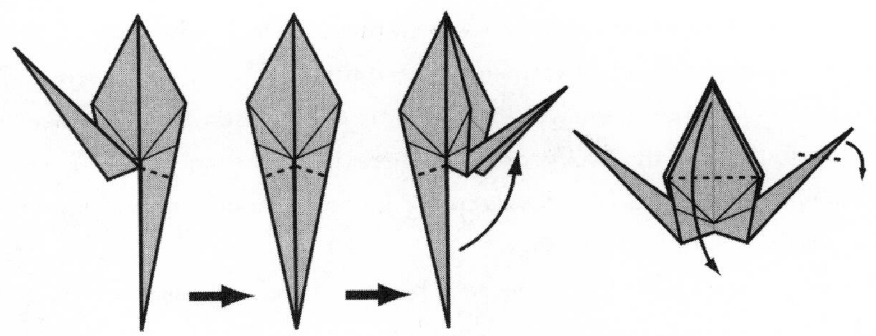

SHELLS

When I found the seashell by my pillow this morning, my first reaction was one of relief: maybe now they'll believe me at last.

The small, round object on the tatami was glistening, wet. I heard a rustling as crabs scuttled to their hiding places. The tide had gone out. Just moments before, I'd been sleeping on a beach, wrapped in my futon.

Our apartment is two miles from the sea. The idea that the tide could come in this far at night is absurd. I don't blame people for thinking it's all a delusion. Why, when everyone else is safely asleep, should I be having panic attacks about drowning in bed? Night after night. And the apartment is up on the twelfth floor. Even if there were a major flood, the water would never reach us here.

My nightmares and constant tossing and turning ultimately made it impossible for my wife to sleep next to me. She kept shaking me awake, but the disturbance continued as soon as I dropped off again. I can imagine her getting up in despair, thoughts of the sashimi knife in the kitchen running through her mind as she stares at me with weary, bloodshot eyes.

Yes, it must have been hard on her. The pain of losing Sayaka was bad enough; for me to go nuts on top of everything else was more than she could take. In the end, she left for her parents' place without a word. I suppose I should be thankful that she didn't decide to put me out of my misery with that knife.

But even she wouldn't deny how wet my hair used to be when she shook me awake. It was like seaweed. I remember her muttering, "God, your sweat stinks of the sea." And now there was the shell by my pillow—something plainer still. If it's real, it'll prove that waves brought it here during the night. You can't have shells without the sea. Their fossils can be found on mountaintops, proof that the area was once underwater.

I lift my head and inspect the shell blearily. It looks absolutely real, quite solid. If I were imagining things, surely there wouldn't be so much detail.

Try closing your eyes and imagining something. The interior of your house, something you saw walking around town yesterday, anything. An image, from memory. How does it look? Not sharp, right, but vague and blurry? "Memories lack detail," as the philosophers would say.

If the shell in front of my eyes turns out to be a hallucination, then I must be as unhinged as everyone says I am. All I need do is reach out and touch it. If my short, plump fingers encounter nothing but bright morning sunlight . . . then, all right, they win. I will have to admit that it isn't proof of the sea at all, but proof that I'm falling apart.

That might not be such a bad thing. Maybe I need to put more trust in people. Maybe I need to stop being so stubborn and loosen up a bit. Unpicking the knots with my clumsy fingers might not be easy, but it would be worth the effort if it meant I could finally stop lying here waterlogged like this.

The moment of truth . . .

My chin still on the pillow, I reach out a tremulous hand. As my fingers are about to make contact, I can't take the strain anymore and I shut my eyes tight. What if there's nothing there? I feel as though the whole world might collapse around me.

But there's a definite sensation of something solid and cold against the pads of my fingers. I'm touching something, no doubt about it, experiencing reality through my sense of touch.

I play with the shell before clasping it in my hand. It feels clammy. The sensation of it in my palm does not fade. Of course, your senses can play tricks, too. But not like this, not a lingering feeling like this. You might sometimes think you've touched something when you haven't. But no illusion or misapprehension could last this long.

People might disagree, but for me this perception of reality is good enough. Things exist in tangible and stable form, as anyone can confirm.

This shell is not a sign that I'm unraveling, far from it. It's the firm knot that will hold me together.

Still lying on my belly, I bring my clenched hand in front of my face, close to my eyes. "Awesome," I whisper. That's what Sayaka used to say.

There really is a shell in my hand: a cowrie with brown markings, about three-quarters of an inch in size, washed up by the tide. I've seen shells like this before. We found one on the beach at Nomozaki the summer before last, when Sayaka was three.

I see her chubby face laughing in front of me. The gurgle of her excited breathing comes back to my ears.

This sadness I feel is not just at having lost her. What hurts even more is knowing that the images I have of her in my mind are fading. Often as I trample through the leaves in Izumimachi Park, where we used to go for our walks together, I think how depressing it is that human memories are so fragile.

Of course, I can remember her running up the steps ahead of me. I remember how she used to turn back and call, "Come on, Daddy—hurry up!" But the love I felt for her then—the best and brightest, the truest feeling I have ever had—has faded. It will never return with the same force again.

It's been barely six months, and already the memory of her smile is starting to go. All that's left is an outline. Sometimes I'm not sure I could remember her face at all without the photos on my camera. Why are we so forgetful?

Maybe it's just another of the symptoms. Maybe I really am losing my mind.

That's why this cowrie is so precious. I can feel Sayaka's presence in it so clearly—her tiny hands, the look of happiness in her eyes, her sweet smell.

But this can't be one of the shells we collected on the beach. I took those from the bottle where she used to keep them and put them in her hand as she lay in her coffin. They were cremated along with everything else. Now nothing of them remains but ash, mixed up with her bones in the grave.

So this must be a different shell. But it still brings back memories—more even than her lunchbox and chopsticks or the beads she wore in her hair or any of the other things I've kept to remember her by. It's as if she's taken up residence in there, like a hermit crab wriggling tail first into a new home.

But there's not just one shell! When I look around the room, there is a whole trail of them scattered across the greenish tatami.

Forgetting the February morning cold, I get out of bed with uncustomary speed. I rub the sleep from my eyes. They're everywhere! The apartment is covered in shells. Not just on the tatami: there are two on the dinner table, one on the quilt, three in the sink—all glowing with a fragile light, as though they might not last, like dew. I walk through the apartment in my pajamas and collect eleven of them before they can melt away.

With the shells clutched tight in my hand, I stand in front of the fan heater and wait for my bulk—all 215 pounds of me—to warm up. Sayaka used to tease me when I was having a lie-in. "If you don't get up soon, Daddy, you'll turn into a walrus."

She loved walruses. It makes me laugh now to remember what she said. As the warm air courses over my body, I open and close my fist several times to check that the shells are still there.

It isn't the first time I've found things like this. I found fish scales in the apartment once. I put them in my pocket to show as evidence but lost them before I could use them. But those scales were like tiny contact lenses; there's no way I'm going to lose a handful of shells.

Ideally, I would like to catch one of the little crabs. They must hide under the pillows or something. A crab or two would clinch the case once and for all. Although, come to think of it, my wife can't stand anything with eight legs—they're all just spiders to her. She'd probably faint if I suddenly pulled a crab out of my pocket.

The phone rings.

"Were you up?" It's my elder brother. "How did you sleep?"

"Much better. Right through till morning. I think the medicine's working. In fact, I think I overslept. And when I woke up, I found a seashell by my pillow . . ."

He has no answer to that. There's silence for a few moments. I can sense his brain at work, assessing my condition.

There's another cowrie on the little table where we keep the phone. That makes twelve already this morning. But I can't afford to get carried away. I need to remain calm. People are keeping an eye on me. It's probably best to keep quiet about the shells for now. Better tell him more about it face to face. Let him see the evidence with his own eyes.

I remember the look he gave me when I spoke to him about it just before I was hospitalized. He let me finish and then hammered me with questions for hours. It was like being battered with logic.

"All right. So tell me, why does nobody drown? Me, for example: I can't swim to save my life. And wouldn't you expect to find at least a few boats washed up on the streets? Is there seaweed hanging from your washing line? Did you find an octopus in the closet? Or do the waves somehow make everything neat and tidy again before they ebb away?"

Even my wife was on his side. "I was awake the whole time. The sea never came near," she said. I felt I was being backed into a corner. I lost control. I charged at my brother like a wild boar and threatened to jump off the balcony.

He doesn't want a repeat of that. So I know he won't argue with me so forcefully this time. Still, I'm only too aware that I can't really explain what's happening. It's just not the kind of thing that can be explained scientifically. It's beyond logic and common sense.

But that doesn't alter the facts: the sea surges inland in the middle of the night, and whole swathes of the city are submerged.

My brother is better prepared now. If I start insisting, he probably won't bother to come around himself; he'll just send a team of white coats from the mental ward. And they won't even argue. They'll listen patiently and act all sympathetic. "Yes, yes . . . You must be feeling very tired. How about taking it easy for a bit?" And they'll scoop me up like a fish in a net. The next thing I know I'll be back in that hospital again.

But there is nothing really wrong with me. And this time I have the evidence, right here in my hand. Let's see him use his logic against that! There may be no drowned bodies in the streets, no fishing boats tangled with the traffic lights, no seaweed on the clotheslines. But I have twelve solid shells in the palm of my hand. You need firm results to prove a theory, and I have them—even though it may mean looking at things in a radically different way.

But I decide to change the subject. The timing isn't right. He would only try to turn his logic against me again, telling me I must have scattered them around myself while I was sleepwalking or something. He doesn't get it. Ultimately, it comes down to a simple lack of trust.

Creed, faith, conviction, assurance, trust . . . all the words you find listed under "belief" in a thesaurus are a vital part of human life. Once you begin to doubt, the world starts to blur like a mirage. You lose sight of God, lose friends, lose the ability to deal with other people. In the end, even crossing the street is beyond you.

I don't have the energy to argue with him. We would only end up going around in circles again and wearing ourselves out.

"How are things at the office?"

"Busy. Lots of inquiries about renovations."

"I'm sorry this had to happen at such an awkward time."

"Don't worry about it. You just rest up and make a full recovery. Dad's helping out. We'll manage."

The thought of my father bent over plans and diagrams at his age makes me sad. He started the firm as a young man. But he's in his seventies now, and it's painful to think of him struggling to get to grips with computers and modern equipment when he's supposed to be enjoying his retirement. He had an operation for cataracts two years ago. The glare of the computer screen can't be doing his eyesight any good at all.

I sometimes think Sayaka's death hit him harder than anyone else. He has always loved children. When my brother and I were small, he used to take us with him to all kinds of exotic places: Hawaii, Phuket, Okinawa . . .

He must have been busy, but he always kept his promises. It was only after I started working and had a family of my own that I realized how impressive this was. Sayaka never got to meet Hello Kitty with me.

My brother's two kids—Takashi and his sister, Hiromi—are in high school now and don't have much time for their grandfather. He used to dote on Sayaka.

"I want to get back as soon as I can," I tell my brother. And I mean it.

"There's no rush. That's one of the benefits of working for the family firm. Anyway, first things first. It's Wednesday today. Don't forget to take out the trash."

This is his way of looking out for me, trying to make sure I keep my life in order. Take out the trash, eat a hearty breakfast, and remember to take your alprazolam. And walk as much as you can around the neighborhood. No napping in the afternoon—if you start to feel tired, do some push-ups and sit-ups. He reminds me to buy healthy stuff at the supermarket like eggplants, cucumber, and shimeji mushrooms. Cut down on the meat, he says. Eat low-calorie meals, keep the apartment clean and tidy. Aim for regular bowel movements, don't forget to gargle, and have a long relaxing soak with bath salts every night before bed.

He's obviously worried that if I don't take care of my health and stick to an orderly, sensible lifestyle, I might fall to pieces. I'm grateful, really. A lot of people would have given up by now.

So I decide to follow his advice and deal with the garbage before having any breakfast. It's the first item on my timetable for Mondays and Wednesdays. I even separate the non-burnables and the recyclables, after I got a lecture once on the subject from my wife. Let the little things slide and your whole day can get messed up.

In any normal business, I would have lost my job a long time ago. Even if there were nothing else wrong with me, there's the way I look: a fat, clumsy-looking man is hard to take seriously as an architect.

I think I may have put on a bit more weight again. My underpants, which are forty-three inches at the waist, feel a little tight. I just about manage to squeeze into my brown corduroys, but my thighs bulge so much that I'm worried the fabric might burst. It's a mystery to me where it all comes from—especially since I've been avoiding fatty foods like pork cutlets and Korean barbecue recently.

There is the beer, I suppose, but even that I'm limiting to one small can of a low-calorie brand. Because of the side effects of the medicine, though, one can is enough to get me drunk. Sometimes I sit and cry late into the night. I find myself wishing the waves would sweep me away.

Ideally I'd prefer not to let my doctor know about this sort of thing, but he seems to be able to read my mind. It's as though he has some kind of device attached to the tip of his silver-framed glasses, constantly decoding my thoughts via electromagnetic waves. So the beer is probably an open secret.

Once I've warmed up, I put on a white turtleneck sweater my wife knitted for me and pull the zipper of my moss-green jacket right up to my chin. Sayaka's pink flip-flops are arranged neatly by the door. She still lives on in the things she left behind. Just remembering her ankles, plump like mine, makes me tear up.

Kakino-san is always telling me that I'll have to steel myself to get rid of these things soon. But "soon" is not yet. The moment never seems to come—like the moon in the children's song, always skipping one step ahead.

I think it's the flip-flops I would find hardest to give up. I can't even touch them. It may sound weird, but I can't bear the thought of anything new being laid on top of the image I have of her running on the beach, her heels bouncing on the sand. I'm worried that the memory might fade if I move them. It would be like new paint applied to an old canvas.

The same goes for the other mementos, like the place near the doorknob where she drew a tulip on the wall with a marker pen. I look away from it. I don't want to lose any more of her. But part of me hopes Kakino-san is right. Perhaps "soon" is not so far away after all. I feel hopeful that this special day—the day the shells appeared—marks a new start.

I get another fillip in the elevator, where there's a cowrie on the floor. I feel the tug of gravity as the elevator descends, but my spirits are buoyant. When the doors open, there are three more shiny shells on the floor of the lobby.

The unmistakable tang of the sea floats up from inside the mailbox. On top of a flier offering a five hundred–yen discount at a local pizza place are two cowries, shimmering there like a special free gift.

Out through the glass doors, I stroll past the orange osmanthus in the garden. The bush gives off a wonderful smell in autumn. When I discover another shell winking at me from the foot of the gatepost, almost as if some of the neighborhood kids had put it there as a joke, I can't stop a smile spreading across my face. A charge of excitement runs through me. I imagine a trail of them leading right to the shoreline, hinting at hiding places along the way and beckoning me on.

For days now, I've been able to sleep without any fear of drowning, and I wake up feeling quite light and refreshed. It's as though I've moved closer to the sea. Sometimes I have this odd feeling that I might be growing gills—evolving into some kind of merman.

How can any of this be happening—and why? My brother doesn't need to plant the questions in my mind. Why does no one else drown? Why does no one even notice the waves? I'm not an unscientific person. For a while in college before opting for engineering, I thought seriously about majoring in one of the pure sciences.

Maybe I have developed gills. Humans and other animals with lungs aren't aware of the air around us all the time, just as fish are presumably unaware of the water. Maybe there's a hidden organ somewhere on my body that allows me to breathe underwater when the waves wash over the city. After all, the human body is still largely terra incognita. Maybe the gills have something to do with my illness.

Or is this all just too crazy? I can't make any sense of it myself.

Whatever the explanation may be, the fact is that I no longer thrash about at night. In that sense, there's no reason why my wife shouldn't come home. But I haven't managed to put that to her in so many words yet.

I've got a bag of recyclables, mainly empty beer cans, in my left hand and one full of plastic stuff in my right. There's a good balance between them today. Sometimes the cans weigh so much that I tilt slightly to one side as I walk.

I also have the reassuring weight of nineteen cowrie shells jangling in my pockets. The morning's catch makes good ballast and—better still—proof that I'm still sane.

They might not be as persuasive as seaweed or an octopus, but there's no denying where they came from. I can't wait to show my brother. "Here, look at these," I'll say. "Now do you believe me?" People like him don't trust things they can't explain, unless you confront them with hard evidence.

It's a bright morning but cold enough to turn my breath white. Not much above freezing. My fingertips tingle as I walk down the hill from the apartment to the three-way junction where the garbage is collected. One regular from the neighborhood is already there. I haven't seen him for a while.

It's almost 8:30 by the time I turn up—much later than usual after my lie-in. There is no sign of his wife; normally, they do this together. Dressed in a thick, navy blue, hooded parka and work gloves, the old man is quietly sweeping up scattered bits and pieces and broken garbage bags.

I call out "good morning," but his tight-lipped face doesn't move. He glances at me but otherwise gives no response.

He is a heavy-set fellow with bushy eyebrows. My wife told me she got a stern telling-off once for putting out the trash without making sure the bag was properly tied. This must be him. He certainly looks like a bit of a stickler, though I have to admit he does a good job of keeping things tidy. He's obviously fit for his age. We're lucky to have someone like him living in the area—even if he isn't exactly what you'd call cheerful. Apart from acknowledging me briefly with his eyes, he carries on working without a word.

From the way he looked at me, I can tell he's suspicious. He probably thinks I'm going to dump everything without even bothering to separate the kitchen waste from the plastic packaging.

Or else he's one of their spies. This happens sometimes: I become convinced that people are watching me. He could be in league with my brother and the doctors; they might have arranged for him to keep an eye on me. But then I remember when I began thinking that even my wife was part of the conspiracy—which makes me cringe and brings me down to earth.

Let's face it, I'm a hypocrite: lecturing my brother about the importance of taking people at their word when I'm riddled with suspicion myself. And it's such a crisp, clear morning, a once-in-a-thousand-years kind of day. So again, I resolve to take the world and the people in it as they come.

The old man and I have known each other by sight for years, but apart from the occasional hello we've hardly exchanged a word. I don't even know his name. I did see him smile once, though. Sayaka was watching him work once, when she shook her head and sighed like a grown-up: "Oh dear, what a mess!" I remember thinking: So he does know how to smile, after all. That must have been in early spring last year. Of course, I had no idea then that it would be our daughter's last spring.

There are just a few brown and yellow leaves left on the old cherry tree that stands where the three roads join. Every winter, I worry that it won't survive, only to be pleasantly surprised when new buds appear on it again in spring. I'm always amazed by its life force. It has the most delicious, bewitching blossoms of any tree I know. Sometimes, if you look at the flowers by moonlight, there's a sense almost of madness about it—the sheer vigor of it, perhaps.

I can still see Sayaka playing here when it was in flower last year. There's a phone booth by the tree on one side of the intersection, and she went darting in and out of it with squeals of excitement, scampering after falling petals.

When she was born, I felt I had been born again too. Everything looked new. The world shimmered with fresh life. The clouds, constantly changing shape as they drifted across the sky, the clean shirts flapping on the line, the small black spider skipping down the windowpane . . . The whole world glistened as if it were fresh from the wash. Her eyes used to widen with delight when she discovered something new. "Whad dat, Daddy? Whad dat?"

I would do my best to explain things in a simple way so she could understand, but I often found myself at a loss for words. All I could do was stand and share her wonder. How precious those moments of peaceful silence were when it was just the two of us. She was my new eyes, ears, and hands.

Our universe is an accumulation of minute lives, each like a pinprick of light. And yet we are blind to so much of it, stretching out around us: strange creatures that only children can appreciate; visions of the past inaccessible to young eyes; truth, goodness, and beauty that only the insane can understand.

But something in the corner of my eye interrupts this daydreaming. I turn to look. There on top of an old wooden chair that someone has dumped at a corner of the intersection is another shell, looking wet and shiny, as though only this moment left there by the sea.

It's as if Sayaka is trying to send me a sign. I can't help looking behind me. I remember, when she was delirious with fever, her repeating through swollen lips: "Let's go and collect shells at Nomozaki again, Daddy." We had taken her swimming there one summer's day when she was three.

I look down at the shell. It gives off a cold, bright light under the white glare of midwinter. My eyes are still hers. Inside me, I can feel her delight in it.

Maybe it won't matter if I clear those flip-flops away. As I stand there in the morning light, I almost expect to catch a glimpse of her playing hide-and-seek behind the trees. I shut my eyes and pretend it's my turn to be It. "Ready!" I call under my breath. The old man looks in my direction.

I bend down and pick up a few instant noodle wrappers and stuff them inside my polythene bag, then tie it tight again. Part of me is still reluctant to head back home. I can't shake off the feeling that this suspicious old man won't be satisfied till he's gone through my garbage after I leave.

Why is there always so much rubbish strewn about the place? Maybe that, too, is the tide. My fingers are growing numb from the cold, but I hardly care.

My wife used to say how much she liked my pudgy fingers. I've always been chubby. No girl had ever taken an interest in me before, so when this smart, sophisticated woman five years my senior took the initiative, my heart just about burst with excitement. That was ten years ago.

For the first five years, it was just the two of us. She used to blame me for our being childless. "What's wrong with you—a big man like you?"

She became quite worked up about it, and it began to weigh on me. Then, when I was about to go in for tests, we found out she was pregnant. I felt I had finally managed to do my duty.

She was thirty-six at the time, so I suppose she was starting to panic a bit. Yet the idea of having a baby at her relatively late age didn't seem to worry her; even after Sayaka was born, she would often rouse me in the middle of the night, saying, "Let's make a little boy this time." But in the end, we had only one child. She may have been right—perhaps I was lacking in that department.

She started calling me Papa even before the baby arrived. She'd only ever used my first name, Hiroyoshi, before. It felt a bit like getting a promotion.

I blow on my fingers to warm them, feeling that Sayaka would have done the same. Then I decide to give the old man a hand. Initially I get a glare from him, but once he realizes I'm not being a nuisance, he goes back to just ignoring me. I'm soon getting into the swing of it. After a while, the garbage truck arrives, and they start tossing the bags into the back in that smooth routine of theirs.

The old man takes out a pocket ashtray and a packet of short Peace cigarettes and lights up. Puffing away, he glances in my direction occasionally.

Maybe he's shier than he looks. He might want to thank me but doesn't know how to start. I decide to help him out.

"It's probably students who make the mess. A lot of them live around here," I say.

Actually, I want to talk about the tides, but I opt for a safer opening. I used to have a habit of jumping right into things without stopping to consider what the other person might be thinking. My three weeks in the hospital helped enlighten me a bit on that.

He answers with a grunt.

Whether students are really to blame, I have no idea—though there certainly are plenty of them about. Our two-bedroom place is in a building whose first ten floors are mostly small apartments, many of them rented by students. They often congregate here on this patch of land on their way home at night. The racket they make reaches all the way up to our floor.

One time, they were carrying on outside into the early hours, singing some endless song about dancing rabbits. Eventually, my wife had had enough. She jumped out of bed, ran over to the window, and screamed: "Will you shut the fuck up!" Sayaka came and squeezed herself against me. "Mommy's scary when she's mad."

Sayaka hated being around people who were drunk. She would cover her ears, a look of obvious distress on her face. But nothing frightened her more than her own mother when she was angry. To tell the truth, I was a bit scared of her too. Sayaka was much closer to me in personality than to her mother. I've never had that argumentative streak. It upsets me to see people fighting. I don't like competitiveness much, either. I suppose I'm what you'd call peace loving. I think Sayaka was similar. When her preschool group had an acorn-collecting competition, she made do with just one acorn. She looked so pleased with what she'd found. If there were more people like us, there wouldn't be so many wars.

"No one tells them the rules. What to do with their rubbish," the old man says. At first I don't know what he's talking about and stare back at him vacantly. "The students," he says.

Quite a lot of them in our building are foreigners. I don't know where the landlord lives, but it's not here. We've been here for ten years, and we haven't seen him once. A real estate company deals with any problems that arise, but it's probably true that no one ever bothers to explain the local regulations.

The phone booth by the junction takes the silver IC-chip cards that can be used to make international calls, and I've often seen young people from Southeast Asia waiting there to call home.

"Anyway, thanks for always keeping things tidy," I say. He gives another grunt of acknowledgment.

Squinting against the smoke, he stubs out his cigarette in his ashtray and slips it into a pocket. He stands there for a few moments in silence, looking me up and down. I begin to think he's going to give me some unasked-for advice. It's not good to be so fat, you know. Think of your heart. You want to get some exercise. Why not take up walking or something? As if he can talk, with a cigarette always at his lips. I'm about to turn and go home when he finally speaks up—but it isn't my physical fitness he wants to discuss.

"What happened to the little girl? Haven't seen her for a while."

"The girl?"

"Yeah. Sweet kid, big round eyes, bright as a button. She used to help us out sometimes. Haven't seen her around much recently. I thought maybe she was your daughter."

Sayaka? Didn't he know she was dead? I wasn't expecting this. I can't think of what to say.

"Our daughter?"

"Well, she did look a bit like you. Kind of plump. Sayaka, I think her name was. Yeah, that's right. Often used to lend us a hand. Your wife used to come and fetch her."

There was no doubt about it: the old man knew her. So it wasn't only us who remembered her, but a relative stranger.

I feel a wave of sadness. Why didn't I hug her tighter when she cried? I could have done more when she was upset. I could have stroked her hair and patted her on the back and told her everything was going to be all right.

I can't get the words out. He's looking at me with a puzzled expression on his face.

"She . . . died. Last August. From pneumonia." And then the words dry up again.

His face turns bright red. "Dead? But she was just a child." He sits down heavily in the chair.

"I'm sorry," he says, looking up at me. "I had no idea." I notice the white hairs in his nostrils. The days when he might have bothered to trim them are long gone now. They look like grass coated with snow.

"Please—don't apologize. It's just something one has to accept."

His shoulders sink. He looks so upset that I feel I should be the one consoling him. Despite the clear skies, it's still winter. I long for spring, the way people in the snowy north must do every year.

He takes a packet of tissues from his jacket pocket and blows his nose so hard that I can feel my own nose start to tingle.

"I didn't know she used to help down here," I say.

He wipes away a tear. Set deep in his rugged face with its prominent cheekbones, he has round, beady eyes like an elephant's.

"It was the start of the rainy season last year the first time we saw her. We were tidying things up here as usual when she came toddling down that slope and started to help."

Normally I used to leave the house at around 7:40 in the morning. I'd never passed the man and his wife on my way out. They probably started after eight—I remember seeing them a few times when I was running late for some reason or had taken the day off work. But I had no idea that Sayaka joined in. I suppose my wife must have known, but she'd never mentioned it.

"We don't get many cars here, but every now and then they come through at crazy speeds. Since there are no traffic lights or a proper crossing, we always told her to look carefully both ways. 'Right-ho,' she said, and did it with her arm held high."

One of the three roads leads to the bypass and on to Isahaya, where my wife is now. Another follows the river up National Highway 206, over Saikaibashi Bridge into Sasebo. The third goes through Matsuyama-machi, close to ground zero, and into the center of the city. This is a popular shortcut, especially when the other roads are jammed during the morning rush hour. They come hurtling past sometimes; in fact, since there are no traffic lights, this quiet street might be more dangerous than the highway, even though there is much less traffic.

We always drummed into her how important it was to look both ways before she stepped into the road and to lift up her hand to signal that she wanted to cross. She was an obedient child. From what the old man is saying, it sounds as though she really did thrust her little hand into the air and check carefully left and right.

She flashes in front of my eyes again. I feel she might come and start picking up stray bits of rubbish. I shut my eyes, and there's a sting against my eyelids. She's not here anymore, I tell myself. But each time I whisper the words, her image flickers before my eyes again.

Words can't cancel out my imagination. It doesn't matter how often I remind myself that she's not here with us, that she's dead—she still returns. I dream of another world where Sayaka is still alive. It's as if the images of things we've lost are swept away on the tide inside our heads, to wash up on a distant shoreline somewhere deeper inside us. People have always been driven to imagine this other place—the other side, the world beyond, Paradise . . . It's the rift between two functions in our brains: imagination and rational thought.

I can feel my own brain starting to overheat. I want just to sink into the cool water of my sadness—the calm inside an empty seashell. But my mind keeps churning with questions that have no answers. I can't stop it.

Why was she allowed to live for only four years? When my wife called before lunch one day to tell me that Sayaka was running a fever, I assumed it was nothing to worry about. I remembered the last big panic when she'd come down with chicken pox. I was getting used to children's illnesses by now. They often get a temperature for no obvious reason.

Even when she phoned again in the afternoon to say that the fever was worse and she was thinking of calling an ambulance, I brushed it off and told her to take a taxi . . .

How many times have I regretted giving that advice, something I will go on regretting for a long time yet. My wife was right: it was my fault. I was too slow, too indecisive.

The air here is cold and clear as water. I can see drops of dew glistening on the bare branches of the cherry tree. I take a deep breath and try to shake these thoughts from my head. I mustn't let myself drown in memories. The world looks refreshed, still dripping wet. She was lucky to have had four happy years in such a beautiful place. Perhaps being born at all is blessing enough. Why worry about how long or how short a person's life is? Four years, a hundred . . . they're both just a tiny flicker in time.

"I hope she wasn't a nuisance," I say.

"Far from it. Always a real pleasure." He takes out his tissues again and dabs at his nose, which is cherry-blossom pink at the tip, with its white sprouting hairs. "She always listened to what she was told."

"Your wife isn't with you today," I say, bending down to pick up another cowrie shell I've found among the withered grass at my feet. The man pays no attention to what I'm doing. He's lost in the past.

"She's not my wife. My wife died a long time ago. That was my sister."

"Your sister? Well, that would explain why you always seem so comfortable together. I thought you were an old married couple. Is she away somewhere?"

"She died, too. Last summer."

Now it's my turn to fall into an awkward silence. I never know what to say in situations like this. I stare at the raw-looking sky.

"Collapsed one day just before lunch. A brain hemorrhage . . . She never came to. She died that night."

"Sayaka's fever came on around lunchtime, too. By that night, she could hardly breathe. There was nothing we could do."

I look into his eyes for the first time. They are clear and deep, like the eyes of a man who has spent his life staring out to sea.

"Was it in August?" I ask.

"Yeah. One of the hottest days of the summer . . ."

He breaks off and turns to look down the road that heads upriver. An old black Toyota Crown is approaching at high speed, the sound of rock music blaring from the stereo. For some reason, the speakers must face the street. The car races toward us. The chassis has been modified so that it hulks low on the tarmac like a toad.

Even when it reaches the junction, it doesn't slow down. As it passes us, a man with a pale face and shaved eyebrows looking like a Noh mask leans out and tosses a beer can from the passenger-side window. The can arcs through the air and bounces heavily twice on the black surface of the road. A few spurts of foam and brown beer spit onto the tarmac as the can rolls to a rest.

The old man leaps to his feet and shakes a fist above his head as though trying to fling something with all his strength.

"Who the hell d'you think you are, you son of a bitch?" he yells. The roar of his voice takes me by surprise, and I clutch the shells in my pockets. He obviously has the same kind of personality as my wife. They're the sort of people who make world peace an unlikely prospect.

"You won't get away with this, you bastard!"

He's still pacing and stamping, his shoulders heaving with anger. He glares up the road leading toward ground zero. I'm a bit worried that the driver might see him in the mirror and come back for more.

He lumbers over and picks up the can, pouring the dregs of the liquid in a stream onto the ground. There's a stale smell as the beer soaks into it. It's a night-time smell, not the kind of thing you want to inhale with the clean morning air.

When he rattles the can, a brown cigarette butt emerges from the opening. He pulls it out and, scrunching it up in a tissue, adds it to the collection in his ashtray. The can goes into a bag on the chair. No doubt he'll take it home and put it out with the rest of his trash next Wednesday.

"Because the bags are close to the roadside, some people think they can just chuck stuff out of their cars as they drive by," I say in an attempt to calm him down.

"I don't know what the world's coming to," he mutters. But I'm not ready to join him in dismissing a whole generation. There always are a few bad apples. And some red-cheeked ones. I feel another tug of nostalgia. Since my wife moved out, there's been no one I can share things with. But I don't want to argue with him and sour the morning with bitterness and anger.

"I'm sorry for shouting," he says, almost as if he's read my mind. I notice his shoulders relax.

"My sister and your kid used to talk about some funny stuff together here."

For a moment, this suggests a faded picture to me: of an old lady and her granddaughter gathering fallen nuts under some trees.

"My sister used to say it was the sea that washed up all the trash. She said that waves washed over the city in the middle of the night."

I look into his wrinkly face, and he gives me a sheepish smile—probably the first I've seen from him since that day with Sayaka.

"Funny kind of thing to say, isn't it? Of course nobody took her seriously."

"Did she really believe the sea comes in this far?"

"I expect she was thinking of that big tsunami a couple of years back, in the Indian Ocean. But even something like that wouldn't reach us here."

My heart is pounding so hard that I can barely breathe.

"But there was no doubt about it in her mind. She was quite insistent. Said the sea came in during the night and washed right over where we're standing now. Actually, I don't think it was so much a tsunami she had in mind—more like a regular high tide. She must have been going senile. She used to say that's why there's always so much rubbish around. Brought in by the waves, you see. Bits of wood, cup noodle packets, plastic bags, empty soda bottles—all brought in on the tide, according to her. Anyway, she was right about one thing: the pollution's getting so bad the whole coast is like one big refuse dump nowadays."

Suddenly, I see the area around us as a long expanse of shoreline and Sayaka walking along the sand, strewn with flotsam. She has a straw hat with a red ribbon pushed low over her face, her hands held behind her back like a little professor.

I remember the way she moved forward along that stretch of beach, looking down, her flip-flops squeaking as she walked, not caring about the hot sun. I reached out a hand to replace the towel that had slipped from her shoulders.

She kept picking things up—not just shells, all kinds of stuff. Most of it looked like junk: fish heads, wine corks, the metal handles of broken mirrors. Every time she made a new discovery she would hand it to me for inspection. "Whad dat, Daddy?"

For her, everything glowed with mystery and the magic of the sea. Later, when we got home, my wife told her crossly to throw her collection away. "They're dirty. Nasty," she said. But they never seemed dirty to me. Everything had been washed by the sea, rubbed clean of the stains it had acquired in the human world. The objects were quiet and plain, like the faded images in old photographs.

I loved to see her so cheerful and innocently curious about the world around her. Sunlight streamed down on the beach. A yacht's sails showed white on the horizon. But the happy moment didn't last.

For some reason, I began to doubt the reality of what I saw. I imagined a tiny fraying hole in the fabric of it and the hole widening . . . Then, just as I was thinking this, Sayaka held up an empty bottle of laundry detergent. "Whad dat, Daddy?" I looked at the label, but to my horror I found I couldn't make any sense of it. What were presumably just ordinary letters had taken on bizarre, distorted shapes. They meant nothing to me. It was like trying to decipher writing in a dream. The world slipped out of focus. I panicked and flung the thing away from me with a yelp.

When Sayaka started crying, I held her close and tried to laugh it off. But I couldn't forget the fright I'd had. Then my wife picked up the container where I'd thrown it. "What's wrong?" she said, looking at the label. "It's Korean. It must have come from one of the ships." And she strode away across the sand . . .

"Yeah, she used to say the funniest things," the old man goes on. "All this mess was the work of the tide. She was an innocent soul. It wouldn't have occurred to her that there are people in this world who toss beer cans out of a car window without giving a damn."

I feel I'm about to make a connection no one else can see. It's a sense of something impending—not quite like the intuition of someone about to hit on a brilliant new theory, perhaps; more the indefinite but unmistakable premonition you sometimes have before you think of the solution to a puzzle.

"But this isn't the Ariake Sea—even in the harbor here, there's not that much difference between low and high tide. No, she was going senile. That's the only explanation for it. Most of the time I didn't bother to answer. I mean, what's the point in arguing, right? If that's what she wants to believe, let her believe it. That was my policy."

He has a good-natured, understanding side to him, unlike my brother. He's not one of those scientific types who insist on pursuing things to their rational conclusion. But he isn't exactly a pious liberal, either.

"Did she ever say anything about this theory to Sayaka?"

"Oh yes. Your daughter was nice and polite. She took in all the nonsense my sister threw at her. She just nodded and sounded amazed by it. The sea comes here at night? And fishes? And shells and octopuses? There was a real sparkle in those big round eyes of hers."

I feel a warmth spreading through me. I'm sure my wife would understand if she were here.

The grass is wet with dew, the road shimmering in the sun. I can see clouds reflected in the bluish glass of the phone booth. And Sayaka still alive inside me.

I have a vision of waves overflowing the cherry tree and phone booth, and bags of rubbish pitching in the water. An unseen tide surging in at night, submerging the city. But this isn't the ordinary tide that fills the harbor. It's more of an effect, like a wash on a watercolor or the aura around the edges of a solid object.

When I arrived at the emergency ward, Sayaka whispered to me from deep in a fever: "Let's go to the seaside, Daddy." They'd taken her there in an ambulance from the children's clinic. I held her burning fingers in my hands. "As soon as you get better," I said. "You hurry up and get well, and then we'll go and collect shells."

But her fever didn't break. After a while, through labored breaths, she said, "The sea is really coming, isn't it, Daddy?" She was still a child, so I was used to her sometimes not making sense. But now, looking back, I can begin to understand what she was telling me.

Of course, finding out that someone else knew about the night tides does come as quite a jolt. But that isn't all. It occurs to me that the old woman was the first to notice. Then, through Sayaka, her discovery was passed on to me. And the solid weight I can feel in my pocket is the proof.

"I used to lose my temper with her sometimes," he says. "She went on and on about it. It made her cry when I snapped at her. I should have been more understanding."

"Oh, I'm sure she knew you didn't mean it." I feel I should say something reassuring, even though of course I have no idea if it's true or not.

"Maybe so. But she was pretty far gone by then. Always doing silly things. Trying to make tea with cold water, putting her gloves in the fridge. And looking for things she hadn't even lost. In the middle of the winter, she'd be walking around muttering, 'Now where did I put that watermelon?' I lost my patience with her sometimes."

"Everybody boils over now and then. I was the same with Sayaka."

If only I had held her tighter when she cried.

"How old was your sister?" I ask him.

"Sixty-seven when she died."

"People often do get a 'second childhood' around that age."

"I wouldn't mind, myself. Less responsibility."

"I think it's more or less inevitable if you live long enough. Everyone who lives to be a hundred is like that, more or less. Some of us go sooner than others, that's all."

“She really was like a child sometimes during the last few months. One day when that cherry tree was out, she just stood under it with the petals falling on her face. I’ll never forget how happy she looked. It was last winter that she really started to lose it, always forgetting things—and that’s when she came up with these funny ideas.”

“Did you take her to a hospital?”

“She wouldn’t hear of it. She was too proud. And most of the time there wasn’t really any problem. So I didn’t press her. I was afraid of the reality, I suppose. I didn’t like to think of her getting like that before me.”

Intermittent senility. The term pops into my head. I suppress it and decide to introduce myself at last. “The name’s Takamori, by the way.”

His turns out to be Nagai. The sister was Momoyo, written with characters meaning “hundreds of generations.” It’s the kind of name a high-class geisha might have.

“She was always neatly turned out. Not like me. And always determined to do the right thing. She moved in when my wife died, said I was hopeless on my own.”

“Are you managing all right now?”

“Most of the time.”

“It’s not easy, is it? My life’s been a mess since I’ve been on my own.”

“What happened to your wife? Don’t tell me she . . .”

I wish I could keep my big mouth shut. I’ll have to tell him the whole story now.

“Oh no, she’s fine. She’s gone back to her parents’ place for a while, that’s all. But I’ve not been myself since she left. I’ll be in a real state if she doesn’t come back soon.”

I clam up after that. A strange kind of panic comes over me. This happens sometimes: I get the feeling that people can see through me as if their eyes are like X-rays, boring right through to my bones.

“You should take care of yourself. It’s a tough time for you. You and your wife need to support each other and get through this together. With relationships, you never know when things might start unraveling . . .”

“Unraveling?”

Maybe he really is reading my mind. I try to resist the suspicion and resentment I feel. Faith, trust—I have to start from there. Once I begin doubting everything, I’m heading for isolation.

"Unraveling, bit by bit . . . Like with my sister. Always tugging at loose threads. Physically, there was nothing wrong with her. She had a good posture right till the end; looked like she had a ruler down her back."

I squeeze one of the shells in my pocket. This is no loose thread. This is a good, solid knot that's going to help me keep a grip on reality.

"She literally couldn't resist picking at loose threads. She'd tug at a little tear in the pillow until the insides spilled out all over the futon. She picked the cotton stuffing right out of her padded jacket. And she was always worrying away at her fingernails."

"Fraying at the edges . . ."

My mind is drifting again, off on another of its word-association games. Frays, raise, in praise, happy days . . . My mind runs away from me sometimes, skipping and jumping from one thing to another, free-associating until it tires itself out and goes blank. If my wife and brother do put me in an institution, I won't have any real grounds for complaint.

"She even used to pull at the stray bits on her own body."

I have a bad feeling about what's going on in my head. Really I should be getting home, but the old man is obviously lonely and glad to have a bit of company. I feel I owe it to him to stay and hear him out. His sister and Sayaka were a team. Maybe he and I are going to be partners, too.

"You know how your lips get dry and the skin starts to peel? Well, she used to pick at her lips till they bled. Must have hurt like hell, but she couldn't stop. I used to tell her not to do it, but she didn't seem to hear. It was like she was unraveling her own thread."

I picture the old woman's cracked lips, blood seeping from the flaky skin. In my mind's eye I see a squid being peeled and white flesh spilling out . . . The thought short-circuits with a fizz. Nagai is eyeing me a bit suspiciously.

I hold my hands to my chest and wait for my racing mind and pulse to settle. Something about the gesture seems to catch Nagai's attention. "Are you a Christian by any chance?" he asks.

"No, why?"

"I just wondered . . ." He gives me a searching look again, and we both are silent for a few moments.

"Would you mind," he says, "if I said a prayer for your daughter?"

"You're a Christian?"

He nods.

"There's a Buddhist altar in the apartment. Would that be all right?"

"Of course."

Thanks to my brother, the place is fairly presentable, so I don't feel too awkward about inviting him over. And it's time I was heading home anyway; I need to take my medicine.

"Yes. That would be nice. I'm sure Sayaka will be happy to hear from you again."

We make our way slowly toward my apartment in the morning sunlight.

"It must have rained during the night. The road's still wet."

Sunlight bounces off the tarmac. It's as bright as a spring morning, with snow melting in the sun. But it wasn't rain that made the road wet, it was waves. I can see them clearly, washing over the utility poles and the phone booth. But it would only confuse him if I start blabbing about it now. There's no need to rush into things. I'll break it to him slowly. Eventually, he might come to accept the discovery his sister, Sayaka, and I have made. Keep calm, that's the main thing. I'm beginning to get jumpy.

It's just us in the cramped elevator. The silence starts to feel awkward. What are two men like us supposed to talk about? I have no idea. Nagai watches the numbers as we ascend. His nose twitches, and he turns to look at me. Maybe asking him over wasn't such a great idea after all.

"Is it just me, or is there a smell of fish in here?"

My suspicions return. Is he planning something? Or is he coming closer to my way of thinking? I feel a strong urge to tell him everything. We're not enemies; we're almost fellow believers, with the same faith burning inside us. He probably knows all about it already. He must know that what his sister told him could be true—that the sea really does roll in over the city at night, waves drenching the buildings, roads, and cars . . .

The words are on the tip of my tongue, but I clam up again when I notice his Adam's apple bobbing up and down as though there's something stuck in his throat.

"No doubt about it," he says. "There's definitely a whiff of something." He starts sniffing at the collar and sleeves of his navy blue jacket.

"I used to work at sea. Tuna trawlers . . . They were still made of wood in those days. We used to go way out into the Pacific. This is fifty years ago now.

When I gave it up, I had this jacket dry-cleaned and put it away, then I found it again recently in an old chest of drawers. Nearly half a century later, and it's as good as new. It's true what they say about paulownia wood: it really does keep the insects away."

So he was at sea. That explains the faraway look in his eyes.

"I knew you had something of the fisherman about you."

"In my younger days . . ."

I want to ask why he decided to give it up. There's a hint of painful memories on his face as I look at him from the side. It's easy to imagine how a stubborn character like him might have struggled to get on with people when he was young.

"Did you ever see a walrus?" I ask, mostly for the sake of something to say. I'm letting my thoughts run away with me again. It probably wasn't the brightest thing to say, to judge by the odd look he's giving me now.

"Why do you ask?"

"Oh, Sayaka loved walruses. She used to put her arms around me sometimes and say: 'My big daddy walrus.' Since I'm so fat, from behind it looks like I've got no neck. It's worse from the side. It looks like my head just carries on straight into my back."

I try to make a bit of a joke out of it, but Nagai seems to be taking my question seriously.

"We often used to see dolphins and whales, and I think I saw a sea lion once. But walruses? I'm not sure. I mean, I've seen them in aquariums . . . We used to go quite far south, but I don't recall ever seeing a walrus. Could be I did see one and I've just forgotten. Maybe I'm losing it too."

His eyes remain fixed on the progress of the elevator display while he speaks. He falls silent, and the usual scowl returns to his face. The air grows heavy, and I can sense the distance growing between us. The elevator must be moving at the same speed as ever, but the force of gravity seems to be increasing. There's no way of judging, of course, but for a moment I clearly feel I'm being vertically compressed. Time has slowed down.

"You live on the twelfth floor? That's pretty high up. The apartments get more expensive the higher you go, don't they?"

"Not here. Most of the building is one-room apartments for students. Our place is just two bedrooms with a tiny living room. It's nothing special. We don't pay that much really."

"You're renting?"

"Of course."

"You must have a good view."

"Not bad. But there are so many high-rise buildings around nowadays, you can't really see that far."

"Can you see the sea?"

"No. We can make out the big apartments by the harbor, and a bit of the bridge. But not the actual sea itself."

"Even if there was a big tsunami, there's no way the waves could reach this far inland, is there? It's just impossible."

But the flood I'm thinking of has nothing to do with tsunamis; it's more like a quietly rising tide. The waves move inland, sea bleeding into sea, silently flooding the roads, engulfing the cars—and most people keep right on sleeping and don't notice a thing. All in absolute darkness, like a lunar eclipse.

"Tens of thousands of years ago," I say, "this might have been part of the bay. It's possible it could happen again if the polar ice melts. They're always finding sea fossils high up in the mountains."

"Human beings were still monkeys back then."

"You believe in evolution, then—even though you're a Christian?"

"Even the monkeys know that much. They're always showing programs about it on TV. Even monkeys watch TV nowadays."

"How long is it since we branched off from the apes—about five million years?"

"Not so long ago when you think about it. And according to my sister, the sea covered the streets of our neighborhood only last night."

Once again, I'm seized by an urge to show him the shells and tell him everything. But as I'm mulling it over, the bell pings and the doors open. The moment passes. But there's no hurry. I have the evidence in my hands. I will reveal it in good time.

"Do you mind if I wash up first?" he says as we take off our shoes in the entrance. "It wouldn't feel right to say a prayer with dirty hands. Not after handling all that garbage."

I show him to the bathroom. I'm a bit embarrassed to notice that the blue plastic basket by the washing machine is still full of my underwear. But then an even more worrying thought comes to mind. As my brother never tires of pointing out: if the city is submerged night after night, why are the clothes and the bathmat always dry? I feel slightly rattled and squeeze the shells in my pocket to reassure myself. I'm scared they might melt away, like a dusting of snow.

Nagai takes off his coat and kneels down at the little altar with Sayaka's photograph on it. "I'm sorry," he says quietly. "It should have happened to an old man like me." He crosses himself, and I notice he's crying. The tears look out of place on his stern features. I sit down on the floor behind him in the sun to watch. I'm sniffling too before I know it.

Sayaka only ever made friends with gentle people. She seemed to know immediately if someone was nasty. If she took a dislike to someone, she would turn her back and refuse even to say hello. She was a good, honest girl. Nagai is a bit rough around the edges, but there is a softness inside that prickly exterior. He reminds me of something in a rock pool, crusted with barnacles.

"Such a shocking thing to happen," he says, his forehead touching the floor as he finishes his prayer.

Still sniffling, I move to position myself across from him and bow my head. "Thank you. I'm sure somewhere up there Sayaka appreciates your taking the time."

Some decorations from the Tanabata festival still stand in a vase in one corner of the room. Nagai crawls over for a closer look. They're a relic of last summer's festival—the last we spent together. How could we have known she had just a month left to live?

He picks out one of the votive slips and reads it aloud. "'My wish: please don't let Daddy's boobies grow any bigger.'"

"My wife wrote that," I explain, when he looks at me quizzically. "She's always poking fun at me for being so fat."

My whole body overheats when I'm embarrassed, and I start to sweat. There's nothing unusual in that, of course—except that it goes on. Even in midwinter, the least little thing can trigger it. I sit there feeling like a toad as the greasy moisture seeps out.

The smell of it starts to bother me. My wife has warned me repeatedly about my body odor. I can't get by without a deodorant, even when it's cold. Maybe it's a hang-up because of this, but I often get anxious if people get too close. Nagai's presence in the same room is starting to affect me. I wish I had never invited him up.

“Sayaka hadn’t learned to write yet. You see the strips of paper next to the bamboo grass, with the pictures on them? That one’s hers—the diamond-shaped one with Hello Kitty on it.”

It doesn’t take him long to find it. As he picks up the crayon drawing of three bearded faces with red hearts dancing around them, I see a tear fall onto the paper; he wipes it away quickly with his fingers.

“I’m sorry . . . It’s a sweet picture . . .”

I never did get to take Sayaka to meet Hello Kitty at Harmony Land. If only I’d taken the time to make her happy when I still had the chance. The opportunity will never come again now.

Nagai purses his lips, still looking tearful. I get up to make some tea.

“D’you mind if I step outside for a look at the view? I could do with a smoke too, if that’s OK.”

“Of course. There should be some sandals by the door.”

He nods and puts on his jacket, then opens the screen door onto the balcony.

There’s always a wind blowing up here; a gust of cold air comes into the room. He shuts the door behind him and stands looking out toward the harbor. He looks tired, and for the first time there is no mistaking his age. I fill a cup from the hot water pot and carry the tea out to the balcony. The wind is chilly as always, but it’s not the kind of whipping gale we sometimes get. The slopes of Inasayama are just about visible through some mist. It’s a view I’ve seen thousands of times. There’s nothing different today—except that everything seems to have a special glow as if the world is suddenly revealing the light that’s always been hidden inside.

“This must be where she used to sit?”

Next to the aluminum table and the two chairs my wife and I use is Sayaka’s high chair. I ought to have tidied it away by now. But just like her flip-flops, I can’t bring myself to touch it. I’m frightened of wiping out memories. Its feet are rusty, and the rest of the silver metal is getting tarnished. “So this is her chair,” Nagai says. The tears are welling in his eyes again.

“We often used to have barbecues out here in the summer. It’s too hot during the day, but there’s a nice cool breeze when the sun goes down.”

“You’re not bothered by flies?”

“How do you mean?”

"I tried cooking in the garden at home once. I thought it'd be like having my own little beer garden. And it was—until the flies arrived. They wouldn't leave me alone."

"Oh, they're not a problem here. It must be too high up."

From a fly's perspective, this must be like a mountaintop. They don't belong up here.

"I bet she wasn't a fussy eater."

"No, she had a good appetite for such a little girl."

An image of her biting into a chicken wing returns. Gnawing at the meat, breathing heavily through her mouth, smearing grease all over her face and hands. She looked ready to gobble up anything. My wife was always telling her, "Slow down. Don't eat so fast." She was worried that she'd grow up to be a fatty like her father. She used to talk about putting her on a diet—even though the girl was only four years old.

"I'm sorry we don't have an ashtray," I say as Nagai takes his portable container from his pocket.

"I'm the one should apologize. My wife didn't mind so much, but my sister hated me smoking in the house. She used to send me out into the garden. I smoke all the time now—I don't care anymore if I get cancer."

"A fatalist."

"None of it makes sense anyway. Why should an innocent kid like your daughter die and an old bastard like me survive, with all my vices?"

He leans over the railings and points a finger. "That's my place over there. You can just about make out the orange tree in the garden and a bit of the roof."

Across from the junction where we put out the trash, a flight of steep stone steps weaves its way up the slope through the houses. At the top is a kindergarten. Nagai's house is to the left, about halfway up the hill. It looks like an old building, with heavy black tiles on the roof. It's hemmed in on all sides; he can't get much sunlight.

"Not much of a view of Inasayama today," I say. "Maybe the sand's coming in from China again." But really I know it's still too early for that. Later in the year, the winds will blow great gusts of sand from the deserts deep inside the continent and carry them across the sea to Japan.

"Your daughter always listened to my sister. I'm glad about that. No one else would take her seriously, but your Sayaka did. At least she found one person to listen to what she was saying."

His thank-you falls like droplets of warm water. Surely I can trust him? I squeeze the shells in my pocket. I'm about to take them out and show him when he speaks up again.

"I always assumed it was just a lot of nonsense. But recently I've begun to think maybe there was more to it than I realized."

So he's started to come round! That makes it a lot easier. No need to rush.

"Down there . . . after the bomb fell . . . the whole area was like a sea of fire. My mother had taken her to our grandparents' place in Shiroyama with our younger brother and sister. That's where they were when it happened."

"How old were they?"

"She would have been seven. Our little sister was four; the youngest, three. The house collapsed, and our grandparents and the two younger children were trapped. Then the fires came. They couldn't do anything. My mother was frantic. My sister had to drag her away. That's how they survived."

What can I say? Living close to ground zero, you sometimes hear stories like this, even now. To me they seem like tales of long ago—legends almost as distant from the present as the persecution of the Nagasaki Christians.

"My mother was badly hurt. I think she was practically delirious. It wasn't easy to get a straight account of what'd happened. But she kept moaning the names of her two youngest kids. That's how I knew: they must have been trapped under the house. In desperation, she went on trying to help them get out."

"What did your sister say about it? They came away together, didn't they?"

"She never spoke about it. I checked with our uncle and aunt later, and they confirmed it—she never said a word about what she'd seen. She kept her silence till the day she died."

"But they were together?"

"I assume so. They must've been."

"Did she ever marry?" It's none of my business, but luckily he doesn't seem to mind.

"There was something a bit different about my sister, something that kept people at arm's length. She wasn't ugly or anything—but I don't think she ever had many suitors."

As he speaks, I notice another shell on top of the overturned plant pot at the back of the balcony. How many does that make now, twenty-two? We were given the pot as a wedding present. It had a begonia in it, which started to wilt not long after we moved in. It was hopeless. We fed it with water and fertilizer and tried everything we could think of, but nothing seemed to work. The leaves turned brown and drooped. I hardly give it a thought nowadays, but when we were first married, it seemed like a bad omen.

"I think what she went through then, escaping through the fire—it marked her forever."

He plops himself down in my wife's chair. I sit across from him in the other one. Next to us is Sayaka's empty high chair. It isn't hard to see her there, leaning her head to one side and listening intently to the grown-ups.

"It must have scarred her for life. She was only seven when it happened."

Sayaka nods sympathetically. Nagai sighs and takes a sip of tea. "Thanks," he says. The wind is not as strong today as it often is, but it's still cold enough to turn his breath white.

"It wasn't just the things she saw. I think she was forced to make a terrible decision when she was still just a child."

"What do you mean?"

"My mother lost her mind. The panic and grief was too much for her. My guess is that it was my sister who made the decision to leave the others under the house. It was the only way they could save themselves."

"But . . ."

"They could hear their voices down there. When they got home, my mother was put to bed, but she kept calling out her children's names. 'Hold on! . . . Help's on its way . . . Be brave . . .' She thought she was still in Shiroyama."

I can only listen in silence. I know what it's like to lose a child. It hurts just to think of it. To tell the truth, I'm not sure I want to hear much more.

"If my mother had been on her own, I don't think it would have occurred to her to leave. She would have died there with them. It was my sister who made her go. 'Let's get out while we can. There's nothing we can do for Mitsuo and Umeko now . . .' And she tugged her away. Just seven years old, and she made that impossible decision to abandon her brother and sister and save their own lives. She practically dragged her across that wasteland. She must have seen terrible things, things no one should ever have to see."

"And she never spoke about it at all?"

"Not a word till the day she died. I don't think she remembered much, actually; the shock was too much. She said it was like something had gone numb inside her brain. Just thinking about it gave her a headache."

There's a gust of wind, and I feel a piercing cold, but I can't stand up. I'm trying to picture his sister clearing up the rubbish on the pavement. But no clear image comes to mind. Perhaps unsurprisingly, all I can recall are vague impressions. I don't think I ever even spoke to her.

Is it true that it's better to forget? If I could forget about Sayaka—if I could somehow forget that I had lost her—would I be released from grief? Possibly. But would it really work?

No doubt it would be a weight off my shoulders. But it's that weight that keeps me anchored to the ground. I think of the reassuring load of shells in my pocket.

"The memories began to come back as she got older, I reckon—as her mind began to go. Not everything, just bits and pieces that were somehow connected to what happened that day."

When you forget, are the memories lost for good? Or do they lurk somewhere inside your mind, forgotten but still alive?

"I'm sorry. This can't be much fun to listen to," he says, breaking off suddenly.

"That's all right. Those memories of hers—were they specifically about the day the bomb fell?"

"No. It was mainly to do with . . . what I mentioned before: that idea she had that the sea comes right in here at night."

I can feel it. It's almost time. Time to tell him about the shells. I take a sip of hot tea to moisten my throat.

"Do you think there's a connection?"

"One night, I couldn't sleep. I was lying there thinking when it suddenly came to me. When you get to my age, all kinds of things go through your mind at night."

I know all about the misery of sleepless nights. The moaning wind, motorbikes revving outside the window, drunken students in the streets . . . all of it disconcertingly close. Once I was positive I heard the sea, sounding like the cold breathing of the night in my ear.

"My uncle found them that night: my mother lying on the ground in a temporary shelter, my sister squatting next to her. He brought them both to my other grandparents' place in Yurino. I'd been evacuated from the city and was staying there at the time. Mother had terrible burns on her face and all the way down her back. We could hear her late into the night, moaning in bed. We were too scared to sleep."

His eyes are turned in my direction, but they don't seem to see me. He is looking into darkness.

"I asked my sister what had happened. How did they escape? I was just a kid—what did I know? But she wouldn't tell me anything. I remember seeing her eyes glinting in the light that came into the room through the cracks in the sliding doors. So I knew she was awake. It's sixty years ago now, and most of my memories are fuzzy. But I can still remember little details like that—the pupils of her eyes shining in the dark."

He sighs and turns away to look out over the city. His jacket makes a muffled sound as he moves, and I catch a faint whiff of fish.

"She never said a word about it directly. But I remember one night not long after it happened. Our mother was moaning in her sleep again, and Granddad was sitting up with her. At some stage he came in to check on us. He pushed back the sliding doors and asked if we couldn't sleep. Then he told us tearfully there was nothing anybody could have done for Mitsuo and Umeko. No one could get through the flames to help them."

An image of red flames burning through the night comes to me, overlaid on the morning bustle of the city center.

"That was the only time my sister spoke. 'I wish the sea would wash over it all,' she said."

"To put out the fires . . ."

"That's what she said."

I can see their grandfather quite clearly, opening the sliding doors with bony hands and scratching his white head as he looks in on the children. Though my memories of Sayaka are starting to fade, I have such a vivid image of this old man from sixty years ago—a man I never met—that I can see the wrinkles on his forehead and the bags under his eyes, caused by tears and worry and loss. I thought you weren't supposed to be able to visualize things in so much detail.

"Where do you think she got that idea?"

"She must've been remembering an old story—something Grandma used to tell us—our mother's mother; she died with the rest of them when they were trapped under the house. She grew up in a fishing village near Fukuda, and she told us how the local Christians came to the rescue of the villagers when the place was about to be swamped by a tsunami. An earthquake had sucked back the sea, and when the villagers went out onto the beach to look, the Christians set fire to their own houses to warn them of the danger . . . In fact, though, there's never been a major earthquake or a tsunami in Fukuda as far as I know."

I can't think of any big earthquakes in that area either. Nagasaki has been razed to the ground by fires several times over the years. There have been volcanic eruptions at Fugendake in Shimabara and flooding in Isahaya—but I can't remember anything about a real tsunami. Probably it happened somewhere else, and the old woman changed the details to make a story for her grandchildren.

"My sister was always bothered by the Christians setting fire to their houses. She wasn't happy about the ending. They'd done a good deed, but all they got in return was some thanks. They still lost their homes. She used to say: 'What happened to the houses? Didn't they burn down? What was the good of that? They lost everything!' I think she couldn't bear the idea that they'd made such a huge sacrifice for so little."

He smiles wryly and takes a drag on his cigarette. A cloud like a lost sheep floats over the peak of Inasayama. Sayaka used to think clouds were smoke.

"Grandma didn't know what to tell her."

"I'm not surprised."

"It was just a child she was talking to . . . so she probably said the first thing that came into her head. She said the sea washed over the land and put out the fires. And God scattered the ground with beautiful shells as a reward to the people who'd done the good deed."

"So that's where the shells come from!"

It's not a fantasy, not something that exists only in my mind but something that has left its traces in the memory of other people across the ages. I'm thrilled. It's like finding new shells—of a shape and color not seen before. The shells are my physical proof, but it's nice to have this piece of local folklore to back it up.

The sea must have been sweeping inland like this since long, long ago—long before I ever became aware of it. It's not some inexplicable mystery that started suddenly one night. It's a universal phenomenon that has remained hidden from human understanding. People just haven't noticed. Like gravity: gravity was always there, but no one knew about it until Newton brought it to our attention.

Rain fell. Waterfalls plunged. Petals dropped from trees and plants. Waves surged in and then withdrew. Hundreds of thousands of shooting stars tumbled from the heavens. The sun and the moon alternated in the sky, but no one realized that the force of gravity was controlling everything they could see. How can anyone deny that phenomena must exist that we can't understand, even though the evidence is there in front of our eyes?

"The answer seemed to satisfy her. Pretty shells as a reward . . . Of course, shells aren't really worth anything, so to describe them as a reward doesn't really work. But it was good enough for a small child. I think she must have remembered the story when Grandpa talked about the fires. She was praying that God would send in the seas again to put them out."

All the shells I've found strewn around today have been leading me here—to the memory of this girl sixty years ago. The wind is picking up and it's colder now, but nothing can cool the glow inside me. I haven't been clinging to a crazy dream all this time. Others have learned the truth before me and put their trust in it. It's no lie. The same truth that consoled that little girl all those years ago is doing the same for me now.

"And you think it came back to her in her old age when she was starting to get confused?" I try to sound as calm as I can.

"That's the only explanation I can think of. She kept a lid on her emotions, but they were still there deep down inside. From under the rubble of the house, she heard her brother and sister screaming for help. But she knew the risk of staying. She must have relived that moment thousands of times. For her, the bomb fell over and over again until the day she died."

Children shouldn't be allowed to suffer. It's our job to make sure they can laugh, and run, and play, and then sleep well at night. "Isn't that right?" I say silently to Sayaka at my side. She's sitting with her head cocked, listening.

Nagai looks up at the sky.

"She blamed herself for what'd happened. But how can a child of seven come to terms with something like that? So she just put a lid on it and tried to forget about it. But it kept on simmering away."

"It must have been a heavy lid."

He nods. His eyes are fixed on the table.

"She was always so strict with herself, so disciplined and proper. And not just because she was a teacher—she taught calligraphy. I think she was always on her guard. She was terrified of what might happen if she let herself remember. She thought she might lose her mind. You know the Bible story about Noah and the ark and the flood to clean up the world? When her mind started to go, right at the end, I think all she really remembered was Grandma's story about the sea putting out the fires and the shells it left behind. I don't think she allowed herself to remember anything else."

The tide must be starting to come in. Is this the moment to show him my shells?

Someone like my brother would probably deny the facts even after you showed him some good evidence. But Nagai is more open-minded than he looks. I can tell he's ready to believe. If I can get the timing right, there shouldn't be any need for further explanation. He'll get it right away. "So what she told me was true," he'll say, sorry that he ever doubted her. An hour ago, I didn't even know his name. I thought he was just a grumpy old man. But I feel a warmth and sympathy toward him now.

"I'm sure Sayaka loved hearing that story from her."

"I wish I'd paid more attention myself. It may have been a fantasy, but it was important to her. It was a real blessing to have somebody like your Sayaka to listen carefully to what she said."

Yes, that was a good deed she'd done in her very short life.

"It's important to believe. I think maybe I allowed myself to forget that."

I feel something welling up in my chest. The moment is here at last.

"Believe . . . Because it's true."

I thrust my hand into my pocket. I let the shells fall through my fingers and then scoop them up again.

"That's what the priest used to tell us. Have faith, and you'll be saved. I don't think I really understood what he meant."

A piece of white ash falls from his cigarette onto his trousers. He pinches it between his fingers and drops it apologetically into his ashtray.

"My sister and her found something at the junction that day. The last time I saw your daughter."

"Do you remember when it was?" I ask. But I'm pretty sure I already know.

"August 10."

"That's the night Sayaka died."

He looks at me meaningfully.

"Is that right? My sister died the same night."

Our eyes meet. We both know it's more than a coincidence. The connection is so clear. His lips are trembling slightly as he speaks.

"It was early on their last day on earth. I remember it well. We'd just had the anniversary of our brother's and sister's deaths the day before. There must have been some kind of karmic connection—isn't that what a Buddhist would say? They started the day quite cheerfully, and both died suddenly the same night."

"What was it they found?" But I already know the answer. I understand everything now.

"At first, I thought it was stray bits of rubbish. But when I got closer, I realized they both were peering at something in the palms of their hands. They called out to me: 'Look, look at them all! Look at all the shells!'"

"Their reward!"

A wave of emotion sweeps over me, and I pull my hand out of my pocket.

My whole body is trembling. "Just like these," I want to say, but the strength has gone out of me and I just sit there gulping air. I can't speak. I open my hand on the table in front of him. But he's not even looking. He breathes out a stream of smoke and follows it with his eyes across the sky.

"They held out their hands to show me. Their eyes were shining. 'Look at them! Look at them all!' they kept saying."

Slowly, he turns his craggy face to look down at the table. I open my palm proudly and present him with the sight of twenty-two sunlit cowries. Believe and be saved! A broad grin breaks out on my face.

The shells gleam like ivory or marble, their openings like white stitching. I can feel their weight in my hands, their smooth, cool wetness against my skin. I am holding things that will keep me bound to the earth.

I lift up my hand as if making an offering. He lowers his eyes until he's staring directly at it. There's no doubt about it. Yet his sunken eyes show no sign of surprise.

"But there was nothing there. They were so excited. They kept telling me about shells shining all around us like dew, but I couldn't see anything. I suppose my faith just isn't strong enough. And in that case," he whispers, "there's no hope for me." His eyes are soft. "Maybe it was a sign that they weren't long for this world. Maybe she'd finally found the fraying seam she was always looking for."

I look around me in alarm. Stretching far beyond my held-out, empty palm is a level wasteland like a vast expanse of mudflats and, at the edge of this quiet, unpopulated world, the white threads of the waves, silently unraveling.

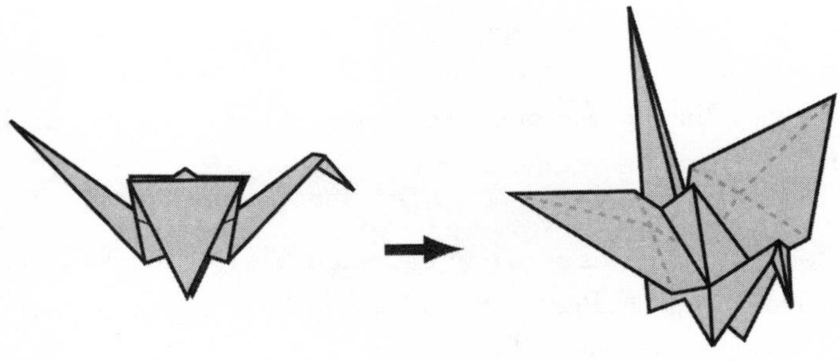

BIRDS

There are two blanks on my family register in the spaces where my parents' names should go. My past disappeared in the shadow of the atomic cloud.

I was rescued from the wreckage immediately after the bomb fell. The woman who picked me up and became my foster mother always said she remembered almost nothing of that day. I was a child crying amid the rubble. She swept me up in her arms as she ran, hardly knowing what she was doing. Later, with me tied to her back, she walked all night in the foothills from Anakōbō Temple out of the city to Mount Konpira.

I don't know my real name or my date of birth. More than sixty years later, I have no way of finding out who I am or where I came from. All I know is that I appeared suddenly out of that white flash of light at 11:02 A.M. on August 9, 1945.

This is the day recorded in my family register under "Date of Birth."

There was a sudden ripping sound, like someone tearing cardboard. I looked up at the ceiling, fountain pen in hand, the ink still wet on the manuscript in front of me. My wife was sitting by my side, pouring tea. Her hand stopped in midair, and we looked at each other.

"What was that?"

She had been listening to some of her favorite old songs on the record player. But there was a look of anxiety on her face now.

"It came from upstairs," she said.

From the black record on the turntable came the sobbing voice of Nishida Sachiko singing the chorus of one of her famous hits. "Dimly lit and lonely, the red hotel . . ." There was no other sound.

"Turn it off," I said.

Hesitantly, she lifted the needle off the record. She liked to take out her old records before bed. "The Red Hotel" and "When the Acacias' Rain Stops Falling" were two of her favorites.

The records were scratched, and the needle skipped in several places when you played them, but she loved this nostalgic music. When she was in a particularly good mood, she used to hum along quietly. She always listened with the volume turned down so that it didn't disturb my writing, but in fact I quite enjoyed having it in the background as I pushed my pen across the page.

With the music gone, silence filled the room. The night seemed to grow heavier, more threatening. Here we were, an elderly couple alone late at night, playing melancholy tunes from forty years ago. "I wish I could die like this / Drenched in the acacias' rain . . ." The lyrics sang of loneliness and heartbreak, but there was something warm and comforting about them, too. They made you feel safe, wrapped around in the plaintive melody.

"It's nothing. Just the wind."

I reached out and took a tangerine from the basket on top of the *kotatsu*. As I peeled it, I listened to our surroundings.

"It can't be the wind. Nothing else is making any noise."

The area we live in is called Kazagashira—Windy Head. In the old days, located high on a bluff and exposed to the bay, this district would have borne the brunt of the winds as they whipped in from the sea. Today, most of the bay has been reclaimed and built on, and areas like Hamanomachi, where the beach used to be, are at the heart of the modern city. But even today, the origins of the name are clear enough when the wind picks up. Often it makes the whole house creak.

The trees in the garden rustle in the slightest breeze. The power lines groan. But there was nothing like that tonight, and when the music stopped, we were enveloped in silence. The only sound was the faint whistling of steam from the kettle on the stove.

"It's nothing."

I held the tangerine to my lips and popped the segments into my mouth. The season was almost over now, and the fruit was soft and ripe. I felt the juice trickle pleasantly down my throat. But my wife was still worried that something wasn't right upstairs.

"Maybe it's something in one of the children's rooms."

"There might be something in the attic, I suppose. A cat might have come in through the roof again."

"But we had it blocked off."

"That was years ago. Another hole might have opened up somewhere."

"That noise didn't come from the roof just now."

"Look, there's nobody there. Why would anyone want to break into a house like this anyway? There's nothing worth stealing. It was just the house creaking, that's all. There's nothing to worry about."

The two-story wooden building is nearly fifty years old; you can often hear the timbers creaking in different parts of it.

"You never know. There could be someone hiding up there."

I knew what was making her so fidgety. A few days back, one of the houses in the neighborhood had been broken into while the owners were away. Since then, she had mentioned several times the unsettling remarks made by the young policeman who stopped by to ask if we knew anything about what had happened.

"Smashed the glass in the porch, apparently—in broad daylight, too. Then just reached his hand through and opened the door from the inside. Pretty rough way of going about it. That's more like forced entry than just pilfering. They were lucky they weren't at home if you ask me." It was quite unsettling.

"Go and have a look upstairs. Just to make sure."

I didn't much like the idea; where we were sitting was the only warm room in the house. "I'm telling you, there's nothing there," I muttered as I got to my feet, leaving a tangerine as a paperweight on the thing I was writing. I pulled on my jacket and pushed open the sliding doors, then stepped into the corridor that led to the entrance. I could feel the cold of the floorboards through my socks, and the chill air sent a shiver up my spine.

I felt along the rough wall for the switch that turned on the upstairs lights. My wife was standing behind me like a little girl. Suddenly, she shouted up at the white walls of the upper floor, tinted yellow by the lights. "Hello! Who is it?" Her voice made me jump. What was she up to?

"You expect a burglar to reply?"

She can be so naive sometimes. We are the same age. When we were younger, she'd been quite an easygoing person, always laughing or smiling. She seemed so happy. Whenever people met her for the first time, it was just a matter of time before they said: "Well, you don't seem to have any worries, do you?" Things changed when we were in our mid-forties and she nursed my foster mother through her final illness. After that, she became stubborn and withdrawn. That might have been that—as far as menopausal symptoms went—but then my foster father fell ill, and she had to look after him, too, for three long years before he died. There had also been trouble with my older sister and her husband. The open and trusting personality she'd had as a young woman is long gone now. Sometimes it's like living with a completely different person.

Her cheeks are drawn, her mouth pursed and pointed like a chicken's beak. Her eyes, though, still shine as brightly as ever. Who is this woman I'm living with, I sometimes ask myself. It's strange. But when I think of what she went through when we were first married, it's painful to remember how much she put up with.

Her distrustfulness made things difficult after the children left home and it was just the two of us again. Things have improved a bit over the past three years, but there's no doubt that the anxiety and wariness have taken root somewhere deep inside her.

The wood creaked loudly as we started up the stairs. It made for an uneasy feeling, as if the frame of the house were being twisted out of shape. Slowly I opened the little sliding door at the top of the stairs and looked into what used to be our daughter's room. Of course, there was no sign of anyone. My wife used the room for storage now. It was full of cardboard boxes containing the children's old clothes, which she couldn't bring herself to throw away. She often took them out of their boxes and put them on hangers, dosing them with camphor and hanging them to air indoors for a few days.

I pulled the cord to turn on the lights. Nothing. And no sign that a cat had been in the room and disturbed anything. We walked down to the room at the end of the corridor, which had been converted into another bedroom, for our son—but of course there was nothing unusual there either.

"Well?" my wife said, pressing up behind me to peer into the room when I turned on the lights. She looked worried sick.

"It's empty . . . naturally enough. All the windows and shutters are locked."

Our son's room faces south, and there are two big windows on the south and east walls. It gets much more sunlight during the day than the girl's room, but at night the air felt gloomy and heavy. When was the last time we changed the lightbulbs in here, I wondered.

"It must be outside then. What about the roof?"

There was no escaping it: I would have to open all the shutters I had closed earlier in the evening.

"There won't be anybody there."

Like the wooden doors, the shutters get stuck in their frames and won't budge without a good deal of jiggling and heaving. Eventually, I got them open and looked outside. Lights from the surrounding houses meant it wasn't as dark as I'd expected. It was obvious right away that there was no one around. If anyone had been hiding there, he would have cleared off when he heard the rattling of the shutters.

The cold roof tiles shone dully like fish scales. The old house seemed to breathe like a living creature.

"There's no one here."

Up the slope stretched a row of lights in people's houses. To the left was a cluster of neon signs—the entertainment district at the bottom of the hill. From windows seeped a pale-green glow, like the eyes of nocturnal animals. Beyond the lights of the town, countless stars blinked in the nighttime sky. It was a scene I had looked out on for sixty years . . .

"It's so cold . . . But what a beautiful clear sky," my wife said quietly. She seemed to have calmed down a little.

In another two weeks it would be the cherry-blossom season, and over the hills in Tateyama, red paper lanterns would be lit again for parties under the trees. But there had been a cold snap in the middle of March; we'd even had snow flurries at the beginning of the week. We were both were a bit anxious about the cherry blossoms this year.

"The house doesn't want us here anymore," she said, hunching her shoulders against the cold and rubbing her bony hands together. She has a way of coming out with things I've been privately thinking myself sometimes. This was one of those times. I didn't want to talk about it. "Come on, we'd better get to bed. It's freezing," I said, bundling her back inside.

Holding onto the banister, my wife took the steps one at a time, grunting slightly as she went. She then got straight into the futon—there weren't going to be any more records, apparently. I refilled the kettle, put it on the heater, and crawled in under the *kotatsu*. The sliding doors to the bedroom were still open, and I could see her eyes blinking up at me from the pillow.

"What is it?"

"Are you going to stay up writing?"

"Yes. I have to give Takiguchi the manuscript on Monday."

"Like a real writer."

"You get some sleep. There's nothing to worry about. I'll keep an eye on you from here."

"Ah, that's nice. You're being good today."

"But you won't be able to sleep with the door open. Here, let me close it."

"Leave it. That way I can keep an eye on you, too," she said, burying the right side of her face in her pillow and looking at me with a soft, girlish expression.

"I feel ticklish when I know someone's looking at me."

"Don't think about it then."

"I can't help it. Aren't you cold?"

Her eyes were now shut. She was lying with her lips slightly open, her hands folded across her chest as if in prayer. The trace of a smile on her lips gave her an innocent, peaceful look; the taut, nervous expression she'd had earlier was gone. Finally I could relax. I picked up my pen and began to fill the square boxes on the sheet of paper in front of me.

It took my foster mother a whole day and night to cross Nishiyama. When she finally got home to Kazagashira, she sank to her haunches in the porch, exhausted. Even Kazagashira, more than two miles from the epicenter of the blast, had been torched by the atomic wind, and several places in the neighborhood had been razed to the ground. Her parents-in-law, who shared the house, had been frantic with worry and were overjoyed to see that she was safe. Her five-year-old daughter leaped into her arms and hugged her tight—until she noticed the nursing infant strapped to her back and asked in surprise, "Who's that?"

"I don't know where he's from," her mother told her in a whisper. "But what else could I do?" And with that she collapsed and didn't get to her feet again for another month. Even after she recovered, she had no clear memory of where she had picked me up.

Apparently, I rarely cried as an infant, clutching my foster mother's skinny breasts like a baby monkey and spending most of the day asleep. If anyone tried to separate us, I would open my eyes wide and let out a surprisingly loud scream. With her own eyes open just a crack, the woman who rescued me would shake her head feebly and say, "Let him be. He's my guardian angel." And so it was that the two of us, with no blood relationship to bind us together, spent the rest of that hot summer locked in a sweaty embrace.

Her mother-in-law used to go from door to door down the narrow alleys of Kazagashira in search of nursing mothers and beg them to spare a little milk, which she then spooned into my mouth. "We felt sure your mother would die too if you didn't make it," she often told me later.

I have no idea what made her so convinced that the fate of her daughter-in-law was tied to this child who had turned up from no one knew where. It seemed like a survival of some older way of thinking, some ancient faith that was revived when people were caught up in a disaster on a scale beyond human understanding.

It would be a mistake to dismiss it as superstition. Even today, we are not as rational as we might like to think, and it may be that the fundamental things that govern our hearts and minds are still influenced by this older turn of mind.

When autumn and its cooler air arrived, my foster mother began to get better. Then, toward the end of October, something mysterious occurred. There's no other way to describe it. Her breasts began to swell, although she hadn't given birth to any child, and one day they overflowed with milk.

That, perhaps, was the day our lives as mother and child really began.

I think it must have been in September last year that Takiguchi suddenly suggested that I try writing about what he called "your atom bomb experience." "But I was just a baby," I told him. "I don't remember a thing." I folded the estimate I'd been going over with him and put it into an envelope. We were at his house high up in Yanohira; red spider lilies were in bloom in a corner of the small garden. Down below, I could make out the green sea and the shipbuilding docks, wreathed in mist.

"You're a survivor, though, aren't you?" he said. We were sitting out on the balcony, sipping tea. He spoke slowly.

"I have the papers. But I can't remember anything."

My eyes may have seen the effects of the bomb, but I have no memory of what I saw. What use is that to anyone? When I think back on it, the only thing that comes to mind is the blank space where my parents' names ought to be on my family register. Takiguchi's insistence began to feel a bit unreasonable.

"Who are you really, I wonder?" he asked. "Where do you really come from?"

He had an inquisitive look in his eyes. But I'd never felt any need to hide my past. I'd spoken freely of the circumstances of my birth any number of times over the years—and not just to him.

"You know the facts. I never knew my parents' names. In that sense, I don't know who I am."

"Even so, there must be something you could write."

"No, nothing. I've hardly even thought about it. I've had a peaceful life."

"Well, there you go. That's your experience of the bomb."

Takiguchi smiled quietly like a Zen monk and looked out into the garden, where persimmons shone small and hard on the branches in the slanting evening sunlight. He started to chat absentmindedly about the fruit. "They're not sweet . . . You have to peel them and dry them. But at my age it's more trouble than it's worth. These days, the thrushes are the only ones who get any pleasure out of that tree."

Takiguchi used to be an elementary school teacher. Since retirement, he has been actively encouraging the people who were mobilized alongside him at the end of the war as students to write down their memories of the bomb. He has these memoirs bound and distributed at his own expense.

That's how I got to know him—through my job as head of sales at a small printing company. Over the years, I've come to know quite a few people who put together self-published pamphlets and books. Some of them have become friends, and I have contributed short pieces to their publications myself from time to time.

I've always loved reading. It was this love of the printed word that made me decide to join a printing firm after I left school. Meanwhile, I went on producing occasional pieces of fiction for a local amateur magazine. We used to get together in a coffee shop in Kajiya-machi, with the sultry voice of Nishida Sachiko singing in the background.

I soon forgot all about Takiguchi's suggestion and buckled down to my last six months at the company, where I'd now been working for forty-two years. But then, just as I was beginning to wonder what I would do after I retired, something happened one bitterly cold morning in December: I passed out, in the toilet.

I'd unzipped my fly when I suddenly felt the weight drain out of my body. Everything turned white before my eyes, and I felt myself floating in the air, transformed into something soft and light that I can only describe as "soul-like." My mind remained surprisingly calm. I remember thinking, "Ah, so I'm dying," as I flew on into the white light. I remember hearing a voice asking, "Who are you?" When I came to, I was lying on the floor next to the toilet bowl. I must have fallen hard against the porcelain. I felt a throbbing pain at the base of the scrotum, but had no clear memory of my fall—just the airy sensation of being enveloped in white light.

My foster father had collapsed in the same place fifteen years earlier and never regained consciousness. The coincidence bothered me, and although there was no biological connection between us, I became convinced that I was somehow at risk of the same kind of brain hemorrhage that had killed him. I kept quiet about what had happened—I knew my wife would be worried sick if I said anything—but I went for a hospital checkup at the end of the year. Much to my relief, the results of the MRI scan came back all clear—but then, in March, it happened again. This time, I was sitting down when my head suddenly flopped forward and I fell flat on my face, arms stretched out limply in front of me.

Once again, I was enveloped in white light and floating painlessly through the soft, fluffy air. It was an almost blissful feeling.

I had recently turned sixty, but I felt about ten years younger inside. There had been no real signs of physical decline, and I still had the energy and drive to keep on working. If anything, I found it hard to accept that I'd reached retirement age. I'd been a picture of health ever since I started working, come to think of it. Not once in forty-two years had I been hospitalized. It certainly never occurred to me that I was about to die.

And now, I had lost consciousness twice in the space of a few months. Suddenly everything had changed. The next time it happened, I might never wake up. The thought filled me with dread. Even now, I sometimes wake in the middle of the night, drenched in sweat, the darkness pressing heavy against my chest. It feels as though I'm lying on the seabed with the weight of the ocean on top of me.

Several times I've sat bolt upright in the dark, feeling my chest about to burst with sadness. What is this heartache? This deep distress that clings and won't let go? I can't shake off the idea that I've done nothing to solve the riddle I was given at the outset of my life—those two blank spaces on my family register. My life seems wasted and meaningless. I sit there alone in the darkness, filled with remorse.

And so Takiguchi's half-forgotten invitation to write something began to nag at me. He himself seemed to have forgotten all about it when I got in touch. But the next of his twice-yearly pamphlets was due just before the Golden Week holidays at the end of April. If I could get the manuscript to him in time for that, he said, he'd be delighted to include it.

I sat down with a pad of writing paper that Saturday evening for the first time in ages. I didn't have anything in particular I wanted to write. More than anything, I wanted to impose some kind of order on the fog of emotions that had been tormenting me. And late at night when anxiety kept me awake, I knew from previous experience the peace and relief that could come from getting absorbed in a piece of writing, listening to the soft scratch of my pen as it moved down the page.

I may have grown up not knowing who my parents were—or who I was myself, for that matter—but on the whole, I can't say that this ever caused me any particular pain or regret.

There were occasional exceptions. A few times in my midteens, I found myself wandering around Urakami as if something had drawn me there. It always happened at moments of stress, when things weren't going well with a friend or something had happened at school. Brooding, I would hop onto a tram and end up in Urakami before I realized where I was going. I don't think I went there in search of anything in particular.

I started work and got married; we had a daughter and then a son. I enjoyed the simple pleasures of watching the children grow up. Almost before I knew it, our daughter was leaving home to get married, and two years ago our first grandchild was born. Last year, we both turned sixty—both of us, as far as we could tell, still in good health. Like anyone else, we've had our ups and downs, but for the most part it's been pretty smooth sailing.

I suppose it's possible that the problem of my identity has been gnawing away at me for years without my ever being fully conscious of it. Presumably, at least a certain number of newborn babies were among the 73,884 people who died when the bomb was dropped. I might have been among them. The idea makes me feel ephemeral—like someone's ghost. The last sixty years begin to seem like a shallow dream.

Who am I? I know that my foster parents went to some lengths to find out when they officially adopted me after the war, but they never came up with an answer.

The records and memories of the midwives living in Urakami at the time were lost. And since I was apparently just a few days old when I was plucked out of the rubble, it's quite possible that my whole family was wiped out before my birth had even been reported, along with the neighbors and anyone else who knew of my existence. It was as if I had never been born at all.

Who am I? No amount of puzzling over it will tell me the answer. I came to terms with that a long time ago. But the question may still have been there somewhere deep inside me, like a hidden stream. Perhaps it was no surprise that it finally came bubbling to the surface in the form of that voice calling out to me when everything went white. Probably the same nagging question is the reason why I still feel vaguely uneasy in the house where I grew up with my foster parents and their daughter.

But another factor must be the unspoken feud that existed between my foster father and me. For him, it probably dated back to the very first time we met. He can hardly have been pleased to come home from the war to find a strange child feeding at his wife's breast. His feelings sent out ripples that are still widening inside me even now, twelve years after he died. Now that he's gone, I decided I needed to try to sort out my feelings about him—to untangle the knot—by putting it down in writing.

It was November when he was demobilized and came back from Manchuria.

As far as I know, he never said a word about where he had spent the war, what had happened to him there, or how he had managed to survive. My foster mother often spoke of the shock she'd felt when he appeared at the door unannounced, a skin-and-bones apparition in gray rags, his eyes oddly bright in a sallow face. He had been listed as missing, presumed dead. At first, she thought she was seeing a ghost.

And who could blame him for being suspicious when he found a suckling child in the house on his return?

Over and over, she tried to explain what had happened, but he refused to believe it. His response was always the same. "Then why are you producing milk?" He was a quiet, gentle man by nature. He lapsed into long, sullen silences punctuated by attacks of jealousy when he would suddenly lash out at her. "Whose is it? Who did you cheat on me with?" Of course, they never fought openly in front of me once I was old enough to understand, but she told me later that when I was still a baby, she often had to carry me out of the house in fear for our safety.

One day toward the end of the year, when she had carried me into the garden to escape one of his outbursts, she saw a white bird in the field next to the house. Even now, there are empty plots of land on the hillsides around here. Most of the people in the area are elderly. Young people aren't interested in moving into the old houses up here in the hills. White narcissi are all that remain of homes that were torn down, or forgotten tulip bulbs that flower year after year. In spring, the whole area turns yellow with rape flowers. But not all the plots are abandoned; some of the residents have taken to cultivating patches of eggplants and tomatoes on the empty land. It's almost as if the area is returning a little to the way it used to be.

In those days, there was arable land next to the house, and a small pond. I vaguely remember a pool of pure water where I used to catch tadpoles and little frogs in the early summer.

It was here that my foster mother saw the bird come down to rest. There are four species of white heronlike birds in Japan. The intermediate egret and cattle egret are migratory and visit only during the summer, so given the time of year it must have been a little egret or a great egret.

Afterward, she said that the white bird had looked at me sadly as I lay crying in her arms. Apparently, I fell silent as soon as I noticed the bird and stared at it intently. And out of this little episode she spun a story. She imagined the bird was the spirit of my real mother, who had escaped from the death and desolation of the Urakami River and had come to make sure I was safe.

Something about the story strikes a chord in me. It may be just make-believe, but a tear comes to my eye when I think of it. The egret was my guardian spirit, and I should always make sure to keep it from harm, she told me. I was lucky to be raised by a woman with this sort of belief. Sometimes I think I might have been more inclined to pick away at the problem of my identity if it hadn't been for that story. I might have become obsessed with it to the point of missing out on the little moments of happiness life has to offer.

Later, when she found out about the effects of the radiation, she blamed herself for having given me her milk. She thought her body had produced it as a way of flushing out the toxins. Whenever I came down with a cold or a fever, she would put her hand to my brow and say, "I'm sorry, Ryo-chan. So sorry." As if she had somehow let me down.

Partly because of this, perhaps, she gave me more love than even her own daughter got. This made the girl jealous. "You're only allowed to do that because you were found under a stone after the atom bomb was dropped," she'd say, too young to understand why remarks like this resulted in a furious telling-off. I felt sometimes I'd done nothing but cause trouble by coming here.

The fact that my foster parents never had any more children, even though they were in their twenties when the war ended, makes me suspect that these rifts went deeper than I realized.

"You're still up?"

She may have drifted off briefly into a deep sleep, but my wife's eyes were wide open now, like a fish's. She looked remarkably alert for someone who was just emerging from sleep, her face still half-buried in the pillow. She pulled the blankets up over her shoulders with her pale, thin hands.

"Here, let me close the doors. The light's keeping you awake." I got up to slide the panels shut, but she shook her head.

"Leave it. I don't want to be in the dark."

A bad dream? I decided not to ask.

"Do you want some tea?"

"No, thanks. I'm all right."

"Can you get back to sleep?"

She nodded and turned away from me. It seemed I needn't worry. I decided to go on with my work. I had just picked up my pen when she spoke again.

"That jar we put out to catch the rain—why did it break?" It was as if she were storing up things to worry about, rummaging through them long after they were over and done with. She sat up under the blankets like a mermaid and looked at me with piercingly clear eyes.

Some time ago, when my foster father was still alive, the spout fell off one of the gutters in the back garden. As a temporary solution, he put an old ceramic jar under the gutter to catch the water. As the months passed, though, the need for more permanent repairs was forgotten. Moss began to grow on the jar. Eventually, surviving both my foster parents, the jar came to resemble a large round ball of moss until one cold morning last December, when it suddenly split clean in two like a walnut.

Whether it was the ice or the thick layer of moss that broke it, I can't say. A clear crack ran almost exactly down the middle. Water had pooled inside the dull gold-colored hollow.

It was around this time that I began to notice changes in my wife's state of mind again.

She turned into a worrier. Watching the news, she'd suddenly turn to me and ask, "Could a North Korean missile reach us here?" Every time there was a wrong number, she would be convinced that she was being targeted in some telephone scam. Hardly a day went by without some upsetting event or other. Since the recent break-in nearby, I had an awful feeling that she was heading for a serious relapse.

"It just broke, that's all. An accident. There's nothing to worry about," I murmured. I turned back to my writing. But I could tell she was still looking at me. I could feel her gaze on the side of my face.

"What do you mean, an accident?" she asked.

"It just happened, that's all."

I looked over at her. With her lids closed, small wrinkles gathered around the hollows of her eyes. There was no sign of the girlish look she sometimes had, and the signs of old age were much more obvious. She looked like what she was: a woman past the age of sixty.

"And what about you—was it just an accident that you were picked up out of the ruins and brought to this house?"

"Yes."

"And an accident that I met you?"

"Well, if you hadn't been working in the office when I brought the estimate that day, we probably never would have met."

She smiled softly but didn't open her eyes. "Maybe," she said. Was she remembering the day we met, too? And was it just an accident that we got married?

I remembered nervous hands trembling as we exchanged red-lacquered saké cups.

"No. Maybe it was an accident that we met—but not that we got married. That was more like fate," I said.

She opened her eyes and looked at me with her mischievous, girlish smile again. "Lucky me," she said teasingly. "And was it fate, too, that your sister married that man and left us to take over the house, even though we'd no real connection with it?"

Probably the simmering conflict that had soured my wife's relationship with my sister and her husband was another factor that had contributed to her anxiety. My sister, Keiko, lives in Osaka now and has drifted apart from the rest of the family. The last time we saw her was when she came home around three years ago to visit the family grave. But even then, she didn't stay long. "Well, things have certainly changed around here," she said, bolting down a cup of tea before making her excuses and hurrying off to catch a plane. She never did say what she thought had changed, or how.

The person my sister married was a businessman who made his fortune as a young man and now runs an import business in Osaka that deals in precious metals. He's one of those smooth talkers. I remember the first time we met him: camel-colored suit, a flurry of wisecracks and backslapping, a gold watch and chain on his left wrist.

My foster father worked as a welder in a factory that did subcontracting work for a shipbuilding firm. He was a typical down-to-earth working man who must have found his son-in-law hard to warm up to.

"Daikoku. Like the god of fortune? Well, it certainly sounds like a lucky name," my foster mother said after his first visit to the house. But it was obvious what she really thought.

"Frankly, I don't like him," my foster father said. It was unusual for him to be so blunt.

"I suppose in his line of business you need to be a bit glib . . ."

My sister was looking aggrieved.

"It wouldn't be the first time," my foster father said. "Bringing another little god into the family . . ." I can still remember how that word "another" stung.

"Well, you needn't worry—I won't be here much longer anyway. Ryo will probably inherit the house, and I couldn't stay here even if I wanted to."

My sister was badly hurt by all this. She shut herself away and only glared at me with reddened eyes from then on. I didn't know where to look. I felt horribly guilty.

Now, when I stopped writing and looked up at the ceiling, I saw wooden boards that have turned a rusty brown and walls that have yellowed with age. But it was in this same spot that Daikoku was first introduced to the family thirty-seven or -eight years ago. And the room my wife was sleeping in was where my sister sat and cried her heart out all those years ago.

She married and left home soon after that first meeting and gradually became estranged from the family. It was probably only the distance between Nagasaki and Osaka that prevented a major falling-out. This became clear when my foster parents died and Daikoku showed his true colors in a series of fierce arguments over the division of the property.

Before the seven days of mourning for my foster father were even over, Daikoku was insisting on our selling the house and land as quickly as possible. He had done nothing to look after the old couple while they were alive, and then this—as soon as they were gone. My wife was furious. "What a stinker that man is," I remember her saying. We managed to hang on to the house, but it took all the money we'd been saving up for renovations. I've never forgotten a remark he made when he turned up for the first memorial service.

"You joined this family as an outsider, too, didn't you? And now you've got the land and property for next to nothing. It's turned out pretty rosy for you, hasn't it?"

"How dare he," my wife said. I felt the same way. Even my sister had only a distant connection to the house by then. That was it, I thought—connections, fate.

"Maybe it wasn't an accident, or a legacy either. Maybe it really is fate that connects us to a place," I told my wife now. But she was already breathing deeply, clearly fast asleep. I felt as though I had uncovered a trace of new truth in a tired phrase. I repeated the words under my breath as I listened to the steam hissing from the kettle. It was with a warm, peaceful feeling in my heart that I settled down to my writing again.

My foster father never treated me badly. If anything, he may have been more affectionate to me than he was to his own child. Adoption was nothing unusual before the war, and after the war it was quite common for families without children of their own to adopt someone else's. Several of my classmates at school were adopted, and I never felt defensive or embarrassed about my background. I called my adoptive parents "Mother" and "Father" and more or less forgot that they were not my real parents. But I'm sure that for my foster father, the initial unease he felt about me left its mark somewhere deep inside. From time to time, like a piece of grit in a mouthful of food, something would happen to remind me of the reality of his feelings.

I remember he took me to Urakami one day when I was still in middle school. I was well aware of the significance of the place in my early life—my sister, five years older than me, had a habit of telling me how I'd been rescued there. Urakami. The name itself was enough to arouse a shiver of emotion in me. On a map, it was not much more than a couple of miles from the house to ground zero. But in our everyday lives, the epicenter seemed a world away.

Of course, I had been to Urakami lots of times before. My visits there always resulted in a kind of disappointment. Past Nagasaki Station, the scenery looked no different from that anywhere else. It was just an ordinary provincial town, with trams running along the streets. Nothing like the image I had formed in my mind.

I was already past the age where I might have enjoyed accompanying my foster father on one of his excursions into the city. But when he suggested that we go and look at the newly rebuilt cathedral, I decided to join him. We got off the tram at Matsuyama-machi and followed the gently curving gravel path up the hill to the church.

Yellow rape flowers were in bloom along the river. The water glinted in the spring sunshine.

Suddenly, the cathedral soared upward from behind the one-story wooden houses on the corner. I'd seen the new building on television, but the grainy impression on the black-and-white screen had not prepared me for the beauty and vigor of the new stone against a blue sky. My heart rose with it.

I quickened my pace, jogging the rest of the way up the steep slope. At last, I stood on top of the hill and gazed up at the structure reaching majestically into the sky above me. I pressed my forehead to the glass in the door and peered inside. For an instant, my heart stopped still. A pool of color extended across the floor in front of me as the light streamed in through the stained-glass windows.

A white crucifix hung above the altar. My foster father eventually caught up and stood by my side. "That might be your god up there," he whispered. It was quite possible that my real parents had been Christians who used to pray in this church—but I was shocked to hear him allude to it so openly.

I felt I had finally found my own Urakami.

My back felt cold, and I saw that the flame in the heater was burning low. I removed the canister and took it out to the hall to pump it full of kerosene from the red plastic container. The smell of the fuel stung my nostrils.

According to the calendar, the first day of spring had come and gone, but the nights still were cold—particularly in the hallway, where the wind came gusting in through the cheap glass door. I felt the joints in my fingers turn numb as I squeezed the plastic pump. Was this another warning sign? A brain hemorrhage? I tried not to think about it. I lit the heater and read over what I'd written.

To tell the truth, my foster father had another reason for taking me to Urakami that day: bicycle racing. He was a hardworking man who took pride in his job, but he did have one vice. He gambled.

I remember once watching him absorbed in a card game. This would have been when I was still in elementary school. It was the time of year when the men of the neighborhood got together to build the float for Obon, the midsummer festival of the dead. There's a park on the site now, with a number of cherry trees, but back then it was little more than a vacant lot. A crowd of rowdy young men were sitting on rush matting under the trees, dressed in loose cotton long johns. They were passing large bottles of saké and playing cards. Half-drunk, most of them were past caring about the game. They placed their bets almost at random and tossed their cards down carelessly as they drank. My foster father was different. He alone sat with his eyes fixed on the game. He wasn't drinking at all. "What do you want?" he snapped when I called out to him. The look he gave me made me flinch. It was as if he didn't know me.

As soon as we got off the tram at Matsuyama-machi that day, he set off in the opposite direction from the cathedral, toward the cycling track at Komaba. When we reached it, he bought me some oden stew and a bottle of lemonade and then disappeared, telling me to wait in the cafeteria till he came back. My foster mother had told me in a whisper as we left the house that morning, "Keep an eye on him." She'd seen through his little lies a long time ago. "Make sure he doesn't lose everything." I didn't have to wait long. He was back almost immediately. He must have lost. He always staked everything on one race.

As we left the racetrack, I started needling him. "Mom knows," I said. I was a typical teenager at the time.

"You keep your mouth shut," he said. But I kept on at him.

"Why d'you have to gamble all the time?"

"That's just the way it is," he grumbled. "It's all in the lap of the gods, anyway—win or lose, live or die. Maybe my god's the god of gambling. It's him that decides the numbers on the cards, the fall of the dice."

"If you say so," I said priggishly, puffing out my cheeks.

"What's it matter to you anyway?" he said. We fell silent and turned at last in the direction the cathedral.

This was the context in which he had whispered to me at the cathedral that day: "That might be your god up there." But in the manuscript I was writing, I hadn't mentioned his gambling at all. I thought it would just complicate the story.

Much later, I caught him trying to teach the rules of the *hanafuda* card game to my own son. I remember the angry lecture I gave him in front of the boy and how pathetic he looked afterward, sitting alone on the veranda, his back turned to the room. The veranda is still there. All I have to do is open these doors.

It was after he came back from the war that he took to gambling. He had no contact with his former comrades, and his life in Manchuria remained a mystery to us. Asking him about what had happened there would have been unthinkable. Even his wife never tried.

"You have to read the flow of the game," he liked to say. "The trick is to figure out the odds. Beyond that, all you can do is trust your luck." He was talking about gambling, but it occurs to me now that at a deeper level, it reflected the feelings of someone who had risked his life as a soldier and somehow made it back alive.

I tried to imagine what it must have been like for him. The gap in his life was like the empty section on my family register, destined to remain forever a blank . . .

Suddenly there was a loud thud. I stopped what I was doing and listened carefully, but there was only the nighttime silence that enveloped the house. Not even the wind stirred. I went back to my manuscript, crossing out lines and making additions, absorbed in editing my text.

"Wake up! Wake up!"

The urgency in my wife's voice made me raise my head from where I'd nodded off at the table, my legs still tucked inside the *kotatsu*. The writing paper was still spread out in front of me, and the boiling kettle gave out a tinny, high-pitched whistle.

"Listen," she said. "I heard it again. There's definitely someone up there."

She was standing stiffly in her nightclothes by the sliding doors, listening intently, her eyes too bright for someone who had just been asleep. It made me worried. What if she was finally losing it completely?

"You're imagining things."

"No. There's someone up there, I tell you." She was struggling to keep her voice low. There was something unnatural in her expression. She looked unbalanced. I felt a shudder run through me.

Keeping a close watch on her, I strained my ears for the slightest sound.

"I can't hear anything," I said, looking over at the clock on the wall. It was past three in the morning.

"What are we going to do?" she asked. "Maybe we should call the police."

"Wait. I'll have a look."

She was clearly scared out of her wits.

My socks were rolled up in a warm ball under the *kotatsu* where I had kicked them off while I was dozing. I put them back on and went to get the flashlight. In an old house like this, the fuses are always going, so we keep a flashlight by the refrigerator for emergencies.

My wife was already standing at the bottom of the stairs. "Hello? Who is it?" she shouted up toward the second floor.

"There you go again! I told you, if someone's broken in, he's not going to answer you back, is he?"

As I spoke, I felt the familiar faintness come over me again. Everything got far away. Particles of white light seemed to run down the stairs like water. From somewhere up above me, I thought I heard a voice call out, "Who are you?" It was impossible to tell whether it was a man's or a woman's.

I stood stunned, as if reeling from a blow. The white light was gone now, but my cheeks were rigid. A series of shudders ran up my spine. I reached out my hand to support myself against the wall. My pulse was racing, my temples numb. I turned to my wife. She hadn't moved; she was still standing looking up the stairs and waiting for an answer.

"Did you hear a voice just now?"

She gave me a funny look. "Are you all right?"

"Fine," I said, mopping the cloying sweat off my forehead. "So you didn't hear a voice just now?"

"What are you talking about? You just told me yourself: he's not going to answer back."

Had I blacked out for a moment? Maybe there was something seriously wrong with me.

"Are you sure you're OK?"

I shrugged it off. I didn't want to make her any more worried than she already was. "It's nothing," I said, and started to climb the stairs. My body was heavy, and the staircase seemed to stretch way out ahead of me. I climbed and climbed. I began to think I would never reach the top.

If I passed out again now, I would fall back into a void from which there was probably no return. The thought made my knees tremble. It was as though the old house were taunting me—as if the place my foster father had built were refusing to accept the idea of two people with no blood tie to the family moving in and taking over.

Eventually, I made it upstairs and shone the flashlight carefully around our daughter's room. Naturally, there was no one there. I stepped into the room and turned on the lights, then opened the window to look out onto the roof, but there was nothing out of the ordinary there either. My wife was pressing close behind me and hissing in my ear: "I really did hear something just now."

Once we had made sure our daughter's room was empty, we moved as quietly as we could into the boy's room. But there was no sign of any disturbance there either, and the shutters were still bolted from inside.

"Let's check the roof."

I forced the windows and shutters open. Leaning out, I played the flashlight carefully over the roof—but there was no sign of anything suspicious. Tufts of grass sprouted from between the tiles, making it look strangely like a riverbank.

"Nothing." By now, it might almost have been a relief if there had been someone there.

"He could've run away."

"Well, there's no sign of any break-in, at least."

"Maybe I was just imagining things. But I'm positive I heard a noise."

"There wasn't someone's voice just now, was there?" I asked again. Better to make sure once and for all, I thought. Now I was the one who was hearing things. Maybe my mind was starting to skip like an old record. But I could still feel it echoing faintly in my ear.

"A voice?"

"Calling out: 'Who are you?'"

Her gaunt face blanched. She looked like an old bird. With a pang, I realized that what I had said went right to the heart of her anxiety. I tried to brush it off. "Just my imagination," I said. But I could tell that what I'd said had set off ripples in her mind.

"Maybe something's happened to Hiroshi?" she said. It was only the fact that the noise might have come from our son's room that made her think this. The way her mind was jumping from one problem to another was worrying in itself.

"If something was wrong, we'd have heard."

"Maybe we should call?"

"Don't worry about it. Besides, he wouldn't thank us for calling at this time of night."

Our son had been in his late twenties when he got married, but the marriage fell apart within a year. After quitting his job with a transport company in Yokohama, he moved down to Okinawa and started working part-time as a diving instructor in a resort—his hobby since his student days.

He's well into his thirties now and still drifting. Instead of settling into a proper job, he makes wishy-washy excuses about "living the dream" and going off to "find himself." "Unwilling to grow up" is more like it. He almost never comes home—not even at Obon or New Year's. We didn't even hear from him when we celebrated our sixtieth birthdays recently.

We call his cell phone from time to time, but mostly we get the answering service, though he must know from the list of missed calls that we've been trying to get in touch. If we persist, he occasionally gets back to us, demanding brusquely to know what's wrong. It only makes him more bad tempered if we say we were just calling for a chat. "Look, do me a favor. Don't call unless it's something important. Otherwise, I just think something bad has happened." Like my sister in Osaka, he's drifting away from his family home, leaving the two of us here more alone than ever.

"Come on, let's phone him," she said. She seemed on the verge of tears.

I put my arm around her thin shoulders. "Let's go to bed," I told her in the gentlest voice I could muster. "It's late. We can phone in the morning." I took her by the hand, and we made our way slowly down the stairs.

Eventually, I persuaded her to get into bed, still fretful and muttering "I really hope there's nothing wrong." Then I got in under the futon myself, but the events of the evening made it impossible to sleep. I lay awake listening to every sound in the house. I felt a headache coming on—maybe I was getting a cold. Or was it the first sign of something more serious? The memory of my foster father came back to me again, making me almost afraid to fall asleep.

After a while, she said, "Are you awake?"

So she couldn't sleep either. A breeze was rustling the trees in the garden. Without asking, I could tell that her anxious mind was turning even this familiar sound into something menacing. I could read her thoughts as if they were my own. I suppose most couples are the same. You live long enough under the same roof and you start to resemble each other.

"What is it?" I said at last.

"About you finding another job. What's going to happen?"

So now she was fretting about that on top of everything else. I felt a stab of guilt.

"It'll sort itself out. I told the employment agency I'll take anything available starting from April. The forms are all done."

I was retiring from the printing company at the end of the month, after forty-two long years. I had hoped the company would help me find another position, but with the regional economy still stuck in a never-ending slump, there were no openings anywhere.

My boss liked to boast of his contacts in business and local government. He kept assuring me that someone like me would slot in easily wherever I went next. But so far, apart from a few short-term things, there was nothing doing.

The amount I was due to receive as a retirement bonus had also come as a disappointment. No doubt this was another thing my wife found unsettling. After all the years I'd put in, it was hardly generous, certainly not enough to get by on till my pension kicked in. I hated the idea that I wasn't able to provide enough for us to live out our lives without this additional stress. But what choice did we have? It was just something we would have to come to terms with.

What would she do if I failed to wake up one morning? The thought filled me with dread, made me determined to stay alive, for her sake. Our daughter and her husband were always moving around for his company, so they were unlikely to have her live with them after I was gone. And our son was still bumming his way through life, without even bothering to stay in touch. So he'd be no use. Sometimes I'm reminded of the way I used to feel when I started sleeping alone as a child: a sense of utter loneliness that made me want to cling to somebody—anybody—as hard as I could . . .

I drifted into a dream. An old 78 record is spinning. Someone is singing in a voice that's neither male nor female but a combination of two well-known singers from my youth. It seems to be about all the people who were lost in the last war. When I look more closely, I realize that the label on the record is blank, with nothing to indicate the title of the song or the name of the singer.

After a while, the song changes to a sad little tune that sounds like an old children's song or lullaby. I am an infant again, safely wrapped in a blanket of white feathers. But the needle starts to scratch and skip, and the sweet melody disappears. The skipping of the needle becomes a voice, and the voice calls out: "Who's there? Who is it? Who are you?" Then there's a thump of static, and everything goes white.

Why does it get more difficult to sleep as we get older? Perhaps it's the approach of death that makes us afraid to be alone in the dark. After that disturbing dream, I managed to drop off again, only to be jerked awake much too early to feel rested, mentally or physically. But once I opened my eyes the spell was broken, and I resigned myself to the prospect of another sluggish, irritable Sunday.

Still, the bright sunlight breaking through the sliding doors promised clear skies outside. I could hear my wife bustling about in the kitchen. I remembered how I had gone to bed the previous night worried that I might never wake up again. And here I was, still alive. The thought reassured me a little, and gave me the energy to drag myself out of bed.

"Morning!" my wife called as I entered the kitchen. She was obviously in a good mood. Her ruddy cheeks and cheerful voice made me wonder if all the tensions of the night before had somehow been offloaded onto me. Not that I minded. It only seemed fair that after being a cause for concern myself, I should shoulder the burden for a bit.

"See, there was nothing to worry about after all," I said, stifling a yawn as I spoke.

"I know," she replied with her back turned. There was relief and embarrassment in her voice.

"No need for all that fuss, was there?" I said teasingly, on my way to the washbasin.

While I brushed my teeth, I stared absentmindedly at the little stains and flecks on the white tiled wall next to the basin where the towel hung. Then, raising my eyes, I looked up through the slats at the sky outside. As I'd suspected, there was not a cloud to be seen. I could feel the first signs of spring in the warm morning air. This wouldn't be the first time my wife's anxiety attacks had been triggered by a change in the weather. The forecast was for rain in the afternoon, but I made up my mind to relax and enjoy the sunlight while it lasted.

We sat down to our usual leisurely breakfast: dried fish, *kamaboko*, seaweed, miso soup with clams, and pickled cabbage.

"The cherry trees will be out soon if it stays like this," I said.

"They won't pop out just yet, though. There aren't enough buds on them yet."

"But you know what they're like. They burst into flower as soon as the sun comes out, then lose it all at the first drop of rain."

"Still, it's a bit early for that."

"They've probably finished in Okinawa."

"Yes, but it's much warmer down there."

"Why don't we call Hiroshi and ask?"

She lowered her face in embarrassment. "He'll only start shouting at us again if it's something silly like that." I decided not to remind her of what she'd said last night.

"We could walk over to Kazagashira Park later on," I suggested.

"All right—and see how the trees are coming on there."

Afterward, as we sipped our tea, we chatted about some of the things Hiroshi had got up to as a child. The time he caught a snake and let it curl up on the easy chair; the time he drew a huge pair of eyes and a tongue on the festival lantern with a magic marker, or when he jumped on a bus without any money and then wandered into a police box to ask the man on duty to call us to come and take him home. He'd always had a touch of wanderlust in him. Time and again, he had made us bail him out of some adventure of his—a boat trip to Ioh Island or a bus ride to Sasebo . . .

"He'll call if he needs us," I said. She nodded, as if she too had decided not to think about it anymore.

After breakfast, she went into the garden with a watering can.

"You should come, too," she called. "It's lovely out here."

It was a relief to hear her sounding so cheerful. "I'll join you in a bit," I called back. Even from inside, I could see that the azaleas around the edge of the garden were perking up. It was reassuring to think that the garden would be full of red and white flowers again in just a month or two.

I sat down at the *kotatsu* and read over what I'd written the night before. I was trying to think of a way to finish the piece, when I heard my wife calling excitedly from outside.

"Come here! Quick!"

I looked out to see her pointing toward the roof.

"What is it?"

"Never mind, just come. Hurry!"

I slipped on a pair of sandals.

"It's a bird!"

Something white hung from the gutter like a towel. Its feathers were disheveled and its neck drooped low, the long thin beak slightly open. It was one of those white birds you see strutting on tiptoe through the shallows of a river, hunting for fish. An egret . . . almost certainly a great egret.

Its legs reminded me of the long wooden chopsticks my wife uses when she's cooking. They were twisted at an unnatural angle. When I looked more closely, I realized they were tangled in gossamer-thin threads. A fishing line. It glinted in the sunlight. The bird's body was wrapped in more of the same stuff. Unable to move, the bird looked at us helplessly, a mixture of fear and resignation in its eyes.

"It's still alive."

The bird struggled, but it was clear that it didn't have much strength left.

I ran to get the rusty stepladder from the cellar and told my wife to fetch some scissors. Almost immediately, she reappeared with a pair she keeps in a drawer of the Buddhist altar in the living room.

I climbed the ladder and cut away the fishing line from the gutter and the bird's legs, before taking it gently in my arms.

Terrified, it struggled weakly to escape, but in its exhaustion it couldn't do much more than lift its head, not even flap its wings. I held it as gently as I could.

Despite all its plumage, the bird felt almost pathetically light. It was like holding a fluff of white cloud I'd cut down out of the sky. There were fine lines of blood on the bird's beak, neck, and breast, as though someone had whipped it with a thin strap.

"Over here," my wife called. She had spread a towel on the veranda. I laid the bird on the towel and carefully cut away the other tangled strands. Again, the bird struggled feebly and opened its beak, revealing a quivering pink tongue.

As each strand snapped, I felt it in my heart like a needle skipping on a record. The bird, wreathed in white, filled my vision. I seemed to hear a voice coming from it. "Who is it? Who are you?"

Was this how my parents had died, wounded and in pain? For more than sixty years now, I had barely thought of what they suffered. "Forgive me," I said as I snipped away, with tears in my eyes. How heartless, how unthinking I'd been.

"It must have been calling for help all night," my wife said. She, too, sounded tearful. "You poor thing, you must have been scared stiff," she said, stroking the bird's feathers. The hooks on the fishing line were lodged deep in the purple flesh close to the top of the bird's legs. I did my best to remove them.

The bird opened its beak and bent its long neck back. But even this effort was too much for it now, and its head soon flopped forward again. Although I had been as careful as I could, the barbed part had ripped its flesh and the white plumage was stained with pricks of blood.

"If only we'd noticed sooner."

The bird looked up at me. I could see the light fading from its clear eyes. "I'm sorry," I whispered, stroking the soft feathers.

"We're so sorry," my wife said. "There you were, calling out for help all night long. We're so sorry."

"There's nothing we could have done. It was hanging from the gutter—even if we'd gone out onto the roof we wouldn't have seen it."

In a whisper, she spoke to it. Murmuring, I asked it to forgive me. Our hands brushed against its wings and belly.

After a while, the bird stretched out its neck, raised its head . . . and went limp, the light dying in its eyes. As the life began to leave its body, the claws at the end of its bent legs unclenched. The neck sagged and a yellow liquid oozed from its beak. Its round eyes seemed to focus on some point in the far distance, beyond our world.

And like this, covered in wounds, my mother died in the bright spring sunlight.

Nearly half a century has passed since the day I was taken to see the rebuilt cathedral. I am in my sixties now. Both my foster parents are dead; my children have left home. Even in the Urakami I once thought as my own special place, things have moved on. Today the area is just another ordinary district in the northern part of the city.

I've never thought too much about who "my god" might have been—or worried that I might have rejected him as a child before I ever knew him. I'm not the sort of person to go too deeply into things like that.

In that sense, I have lived my life as a blank, empty space. Nothing as active as rejection or skepticism was involved. I have always been such an unreflective person that, most of the time, it never even occurred to me to be ashamed of this.

And then, this spring, we found an egret tangled in a fishing line, trapped in the gutter on our roof. By the time we discovered it, the bird had apparently been hanging upside down there overnight. Several times during the night, it seems to have tossed about as if calling for help; but although my wife, who is much more sensitive about things like this than I am, noticed the noise and kept insisting that something was wrong, we didn't realize what happened until the next morning.

By then, the bird was already near the end. I hurried to cut it free, but it was no use. The light went out of its eyes, and the strength ebbed from its wings. It died soon after we found it.

While my wife and I stood there in the spring sunshine looking down at its dead body, she said again: "If only we'd noticed sooner." The words pierced me to the core. How cold I'd been.

I dug a hole with a spade and buried it under the azaleas. What had I really buried that day? As I washed the dirt off my hands, I was overcome by a sense of loss. I scraped the soil from under my fingernails, and once they were clean, I put my hands together and prayed. I was sweating—it was a while since I had taken any hard exercise.

My wife knew my past and understood what I was feeling. "It was fate that made this place your house," she said.

The house my adoptive parents left me is showing its age. The cedar boards are faded. The white walls are yellowing, and the floorboards creak when you step on them. It wasn't built to last. Even now, in my sixties, I still feel slightly ill at ease here, but I've felt closer to it since we buried the bird in the garden.

That afternoon, dark clouds covered the sky, and I watched as warm spring rain fell on the azaleas.

No one can say how much longer my wife and I have to live. But almost certainly, our children will never live here after we are gone. Sometime in the not-too-distant future the house will be demolished, and the land will become another vacant lot. We will be the last people to use it. After us, there will be nothing but the azaleas flowering unnoticed, with the bones of the bird lying at their roots.

Our children will never know who their god is. For them, he is dead and buried. But there's no point in wishing that any of this could change; it is something that began here more than sixty years ago.

The places on my family register where my parents' names should go are empty. Nothing is recorded there. My past as a newborn baby when the atom bomb fell lies buried in that empty white space.